D0393898

THE
WHITE MAN
IN THE
TREE

THE
WHITE MAN
IN THE
TREE

and other stories

MARK KURLANSKY

WASHINGTON SQUARE PRESS
PUBLISHED BY POCKET BOOKS
NEW YORK LONDON TORONTO SYDNEY SINGAPORE

A WASHINGTON SQUARE PRESS *Original* Publication

A Washington Square Press Publication of
POCKET BOOKS, a division of Simon & Schuster, Inc.
1230 Avenue of Americas, New York, NY 10020

ISBN: 0–671–03605–X

First Washington Square Press hardcover printing October 2000

10 9 8 7 6 5 4 3 2 1

Interior illustrations by the author
Designed by C. Linda Dingler

Printed in the U.S.A.

The story "Devaluation" appeared in *The Junky's Christmas and Other Yuletide Stories,* published by Serpent's Tail Press (1994).

The lines from "The Peasant Declares His Love" by Emile Roumer, translated by John Peale Bishop from Dudley Fitts: *Anthology of Contemporary Latin-American Poetry,* copyright © 1947 by New Directions Publishing Company Corp., reprinted by permission of New Directions.

To beautiful Marian

"You are the tripe in my pepperpot,
the dumpling in my peas, my tea of aromatic herbs."

—Emile Roumer,
"The Peasant Declares His Love"

Protégeant mon orgueil nu contre
Moi-meme et la superbe des races heureuses . . .

To protect me from my naked pride
And the arrogance of lucky races . . .

—Léopold Sédar Senghor, "Le Totem"

CONTENTS

THE
WHITE MAN
IN THE
TREE

THE WHITE MAN IN THE TREE

Something startled Palle as he floated into the numbness of his afternoon's tropical snooze up on the breezy gallery where the damaging rays of sun just missed his toes. He opened his eyes.

Then he heard it again. A car horn. It was Simpson at the gate. Palle would wait a minute. Someone would open it. He gazed past the drooping white wooden gingerbread to the palm fronds. Beyond that was the sky, a wet, brown tropical sky that looked as if it wanted to perspire raindrops. But a faint fuzzy white sun held its place and the rain would not come. He could see little segments of dark blue ocean. Port-au-Prince was out there too. It would be there when he wanted it. Not this afternoon. Too hot.

The horn droned a long note. Palle realized he would have to do something. So he stood up, causing the white

I

wicker chair to creak. He walked to the white wooden
banister so that they could see him, the white man, standing up.

Little Jean-Jean appeared from somewhere below, running down the driveway to the gate. Terrible to run like
that in this heat, Palle thought. Palle had not asked him to
run. He didn't even like to see it. Jean-Jean struggled with
the meager weight his small boy's body offered and slowly
managed to slide the black steel door open.

Simpson drove his car into the shade of the well-
gardened little circle and, getting out, shouted through the
red hibiscus, as though reading Palle's mind, "Don't even
bother to stand up. It's too hot."

"Come on up," Palle shouted down gratefully.
Simpson, seersucker drooping creaseless from his bony
frame, stepped up to the porch, maneuvered around the
comic Liautaud iron sculpture that greeted him, walked
across the polished dark wood floor to the staircase with
the big colored glass balls on each banister post, climbed
the carpeted stairs, stopped to admire the Bigaud, went
right past the huge green brush strokes of the Philippe-
Auguste, and by the time he was out on the gallery,
Faustin was standing there holding a tray with two
sweaty coral-colored drinks.

Palle settled deeper into his wicker seat. "Faustin, is this
the new punch recipe?"

"*Mais oui,*" declared Faustin, plunging his voice a perfect octave between the first and second word.

"Not the rum punch we had before last week?"

Again the same octave. *"Mais non."*

"Ah, that's good. That's very good," said Palle contentedly, with such absolute faith in his world that he was in no hurry to test it with a sip. The concoction would be dry, sour, cold, perfect.

"And how's life at the consulate?"

"Not like this," said Simpson, sipping his rum punch. "So what is happening, Palle? I have a feeling my big favor was no favor at all."

"Yes, that's right," said Palle, smiling pleasantly. "A complete disaster. Maybe it has ruined my life." He chuckled slightly at the idea of ruin.

"So what happened to . . . What was her name?"

"Lanuwobi," Palle said, savoring the syllables as though recalling something erotic.

"Wonderful name. I couldn't figure out what it meant."

"Doesn't mean anything."

"Neither does 'Simpson.'"

"It came to her mother in a dream. Her mother was pregnant with Lanuwobi and she was sleeping, and the phrase 'La-nu-wo-bi' came to her in her sleep." Palle sipped. The startling acid of fruit juices seemed the only thing in the world that was cool, the only thing with a hard, crisp edge on a moist and heavy planet. Then, slowly, he gave in to the rum, dark and syrupy as the weather. He felt like dreaming. "I suppose I met her because I needed a haircut. Well, it was back when I was staying in the hotel, and there were two of them at the desk, and I always said, 'I need one of you to cut my hair.' They laughed a little. And then one night Lanuwobi said, 'I'll cut it,' and she came to my room and, oh, she was very, very nice."

Palle's eyes were closed and he was smiling.

Simpson finished his punch and put it on the white table and Faustin noiselessly reappeared, replaced it with a full one, and vanished.

"I think we should have one more punch," said Palle reflectively, "and then we should switch to these new rum sours—yes, that will be very good. So she was the receptionist. And she has a very nice voice. You know, answering the phone and so forth. Very sweet. I was there for a long period doing that film. Did you see my Haiti film?"

"No. You should get a copy for the embassy."

"And then at some point I needed a haircut. And I thought it would be nice to have this haircut done by—I had two choices. I had a little problem deciding. At that time we were just flirting. Lanuwobi was very flirtatious. But then there was another girl who was also very flirtatious, Mona. You might remember her. She was small and a waitress."

"Do you often do this haircut thing?"

"No, no. This is new. This was a new idea. And she said yes she would do that. But then I was waiting to see if that would happen. The next night she said that she had bought a pair of scissors. Then it all took place in room eleven. The suite, you know. And that was really the beginning of this affair. I persuaded her to stay for the night, and this was really the beginning. She did a nice haircut, I think . . ."

Palle started remembering those days, sneaking around the hotel like happily worried teenagers. The hotel manager, a drowsy-eyed, light-skinned young patrician, did not approve. It wasn't that she was half Palle's age—the manager's wife was even younger—but his employees were not supposed to be sleeping with the customers. Not being a man of great principles, the manager had compensated by making up a few. Hotel employees should not sleep with guests in the rooms.

At the time, the army was out shooting at night. You could hear the dull crack of gunfire echoing off the mountains—sometimes single pops, sometimes rhythmic bursts. Sometimes bodies were found the next morning. Flies would find them first, later journalists. In the afternoon they would be taken away. Staff on night shift were allowed to spend the night in the hotel because it was too dangerous to try to go home in the dark. Palle could never explain to Simpson—unless he had experienced it, which was hard to say—the romance of lying in bed holding a woman and feeling so completely alive while somewhere out there was death, and the dangerous popping noise could be heard coming through the shutters with the still night air and the croak of tree frogs.

Lanuwobi lived with her mother downtown. What a remarkable scene. He would have liked to have filmed it. The white man going downtown in his white four-wheel drive to pick up his girlfriend, down there where the air was full of steam and rot. Her mother had a small food store not much bigger than a large closet. Lanuwobi's dark turquoise-colored bedroom was only slightly larger than her bed. What always stayed in Palle's mind, aside from the terrible smell from the grayish slime in the concrete sewer ditch that ran along the edge of the house with boards to step over it, was the huge television that no one ever watched because the house did not have electricity. They also had two large radios, only one of which could operate with batteries. It somehow seemed important to have these things even though, after eight P.M., Lanuwobi and her mother were alone in darkness in the little house and went to sleep until the orange dawn.

"I think from the very beginning our relationship was *malvue*. Tolerated but not good."

"You visited the home?"

"Yes," said Palle, thinking again about the television.

"You went there for dinner?"

"No! Never. I would never eat there. This was a small place. Low middle class. But they had servants, of course. What a fantastically complicated system. There is another class that is servants for them. But it was in an area where—it stank. I admired the way these people kept their dignity, but I couldn't eat there. She was a very nice woman, the mother. She looked like Bessie Smith, you know, the blues singer. Very dignified. A nice lady, gray hair. Very beautiful. Her daughter was spending the night

with me. She knew this, but it could never be understood
that way. It was always said that Lanuwobi was staying at
the hotel because it was dangerous at night."

Her mother had warned Lanuwobi that she should get
legally married. Lanuwobi talked to Palle about marriage.
"Yes," Palle had said, "we could consider marriage at
some point."

Then, the first problem: Lanuwobi asked Palle to stay at
a different hotel. She said it was embarrassing to come
down to breakfast together. Palle objected, "But I like this
hotel."

"*Mais, c'est malvue.*"

Palle understood *"malvue."* She was sleeping in a hotel
with a white man. It made her look like a whore. So he
checked into a small hotel in Petionville, a group of moun-
taintops named after a light-skinned elitist general, where
the people with money lived on the hilltops and the people
with none lived in hidden shacks on the slopes and climbed
topside to beg. Lanuwobi spent the night with Palle in the
Petionville hotel. The next afternoon she went back to her
job as a receptionist. Palle stopped by for a rum at the bar
and to visit with her a little. But the pouting manager with
the limp lower lip, a man of about the same age as Palle's
oldest son, summoned him into the chaotic little room he
called his office. He had heard that Palle was sleeping with
Lanuwobi in the little hotel in Petionville.

"Where did you hear that?"

The manager smiled. It occurred to Palle to point out

that none of this was any of his business, but it was all so interesting, the way things worked here. How had he found out, and what was he going to say about it? The manager simply wanted Palle back in his hotel. Very happily, Palle moved back to his favorite hotel, and discreetly, Lanuwobi would appear in his doorway. Night after night he would spend in the breezy hotel suite with her young and generous body and the pop-pop of murder vaguely heard in the distance.

But after a few weeks the manager fired her, saying, "You evidently are no longer interested in the hotel business."

Palle was able to get her a job as a receptionist in another hotel. As he pointed out to the new manager, she had a very nice voice for the telephone.

This feeling that she gave him started in bed, this sense of power, that he was a magical kind of man who could answer all her desires. Whatever she needed to be happy, he could supply it. He could see the appreciation in her young eyes that sparkled like polished black gems. He was neither rich nor powerful, but he had enough money and enough power for anything she needed. She lost her job. He got her a new job. She wanted to speak better English. He taught her to speak excellent English. She wanted to drive a car. He taught her and got her a driver's license.

But Lanuwobi was tired of being *malvue* in the hotel where they slept. She no longer had her mother's approval, because she could no longer furnish her with an excuse for spending the night in that hotel where she no longer worked. The mother did not want to be forced to know about their relationship. Perhaps they should get married? Lanuwobi believed in bargaining and felt that she strengthened her negotiating position by arguing that she had been spending her nights with him in spite of her mother. She had done this for him and was owed something for it.

Palle introduced her to the concept of "vacation." They would go south to Jacmel, to a rustic little hotel with a beach in a rocky cove where the water lay still and opaline blue, sheltered by dangerous, jagged black rocks running to a small sandy beach where no one ever walked. They could take off their clothes and feel alone in the world. Sometimes someone would stare from under a tree by the hotel, someone of such low standing that it didn't matter whether they were clothed or naked in front of him.

Each time they went, she insisted that he drive downtown and see her mother and ask permission. At the age of fifty-six, divorced three times, Palle was learning for the first time in his life to go courting. He felt himself very romantic and picturesque. Though at times courting was inconvenient, the mother always played her part so graciously that he came to enjoy it.

Dinner became very important. If he took Lanuwobi out for dinner and they didn't get back until morning, that was acceptable because they were out for dinner, which offered the possibility that it could have gotten too late to get back. He would drive his white car down to their home in the stinking neighborhood, and she would be waiting, in a new and wonderful dress. Palle was always amazed at her dresses. Where did she keep them? Some were sent by her sister in New York. She always looked beautiful. She always had colors and fabrics that showed off the soft blackness of her skin. When they left, he would explain to her mother that if it got too late, they would "wait until morning to get back" rather than risk it in the night. And the mother always nodded.

Lanuwobi had gone to hotelier school and learned flawless restaurant manners, and she could speak in beautiful nineteenth-century French, much finer than Palle's own awkward Scandinavian-accented French. Palle liked being in overdone Petionville restaurants with this strikingly beautiful, perfectly dressed woman with lovely manners.

Occasionally Lanuwobi would mention something about marriage, and Palle started discussing it with his friend Ernesto. Ernesto was a South American, a political refugee, it was always said. Ernesto also was taking out a black woman, though from a slightly lower social standing than Lanuwobi. Ernesto's face—his delicate smile, his dark, molasses-colored eyes—was a caricature of good-natured innocence. He was gallant. He also had to court his young woman, but he took to the role with a natural grace that Palle could not totally master. Ernesto had courted before. Palle's deeply curious, intelligent face always looked as though there was a suspicion of silliness.

He was always a film director, a slight distance away from himself, viewing the scenes of his life, watching the white man. And he was not sure that these courting scenes were working. But Ernesto courted as if he were gliding through the steps of a well-rehearsed classical ballet. No outsider observing Palle and Ernesto would have guessed which one was the romantic and which one was the cynic.

Ernesto could make Palle laugh. "Palle," he would say, "the Haitian bourgeois all want these light-skinned women. But you and I are so white we can have the really black ones." They both smacked the table gleefully.

Before each move, Palle would consult Ernesto. "Palle, you must keep her family away. Keep them away from your doorstep, Palle." Neither of the two friends seemed to notice that Palle very rarely took Ernesto's advise.

Ernesto advised Palle that he should marry Lanuwobi, but that he absolutely had to make a prenuptial agreement. "You have to protect your property, Palle." Ernesto could not understand that Palle had no property. Only the rights to a few documentary films in Danish.

Ernesto had an airtight agreement drawn up with his young woman, and then they were married at a seaside resort north of Port-au-Prince. Palle was the best man. When he drove downtown to take Lanuwobi to the wedding, he did not want to get out of the car with his white linen suit and white shoes. But it had to be done. He had to step over the sewer and go to the door and chat with her mother. He stepped carefully. Lanuwobi was also dressed in white, but she didn't change to her white shoes until she got into his car.

At the wedding, Palle, the best man, delivered a speech in French, which he was a bit shy about. It was difficult to hear because a scuffle broke out while he was speaking. Ernesto had provided T-shirts to commemorate his wedding, and there did not seem to be enough of them, or some people were taking more than one. The food went the same way, Creole food for two hundred people consumed by fifty in a matter of minutes. The guests who were fighting about the T-shirts—some shirts got torn in the tugging—missed out on the food.

But to Palle and Lanuwobi it was a moving afternoon that made them think even more about getting married. Palle was hesitating. He certainly would have no prenuptial agreement. That was no way to have a romance. He would not even mention such a thing to Lanuwobi. But Lanuwobi would not have been shocked. She knew about prenuptial agreements. She studied every detail of Ernesto's carefully worded document. She was ready to negotiate.

At some point, they should get married, Palle thought. Palle had been best man for Ernesto, and Ernesto was to do the same for Palle. But for now, more interesting projects could be undertaken. "You know, Lanuwobi, with your intelligence, there is no point in these low-paying hotel jobs. I could help you do something else. What would you like to do?"

"You know what I would really like to do?"

"What?" Palle asked confidently.

"I have always wanted to own my own beauty salon."

Palle did not know anything about beauty salons. He asked Ernesto, who said, "Excellent idea. You should set her up in her own beauty salon. That would be a good move, and it would only cost you maybe five thousand dollars." Palle did not have five thousand dollars at the moment, but there were times when he did. Next time he did have a few thousand dollars extra, he could do this. He told Lanuwobi that he had decided that at the first opportunity he would get her a beauty salon. Another wish granted.

THEY MOVED ON TO RUM SOURS. They were better, more tart. The air was hot, sweet, and sticky. Rum sours were cold and acrid. Palle sipped, and the muscles in his neck pulled the skin tight across his face. Faustin was standing next to him with the tray in his hand, as though waiting for this facial expression.

"Faustin, these sours are very sour. *Trop aigre.*"

In Palle's household, full sentences were only whispered in the garden and the kitchen. Palle and his staff had no common language. He spoke in truncated French expressions and they replied in equally abbreviated Creole. Between statement and reply, a few seconds lay for deciphering—just enough time to convince each side that the other was a little slow. Palle would quickly lose patience with this torturous exchange and break into longer sentences even though he could never be sure if such statements were understood. But his staff never made that mistake.

"*Mais oui. Twó. Twó,*" Faustin agreed, and shook his head disapprovingly. "*Pa sik.*"

"*Pa sik!* There's no more sugar? But I just . . ." Palle slowly got up and walked lazily into his bedroom and came back on the gallery with black-market Haitian bills, which he handed to Faustin. Wearily, as though reciting someone else's lines, he said to Faustin, "Now this should be enough for a month's sugar."

"*Oui, Mesié.*"

"And you know I will be very angry if we are out of sugar again before the end of the month."

"*Oui, Mesié.*"

Simpson reflected to himself on how Europeans seemed to be born with an instinct for colonialism. Americans had to learn it.

"This was when you helped me with my big mistake," said Palle to Simpson with a wry smile.

"Why did you want the visa?"

"She wanted it. I could get her the things she wanted. That was the relationship. Ernesto said no. He said they are better with no visa. Ernesto is really tough, you know."

"But I remember she was entitled to a visa. She had a father in New York."

"Yes. She had never met him. She had just learned about

him, the long lost father, and she wanted to visit, and for some reason they wouldn't give her the visa."

"I remember. Just an INS screw-up," said Simpson.

"Yes, but I waited too long. I should have married her. She always warned me about that. But I thought I had all the cards. Ernesto knew."

Lanuwobi was not worried about getting to New York to see her father. She knew Palle would get her a visa. He could always do these things. He never said he could do something and then failed. The *blans* could always arrange things between each other. She understood that this visa would be her card to play, not his. And she warned him, "We should get married now. After I go to New York, things will be different."

Palle thought that if she had a visa, he could take her with him to New York—when he wanted. They would not be limited to trips to Jacmel anymore. Through Simpson he had contacted a high official in the INS who had come to Haiti for one week to "look things over." Palle could do this for her. Take it right to the top. She had been applying for two years. He could have the case moved up in a few weeks.

"Thanks to you, of course," he told Simpson.

Simpson nodded and sipped.

"I thought it would make life easier. I was very naive there."

It was springtime and Palle was going to Europe. He always spent spring in Europe doing film business, visiting friends, visiting his sons. He called her from Spain and reassured her.

"Don't worry. I think they will move it very quickly."

"Yes, I have already received word that my visa is ready."

"Really."

"I only have to go to the embassy to pick it up."

"The consulate."

"Yes, as a matter of fact I am going to New York next week."

"Really?"

"Yes, it seems I have an uncle there, and he is coming down, and he'll take me."

"Well—that is very—that's very fast."

Uncle Edner came to Haiti and flew with her to JFK airport, where they displayed their documents, his green card and her new visa. They entered the U.S. with dizzying ease. Then he ushered her into his waiting taxi—an orange-yellow Chevrolet. It was his. "My medallion," he said, and in time she learned that this was a country where having your own medallion stood for something. It was quickly clear that he, and not her father, was the real power in the family, and the source of this power was the fact that he owned a taxi medallion.

Her father lived in Brooklyn in a small apartment that was dark and rented. Lanuwobi had always heard of this man as Uncle Lionel. Now, after she had fitted together numerous pieces of history, Uncle Lionel, the unknown man who sent money from Brooklyn, was gradually revealed to be her father.

She had always thought of Brooklyn as a wonderful place, a place from which money came. But now she could see that the place called Queens was much better. Uncle Edner lived in Queens, and he took her to his home to live. At first she was uncertain, because although Brooklyn was a disappointment, Edner lived in a place called Jamaica, which sounded as if it would be worse. But Brooklyn was old and dark and Queens was new and low to the ground, which gave it much more daylight. When Palle called, she described Uncle Edner's house as "a large home that he owned himself—very new and modern and filled with new furniture." It was a new, two-story house in a neighborhood with a great many other new houses. Everything about the houses was clean. The sides of the houses looked like painted wood, but they were smoother and shinier and they washed completely clean when it rained. Edner had explained this to her. Sometimes when it didn't rain, he would spray a hose on the white sides. It was a washable house.

Uncle Edner had a potbelly that pressed so round against his shirt that she was sure if she touched it, it would feel perfectly hard, like a tightly inflated plastic ball. With his thick balding head and the rolls on the back of his neck, he had the kind of tough and well-fed look that in Haiti would have immediately been recognized as a Macoute look. But he was not a Macoute. He had left in the 1960s to escape Papa Doc. Here in Queens you did not have to be a Macoute to get a potbelly.

Edner looked the way Lanuwobi had imagined her father, whereas her father, Uncle Lionel, was a very lean man with a chronically worried face beneath oblique eyebrows. From the beginning, everything about the two uncles seemed to get reversed. Instead of Uncle Edner and her father, Lanuwobi started referring to them as Uncle Lionel and her real uncle.

Her real uncle and her father settled her into Edner's house with no discussion of how long she would be staying. Edner explained to her, "You're in America now. See what you can do with it."

"Do with it?"

"Yes. Everybody gains something from America. What are you going to do?"

Palle would call her in Queens from Europe—the different capitals—and would nervously talk about his schedule. How he hoped to get back to Haiti by late June. July at the latest. Something had already changed. Before this, when he went to Europe he offered very little information about when he planned to return. Now he was proposing a schedule for meeting back in Haiti, and she responded with phrases like, "Yes, but it's a problem now." Or, "It is not so easy anymore."

Palle called up Ernesto in Haiti and asked him what he

thought these statements meant. Ernesto explained that it was more important than ever to keep the family at a distance.

Palle was beginning to worry that she would not be back in Haiti when he got there. He finally said, "I will be back on June twenty-first." This was unusually blunt. She responded softly in that wonderful voice, "I don't think I can go then."

"Why not? What are you doing in New York?"

"It's just not that easy. You have to get something from being in New York. I haven't gotten anything yet."

"What do you want to get? We can get it."

"I don't know yet."

Ernesto had warned him to save this next line for a desperate moment. It seemed to Palle that this was that moment, and he said it. "Remember, Lanuwobi, I helped you get this visa."

Calmly, in her lovely voice, she replied, "That is not the way they see it."

"Your family? Why don't they see it like that?"

There was no sound at all on the telephone line, and then he heard her say, "They would never believe that. Never."

"You must tell them. Have you told them?"

"Yes, but they said that was not how I got it at all."

"You must tell them. Explain about my friend Simpson in the consulate and the man from Washington. Tell them."

"Oh."

She did explain it to Edner, but he explained that this was a trick the *blans* have. They always say they made a telephone call and made it happen. He told her the story of a *bokor*, a master of Voodoo magic, in Croix des Bouquets. Anytime anyone in the village wanted something, he always said, "I will mix you a powder." If it didn't happen, the *loas*, the spirits, were against it; if it did happen, he would soon appear and say, "Don't forget, it was I who made the powder."

He was going to lose her. Somehow—maybe because he had not listened to Ernesto—somehow he had played it all wrong, and now he was going to lose her. He paced a gray carpet on a gray afternoon in a Paris hotel room. How could he keep her? He had to do something. He sat at the small writing desk.

"Things have gotten far from what I intended—things are becoming terribly wrong and misunderstood. We must undo everything and get back to what we had. Back to Haiti. We must both go back to Haiti and be together, and this time I realize that you are completely right. Our lives should be together. We should get married there as soon as possible. A big wedding. I love you."

He mailed it and anticipated her excitement in their next phone call. But instead he heard frustration in her voice. "Why don't you see it? It is not so easy now. You should have married me before I went to New York. I told you that."

"I will marry you now. We can go back to Haiti, be like we were and get married."

"Now it is much more complicated. You better come here."

He was the director, and now this film was drifting out of his control, or as he put it in his peculiar linguistic blend, "The story is escaping my mise-en-scène. I can't bear that." But he was in production for two films, and he was not able to take even one week off from March until the end of October. Self-torture became his mental pastime. He imagined her meeting someone else. Someone who was still older than she but a little younger than he was, or someone who was really rich, someone who had the ability to spend money with truly dazzling abandon. He imagined her falling in love with New York. He had heard of such things happening. People sometimes fall in love with places even when they are awful. He understood this. He had even done films with this idea.

This was not the way life was supposed to be. He wasn't supposed to be imagining all of these unpleasant scenarios. He was supposed to know what would happen next. He was the director.

He called her as often as he could. He sent her letters so that she would understand that their relationship was something solid—that she could count on it. He told her how much he loved her, how good his intentions were. In his interviews with the Danish press he always mentioned her in ways that made them seem very much a couple, and he would clip these articles and mail them to her. All of Denmark knew that he and Lanuwobi were together. But he was not sure. This was a very long and dangerous period of absence. He must do something—something radical.

He telephoned her with the news. He had decided that she should go to Denmark. She should join him for the summer in Denmark.

"I don't think they will let me."

"Who?"

"Things are more complicated now. If we had been married in Haiti, this wouldn't be a problem now. But we didn't. Now you must talk to my uncle."

"Your uncle?"

"Yes, my real uncle. We can work out a time to call. Then you call. I will tell you what to say."

"And what am I supposed to say?"

"First you have to say that you intend to marry me."

"Yes, that's all right."

"If he asks if you have been married before, tell the truth."

"All right."

"But not all of it."

"Which part?"

"You can say that you were married once and then divorced. But don't say that you have been divorced three times. And don't tell him that you are fifty-six years old!"

"How old should I be?"

"Fifty. Only fifty. And you have three children but not four. Four is too much. And these are all things that you should not mention at all. But if you are asked, then say you are fifty, divorced once, and three children. This is important. Don't forget to say you were divorced."

"It seems complicated."

"It is complicated. That is your fault!"

But she said all this in her lovely voice. He still thought she had the most extraordinary telephone voice—husky and rich like the soft middle range of a cello. And her English was very good now. She had him to thank for that.

He called the uncle at the appointed time. To his irritation, Palle noticed that he felt very nervous about this telephone call. Here he was, fifty-six years old, or fifty, whatever it was, an international filmmaker, and now he was getting little flips in the center of his stomach because he had to call his girlfriend's uncle and ask to take her on a trip. He had to call this man he had never seen. In Queens. A taxi driver in Queens. He tried to picture the uncle in his house with his new furniture, this taxi driver in his modern palace.

He telephoned from his hotel room in the sixth arrondissement of Paris. He told Edner who he was and even described his last three films. Edner interrupted to ask, "How old are you?"

"I am fifty years old," said Palle flawlessly. And then he could not resist asking, "How old are you?" Edner didn't answer. It was a mistake. Palle knew it would be, but he couldn't resist. It was just a small one. The rest of the conversation seemed to go well. He told Edner that he loved Lanuwobi. Well, not "loved," but "cared for," and wanted her to join him in Europe.

"That is absolutely impossible," said the unknown taxi driver in Queens. Palle noticed that Edner also had a very nice telephone voice. "We do not do things this way in our family. You may marry her. That is for you and her to decide." Then his tone of voice changed, became a little tighter in the throat. "After you are married, you decide, not her. You understand, yes?"

"Yes, I understand," said Palle.

"I am not against your getting married. We can talk about it when you come to New York. We can make plans. But going to Denmark now is out of the question. We don't do things like that."

"You realize of course that Lanuwobi and I, we—we know each other well. We stayed with each other in Haiti. I mean . . ."

"I don't want to hear about this. I never agreed with her mother about this. We will talk more when you come," Edner said warmly. It was an invitation.

Finally, in October Palle flew to New York. Everything was to be done in the proper way. Palle would stay at a Manhattan hotel, and Lanuwobi would stay out in Queens, and they would not spend their nights together.

Lanuwobi met him at JFK airport. She was with her sister, who was plumper and had neither the powerful black eyes nor the soft voice. She also had a more direct manner, and Palle could tell that she had spent more time in New York than Lanuwobi had. The three of them rode together in a taxi to Manhattan and up the elevator to the third floor of the Gramercy Park Hotel, to the moss-green suite where he stayed in New York. Lanuwobi and her sister padded over the spongy green carpet and tried out the green upholstered furniture and examined the view of Lexington Avenue while Palle sat on the edge of his queen-size bed and realized that the sister was a chaperon. In late afternoon, the two sisters left together for Queens.

The next day, they managed to get a few hours alone at the Gramercy Park, hours spent wrapped together in the roomy bed. Then she got dressed and left. And it remained that way. No evenings. No nights. Always just a few hours during the day. Wonderful little moments, but not enough. Events were inexorably drifting toward what Palle referred to as "a rendezvous in Queens."

Lanuwobi prepared him, cautioning, "You must wear a very nice suit. It must be very good quality. And you must have a tie." After consulting by telephone with Ernesto, Palle bought Belgian chocolates at Bloomingdale's and an enormous bouquet of purple irises and white lilies, and he put on a slate gray Gianni Versace suit and a gray-and-purple Giorgio Armani tie and struggled to slip, lilies and all, into the backseat of a taxi and was nervously on his way to Queens. Somehow at age fifty-six he was the boy-ish suitor he never had been called upon to be in his youth.

Palle and the taxi driver could not locate Edner's address. Many of the houses were new and a number of people looked Haitian, so it seemed to be the right neigh-borhood, but Palle was confused by the similarity of all the streets. "It's very amorphous out here," Palle told the taxi driver, who did not respond but rolled down his window and started making inquiries in Creole.

They found the house because they saw Lanuwobi and her father waiting on the curb. By then the taxi meter was up to fifty dollars. Lanuwobi wore a new silk dress, a coral color that set off her darkness. Standing a little back in the doorway to the house was potbellied Uncle Edner, the real uncle, looking so confident and gracious, so mar-velously in charge that for an awkward moment Palle could not decide to whom he should hand the flowers. He was warmly ushered into the living room, which was, as Lanuwobi had foretold, very new. The walls were a new wooden paneling that it took Palle only half a second to detect as fake, and all the furniture was covered in a heavy, shiny clear plastic. Everything was plastic, even the white siding on the house. Palle had never seen so much plastic.

He was ushered to a red couch, which made unpleasant noises when he sank into it. The plastic was very slippery against the silk-linen blend of his Versace suit. He felt as if he could slide right off if he did not sit carefully upright.

He was handed a glass of wine in a small glass with an elaborately shaped stem and ornate designs etched on the bowl. He thought this a very ugly glass. The wine was very sweet.

Edner and the father sat on plastic-covered chairs very close to Palle. The women—Edner's wife, their daughters, Lanuwobi's sister—distanced themselves toward the outer edge of the room. Lanuwobi had told him of how Edner's daughter had become a banker and how both girls had graduate degrees and even the mother had gone to university. But Palle never talked to them. They remained in the distance and they did not speak.

Palle asserted that he intended to marry Lanuwobi. He knew he had to sell his case, and he looked with great sincerity into Edner's eyes and said, "I love your daughter, and I want to take care of her"—in the distant edge of the room he could hear women giggling—"and . . . and make her happy." Then he remembered that Lanuwobi was not Edner's daughter, and he shifted his weight cautiously on the slippery plastic and looked into the father's worried eyes. "You know," Palle said, "I am quite a respected man in my country. You can verify this. I can give you a number to call at the Danish Embassy in Washington, and they will tell you—You can talk to the ambassador himself. He knows me. He will speak well of me."

Inside, Palle was laughing at the spectacle of himself pleading his respectability. Lanuwobi found a moment to throw her arms around him in the hallway and plant a secret kiss on his lips and say, "You are fantastic! They love this. And you look wonderful in this suit!"

Going back into the living room, he saw a look from one of Edner's daughters that made it clear she had seen the kiss.

In the end, Uncle Edner said, "You can marry her. This would be fine. And then you make the decisions, not her, you decide everything. You understand?"

"Yes, certainly," said Palle.

The worried father nodded eagerly.

"Yes, you will decide everything. But, of course until you are married, things must be done, you know, *comme il faut*. You understand?"

"Yes. I understand, but of course while I am here, I stay in a hotel in Manhattan—"

Edner held up a finger to silence him. He smiled generously and showed large teeth. "This is not how we do it in this family." It was clear that he would not discuss this subject anymore. Palle looked at the father. The father was nodding sternly.

"You are always welcome here to visit Lanuwobi," said Edner, standing up to dismiss Palle. "And let us know about the wedding plans."

"Yes, and then I will decide," Palle offered, trying to be agreeable.

"Then you decide everything," said Edner warmly, and he laid a thick hand on Palle's shoulder. Lionel followed with a light pat and a nod. Edner offered him a ride back to Manhattan in his taxi, which Palle was grateful for, not wanting to spend another fifty dollars. Before they left, Lanuwobi looked at Palle admiringly and told him how fantastic he was. The taxi had the same clear plastic seat coverings. On the way, Edner asked to see a copy of his divorce decree, and Palle promised to produce one, though he was not exactly sure of where to get a copy. After saying good-bye to Edner at the shady foot of Lexington Avenue, he had an odd sense of freedom, as though he had gotten back the right to his own identity. The fine cloth of his suit felt good against his legs. He chuckled a little with a thought, "They probably never even heard of Versace."

Palle and Lanuwobi did not see each other often in New York. He did not like going out to the house in Queens, and for her Manhattan was almost an hour away on the E train—an unkind underground world where people had their own music plugged directly into their ears. They hummed and tapped and swayed to hissing noises she could only guess at, and they never looked into anyone's eyes.

But sometimes Palle and Lanuwobi would have wonderful two-hour afternoons in the Gramercy Park Hotel. He could not remember any other woman making him feel quite so good, so powerful—then he would remember that he could lose her.

"Lanuwobi," he said, holding her, softly inhaling her from behind her ear. "We must undo all of this. Back to Haiti. I'll still marry you. Undo all of this. This is not what I thought."

"I told you back in Port-au-Prince you should have married me. That would have been simple," she said with reproach in her voice. Why had he put her in this impossible situation? she wanted to know.

Palle consulted Ernesto and was told that the next step was to become engaged.

"How do I do that?" Palle asked.

"You must buy a ring, " said Ernesto.

"A ring? What kind of ring?"

"An engagement ring, you fool."

Palle had not bought an engagement ring for any of his three wives. He had bought a wedding ring for his first wife but never an engagement ring. So on his next visit to Copenhagen he called on a friend, a well known sculptress who had exquisite taste, and they went to a goldsmith and had a ring designed—a simple gold band shooting off at a sharp angle toward three small tasteful diamonds. On his next trip to New York, while walking in the shade of Gramercy Park kicking leaves, he presented the ring with appropriate understated theatricality. But she did not open the box.

"What's wrong, Lanuwobi? This is an engagement ring."

"This is not how you give an engagement ring."

"This is fantastic! I never heard these things. How do you give an engagement ring?"

"You create an occasion. Then you give it."

Palle was not angry. When he used the English word "fantastic," he meant it literally, out of fantasy. He loved his life, that he could leave his Nordic world with its simple rules and become enmeshed in a society so complicated that no one could possibly master all its rules. "All right, I will create an occasion," he said agreeably.

But he did not really get to create it. He informed her family, and they arranged it at a family friend's apartment in Brooklyn. Palle, once again, was in a taxi with an enormous bouquet of flowers and once again could not find the building. Somewhere in Flatbush. The Chinese taxi driver was frightened. "Mister, mister," he cried each time Palle said, "Try this street here."

"Dark street. No good! Neighborhood no good." Palle decided he was right, and when they found the building, he paid the driver an extra ten dollars to wait while he made sure it was the right place.

When he entered the apartment, he was overwhelmed by a sense of being in the kind of surreal film he had studied but never made. He reported to Ernesto with awe in his voice, "The apartment was filled with strange objects from a taste beyond our horizons—strange strange glass things and cupboards with all kinds of porcelain."

Everything was large except the apartment itself. One room was almost entirely filled with a massive mahogany table. There were tall vases stuffed with enormous plastic flowers. On the walls were paintings in gold and linen frames of what might have been Paris except the colors were too bright. There were elaborate crystal pieces of no discernable function and chandeliers that perpetually tinkled like wind chimes because the ceilings were too low and there was always someone who had just brushed by. The Haitian woman whose home it was had an enormous, stiff hairdo, like the brittle nest of a large raptor, and could not get past the chandeliers even when she ducked. Her makeup was thick and almost stylized, and her eyes were painted into a shape unknown to nature. Her soft, fleshy arms, skin puffed and tucked like the limbs of babies, were decorated with dozens of bracelets. Even the buttons on her dress contained jewels. The entire home seemed like a huge, overdecorated cake. They sat around a gold-and-glass coffee table and sipped sweet drinks and then ate a dinner of *banane, griots,* and rice and peas—enormous porcelain bowls of everything devoured with the frenzy of the starving.

Then it was time for Palle's speech. Plump, well-fed faces, shiny and a little overheated from having eaten so hard, stared up at him. It was the presentation of the ring. Palle declared his love, which produced no particular reaction, and then his intention to take care of her and make her happy. The faces nodded. Then he took out the ring, and they strained around the table to get a better look. He heard one woman say *"trois"* approvingly because there were three diamonds, but the woman next to her responded with a shrug because they were not particularly large diamonds. Palle expected one of them to put a small scale on the table. But then, they seemed to know their stones, could probably measure without scales. He could see that Lanuwobi was not pleased by the ring. He later asked her about it.

"Well, it is very modern," she said.

"I thought you liked modern. You are always telling me that you like your uncle's house because it is modern."

"I like the ring," she said unconvincingly, and kissed him.

Palle wanted to keep the wedding, his fourth marriage, discreet and, if possible, out of the Danish papers. The Danish Consulate recommended a Danish minister at a church for Danish sailors on an affluent street in Brooklyn Heights. It was a pretty little church with only forty seats. Palle was pleased by the size. He had told Lanuwobi that he wanted a small wedding. "Only your *closest* relatives. Not all these people from Miami and wherever."

The minister was a young man, with great enthusiasm and crisp, open, Nordic manners. It was like being in Denmark. He invited them into a little room for coffee and cake. Lanuwobi was charmed by this coffee-and-cake ritual, but she thought this priest seemed so young and happy and informal and not at all the way a priest should be. The minister examined the divorce decree that Palle's son had mailed him from archives in Copenhagen and declared it "in good order." There was no need for a translation, which Edner had asked for, nor was there any blood test requirement as Edner had insisted. The requirement had been dropped in New York. They had only to set a date.

Palle, who had forgotten Danish ways, was not prepared for this. He had grown accustomed to complications. He started to become nervous. He had to do some filming in Haiti. The date would be after that. He would come back for the wedding. It would be in several months. After the shooting.

He never made it back for the wedding date. His mother died in Denmark, and he had to spend time in Copenhagen with his octogenarian father. Lanuwobi and Edner understood. This was a family matter. Palle had invested time, and he had forged an understanding with the family in Queens.

Palle would have felt less confident if he had ever seen one of the family meetings that Edner hosted every Sunday. Lanuwobi was placed on the plastic-covered couch, with her father staring mournfully at her from one stuffed chair and Edner imperiously from the other. Another uncle seemed to come over for the purpose of drinking beer, and he stood by the doorway to the kitchen to be as close as possible to the source. The women took their places on the outer edge of the room. It was very different from when Palle was there. Now the women weren't giggling. They were gazing sternly at Lanuwobi with their chins held high, so that they were clearly looking down.

"You will marry this white man and he will take you back to Haiti?" said Edner. "He must be insane. Back to Haiti. What kind of offer is this? What is he promising?"

"He wants to marry me," Lanuwobi said unpersuasively.

"But what is he offering?" Edner wanted to know. "Does he own a home in Haiti?"

"He stays in a hotel."

The room filled with clicking tongues and "oh oh's."

"So where does he own a home?" asked the father in a soft voice that still had an impact because he so rarely asked anything.

"I don't really—I'm not sure he does own a home."

"Anywhere?" said Edner, his eyes enlarged with astonishment. The room fell silent—a spell only broken by the hiss of a beer bottle being popped open by the uncle in the kitchen.

"What kind of car does he have?" Edner's wife challenged. The men stiffened and Edner glared but refused to look in his wife's direction.

Lanuwobi, with tears of shame giving a shine to her large eyes, had to admit that he rented his car also.

"I don't like the divorce certificate," the father announced. "I don't like it at all. What kind of language is it written in?"

"It's his language. It's Danish," Lanuwobi tried to explain.

Edner's round face turned to a kind smile. "Yes. It is written in Danish." Then he brought his large cantaloupe-shaped head very close to Lanuwobi and, still smiling, whispered, "How do we know what it says?"

"The priest is Danish too. He could read it. He said it was good."

Giggles exploded in tiny bursts around the outside of the room. Edner explained, "Lanuwobi, this is the way the *blans* are. He finds this priest. We don't know where. He just finds him. And by *co-in-ci-dence*"—he pronounced the word carefully, and not only the women but her father all responded with big, toothy, spitting laughter—"by coincidence, he turns out to be Danish too? And then he tells us that the certificate is good. Who is this priest?"

"Is he Catholic?" Edner's wife asked. This time Edner turned to make sure his wife received the glare.

"Lanuwobi," Edner said, turning back to her with a gentle voice, "don't you see that they are working together? That is the way the *blans* do things. What does he offer your children, this man with the secret language who owns nothing? What is there in Haiti for the children of people who own nothing? You have to stay in New York. You can get an education. You can earn money. Buy a home."

"Lanuwobi," said her father, "if you go back to Haiti, I will not be your father anymore." As he was saying this, Lanuwobi saw her sister in the back of the room, arms crossed, rolling her eyes upward contemptuously. Her sister did not like Lionel and always said that he had no right to call himself their father after all this time. But Lanuwobi liked having a father.

When Palle returned to New York, Lanuwobi reported all this to him. Now Palle understood. The minute he leaves, this is how they talk. This is why Haitian negotiations always break down. It was a mistake to negotiate at all. He could see that now. "I don't want to go out there anymore. You have to deal with them. I am not doing that anymore. I made the effort. I presented myself properly. Now that phase is over. Now we are on to a new phase."

"But what can I do?" Lanuwobi pleaded. "If I do something against them, they will never see me again."

"Against them?"

"Yes, if I go with you to Haiti against their wishes, then it is over. I will not have my family. They will never talk to me again." She stared hard into Palle's pale eyes. "What can I do?"

Palle, who always offered her solutions, said, "I want you to come with me. That is as simple as that."

"If I do that, I can never go back to them. And if you are not there anymore, if you die or leave me, where will I be? I will be in Haiti, left by a white man, with no family in America anymore. What security do I have? *Qu'est ce que je tire de toute ça?* What will I get from this? I started with nothing. I can't end up that way. I have to get something."

Palle understood. This was not a European conversation. It was part of the charm of their relationship. He did not want a European relationship. She expected something, and he could provide something. They each had their roles. That was why Ernesto thought prenuptial agreements were important. "Work out a solid contract," he often told Palle.

She never asked him for money, but they always talked a little bit about it. Edner had arranged for her to train as a nurse, and she was making a modest salary as a nurse's aide. Edner told her to be patient. "Soon you will be a full nurse. You can meet other Haitian nurses and start a fund. Before long you can buy a home. You can have things in this country. I didn't arrive here with a medallion, you know?"

But for the time being, her salary was very low, and Palle gave her money to help her. Whenever he offered the money, she took it. There was never a discussion. It was something she got. He would give her one hundred or two hundred dollars. Once, after not seeing her for a long time, he gave her five hundred dollars and told her to go shopping.

The problem was more complicated than a few hundred dollars. If she went back to Haiti for a visit, she would have to bring presents for her mother, her brother, other people. Good, expensive, American presents.

He could help her with that.

But if she went back to Haiti to live, she would have to bring something permanent with her—a diploma, a marriage to a wealthy man, something she had gotten in America. To go to America and come back no more of a person than when you left would be—it was unthinkable.

She wanted Palle to pay for her education in New York.

"Well, Lanuwobi," he said. "Education is very expensive in America, and I am not a rich man." This statement was a mistake because it meant that if she went back to Haiti, she would be returning with neither an education nor a wealthy marriage. But then he said something that not only made more sense to her but was much more honest. He said, "Besides, if I pay for your education, what do I get out of it?"

She nodded in agreement. He was beginning to understand. "There is another problem. Remember the five hundred dollars you gave me for shopping last time?"

"Yes."

"Well, I didn't shop with most of it. I sent it to my family. I do that sometimes when I can. And this is another problem."

"I don't see the problem," Palle said.

"You see, if I go with you to Haiti, I cannot send money from New York."

"Now, that's true. I can see that," he said, failing to repress an ironic smile. "You cannot send money from New York if you are in Haiti. What kind of money did you send to your mother?"

"I send forty dollars to my mother. Twenty dollars to one aunt and twenty dollars to another. Most months."

"That's not so bad. I could help you with that in Haiti."

She nodded. A problem solved. Although she knew that giving it in Haiti would not be the same, would not be as good, as sending it from New York, this was a workable solution. Both of them felt that a point had been won.

"And you know the beauty salon is still possible. Of course not right now. The embargo and no electricity. It is not the right time to start a business there. But later I think it could be a very good thing."

"Yes, I would like that, but—"

"But, what?" Another obstacle. He would have a solution. "What?"

"If I start a beauty salon in Haiti, I want to have an American diploma in beauty care."

"I see. Well, find out what it costs, for God's sake, find out. Maybe I could . . . But you know, I am not a wealthy man and I have obligations. I have kids in Europe, and I am still paying, and . . ."

"I know. You see, if you did not have all these obligations, I would not have hesitated one moment."

Palle understood this. And he understood that she was troubled by the fact that he seemed to have nothing. These were real concerns, and he would have to work on being more of a man of substance. He would have to offer her a life worthy of her return.

And then it landed as though fallen from a tree.

When he returned to Haiti, he learned from Ernesto that the Whitcomb House had become available. Whitcomb was leaving and wanted to rent his gingerbread mansion complete with staff, furnishings, and the art collection. With gun battles every night, an embargo by most of the world, and rumors of invasion, it was not expensive. Whitcomb just wanted someone to take care of his property. Ernesto made the introduction, and the lease was worked out. With great excitement Palle called Lanuwobi.

"Lanuwobi, I have just rented the most beautiful house in Haiti, the Whitcomb House. Have you heard of it?"

She had.

"It is huge, the most beautiful house in the country, and with servants to do everything. You can be like a queen here, an absolute queen! Come here. The staff will take care of everything. There is everything that you like. You will be taken care of. Waited on. You will be *Madame!*"

"Yes, it sounds like it would be all right."

"All right? Just all right!"

"But you don't own it."

"No," he said quietly.

"And that is exactly what my family would say. You don't own it."

"No, and I don't want to own it! This is perfect for me. It is my ultimate ambition to live in this house, do you understand? It is like a dream. I don't want anything else. I don't want to trade it in for a small house that I own."

"Well, a large house is nice. We will have to buy a lot of furniture."

"It comes with the house!"

"It is entirely full."

"It is perfect. Very nice furniture."

"But if the house is already full of furniture, it means that you can't buy furniture for your home."

"No. The furniture that is here is perfect. There is no need to buy furniture."

Palle did not despair. He had to leave for Europe soon, and when he came back in the fall, she would come with him to his rented mansion. It was a better life than her family could offer her in Queens. The cards were all moving back to his side of the table. He could see that she was growing tired of New York and her family in New York, and she missed her mother. She didn't like her nursing job and not having enough money to pay for an education. By next fall, she would be through with New York. Here they could play the game of living like the rich without any money.

"I think I can offer you a more interesting life, Lanuwobi. You come down to Haiti. I am not going to marry you in New York. I'm through with that now. You come here. I will show you a good life. Then we can get married."

Palle recognized that he was not a young man ruled by passions. He would make this work, or he would give her up. He did not have to *get* this woman. He was at an age when he looked at these things more philosophically. If she decided to stay in New York—which he doubted she would—he was content with the idea that he had experienced this, he had had pleasure with her and he had helped her, helped her in many ways. He could always feel good about that, even if she went on to a different life.

At last, Palle felt in control again.

In Copenhagen, his oldest son was supportive of whatever he wanted to do, but his second son, a law student, had confided in Palle's ex-wife that he suspected his father was being manipulated by Voodoo.

PART TWO: THE WHITE MAN LOVES TOO MUCH

She missed him. She missed her mother even more. And on days when she didn't see the television or read a newspaper, she missed Haiti. The American press was full of Haiti. The military hanging on. Photographs of corpses. Sometimes she recognized the neighborhood. One day she would recognize the body. She couldn't help looking. Haiti, poor Haiti. Edner thought no one should go back. But there was another Haiti she missed—a Haiti in which people knew how to talk to each other. These Americans had no manners. None. And she missed Creole. The people in Queens and Brooklyn had forgotten how Haitians speak, had lost both the poetry of it and the laughter.

As a nurse's aide she could send some dollars home from time to time. But she had to advance. She did not go to America just to change bedpans. Palle had said she should be doing something better, and he was right. Not that she minded changing bedpans. It is not such a big thing when you have lived your entire life in front of an open sewer. The bed baths of the old people were not that bad either. What she hated was the teeth. She would give them their meals. They would eat and then take out their teeth with parts of the meal still on them, and she would hold the teeth in her hand as she scrubbed them with a toothbrush.

Palle was adapting to life in his breezy urban mansion like an actor learning a new role for which he felt perfectly cast. He had his staff—the soundless Faustin, Eva, Jean-Jean, and a gardener he never saw. A "thunk" sound and a falling dead frond was his only knowledge of the gardener. Eva was the cook and housekeeper. She was a middle-aged woman, bony, with an angular face that looked like pure shadow beneath the kerchief that always covered her hair. Seemingly out of shyness, when white people spoke to her, she put her long fingers in front of her mouth and began to giggle. She was a good cook, or at least she knew how to cook Haitian for white people. Not too much pepper. Crushed bananas, the one Creole food the *blans* always liked, and lots of meat. Steak. Filet. They liked filet. Palle liked chicken, but she said, "Oh, no, *Mesié,* you should like filet. *M'fe sa bon.*" She made a good filet.

And so he ordered huge quantities of beef filet. He was afraid it would spoil, but she reassured him that it wouldn't and vanished to her kitchen with a timid giggle.

Sometimes Ernesto would come over for dinner. Sometimes he would bring his wife. Most of the time Palle ate by himself at the long white table on the ground floor porch below the gallery, sitting in the night breeze facing five empty chairs, eating by candlelight because the electricity was out. In the distance he would hear the cracking noises of murder in the slums, the army out for their nightly killing. The sound would make him miss Lanuwobi, and he would call her. It was usually difficult for her to talk in Edner's house, and they arranged for him to call her when she was on night shift in the hospital.

She wanted him to pay for schooling so that she could advance as a nurse.

"I don't think that is good work for you."

"It's the work I have."

"If I am going to spend the money, I would rather send you to beautician school."

"That is more expensive."

"It is a better investment."

She understood. He would pay for education that brought her back to Haiti. Not education that kept her in New York. This made good sense to her. She argued that Haiti needed nurses. This made sense to him.

After the phone call, Palle would go back to his meal at his long table. The house was full of cats and dogs. He did not know whose they were, and although he had never had pets of his own, he enjoyed having them around. They would circle the table and move ever closer until Palle tossed them scraps of food. If they became too annoying, he called for Jean-Jean, who would appear with a long twig that he would scratch along the tile floor heading straight for each animal, and they would scatter in fear. In time, Palle had only to pronounce the name "Jean-Jean," and knowing what was coming, they would all lope off to diverse unknown corners—all except one ginger-colored puppy with ears so long they almost swept the ground and feet like powder puffs that were too large for the skinny body. Palle had no name for this dog, the puppy who did not fear Jean-Jean's stick but loved filet, much more than Palle did. Palle, wishing he had chicken, would cut the beef in pieces and make the dog beg for them one at a time. "Ah, so you are the one who wanted filet."

The dog wagged his tail because he had heard the word "filet."

"If I were Haitian," Palle said, waving the morsel in the long shadow of the candlelit table until he felt the wet suede tongue of the puppy, "I'd swear this was a conspiracy."

These were his evenings—Palle, the five empty chairs, and the puppy in the candlelight, shadows shifting in the merciful evening breeze. Feeling alone, he would think out loud.

"To live alone and work, that's really—I have been

really happy with living alone and working." He pondered as he and the puppy chewed their filets. "There is something in solitude that clears the head. You can really think and do good work. I have been writing again." He cut off another piece for the puppy. "I would never get into a European marriage again. Marriage is only possible here in Haiti, where it can still be a romantic dream—I like the idea of having a black Haitian woman. I like to think of myself as a white man living here with a Haitian woman. Like Gauguin or something like that. The main thing," he said, holding out a piece of meat while the puppy stared at him intently, "is to avoid triviality."

In the shadows stood the quiet, patient Jean-Jean, struck with horror as he watched Palle converse with the dog. There were people who had these powers with animals. Faustin and Eva stayed in the kitchen so that they would not have to see the filet disappear.

After dinner, Palle would take a rum on the gallery upstairs—the puppy would follow him—drifting to sleep as he tried to read in the candlelight, wishing for electricity. Before going to bed, he would always remind Eva that he wanted mangoes for breakfast. Sometimes he would get them—sometimes not. There was never an explanation.

Friends from Europe came to Haiti, and he wanted to throw a dinner party in his splendid tropical home. "Eva, I am having people for dinner tonight. What can you make us?"

"Filet, *Mesié.*"

"Oh, good, very nice. *Nou vlè sank filè.* Okay?" and, uncertain if his linguistic adventure had been successful, he held up five fingers so she would know how many filets to prepare. "And, Faustin, lots of rum punch, okay?"

"*Pa womn, Mesié,*" he said, shaking his head tragically.

"How can there not be rum? I bought two cases."

"*Mais oui, Mesié,* but the rum did not come."

"Why not?" asked Palle, more curious than annoyed. He knew this would not be an ordinary, banal explanation.

"I am too old, *Mesié.*"

"Too old?"

"It weighs too much. *Oooo,*" Faustin said, elegantly tossing a hand in the air while holding a high-pitched note. "*Anpil, anpil,*" he moaned musically while rubbing his back. "I had an operation last year."

"What must I do, Faustin?"

"You must take back Prosper."

"Who is Prosper?"

"He is a very big boy. Very strong."

"No, I don't want any more staff here."

"*Oui, Mesié,*" Faustin said and started to walk away, showing only indifference and looking older and weaker than ever before. Palle stopped him and gave him a thick role of Haitian dollars, which he exchanged downtown every Monday morning from a woman who used to import scotch before the embargo. She made more money now on black-market dollars than she had ever made on scotch. Palle told him to order two cases of rum. "Have them delivered. They will deliver right to the kitchen."

"*Oui, Mesié.*"

The rum never came. Nor was there any filet for the dinner guests. They all went out to a restaurant in Petionville in a caravan of cars that was stopped by the army on the way back down the hill. The army pretended to search the cars for weapons with an exaggerated gravity to compensate for their certainty that nothing would be found. The army claimed to be putting down a rebellion, but no one had ever seen rebels. After a few minutes, they were allowed to continue. Palle got inside his gate before the shooting started downtown.

The next morning there were no mangoes for breakfast and there was no more coffee. Eva could not wash his shirts because there was no more soap. Palle hired Prosper.

As advertised, Prosper was a very large, strong-looking young man. He spent his days slumped in a wicker chair on the far end of the gallery waiting for someone to ask him to lift something. Palle had the impression that he was somehow related to Eva, but he wasn't sure of this.

Things ran smoother with Prosper in the chair. There were mangoes in the morning and rum in the afternoon. But his second dinner party was no more successful than the first. He ordered the filets from Eva, the rum from Faustin. He asked Prosper to open the gate each time a car arrived, because the big steel door was too heavy for Jean-

Jean. Everything seemed set, and yet . . . There was again no food, no limes for the drinks, and no mangoes the next morning. Instead, he was presented with a brick of cream cheese—green with mold.

Palle called Faustin over. "All right, what is the problem?" he asked, slipping a corner of buttered toast to the puppy.

"I run this house, *Mesié.*" Then with great pomp, as if delivering the curtain line of a bad English comedy, he said, "I am the butler."

"Yes, I understand that."

"I have always run this house. Thirty-two years."

"Yes, well, you do a fine job."

"It is my job to say who opens the gate. It is my job to order the kitchen staff."

"The kitchen staff? Eva?"

"*Mais oui, Mesié.* The kitchen staff," Faustin repeated defiantly.

🐓

Palle could not sleep that night. He lay in the dark wanting to read, but there was no light. Naked on an enormous bed in a room full of bright paintings that were now only black patches on a gray wall, he thought about Lanuwobi, about what they would be doing if she were here now. This life, he thought, is perfect, except for the Haitian woman. The white man and the island girl. If Lanuwobi did not want to play her part, someone else would. He should tell her that.

"She should realize that she is in danger of losing me!" he said out loud. His voice stirred the puppy, who stood up reluctantly and wondered what they should be doing now. Suddenly there was an odd hum. Then a breeze. It was the ceiling fan. The electricity was back. Palle reached and pushed the switch in the lamp by his bed. But it was still dark. He tried the lamp on the other side. Nothing. Haitian electricity, he thought. Like Haitian everything else.

Palle's third attempt at a dinner party went a little better. His guest worked at the shop that used to sell scotch and now sold dollars. She dusted the sample bottles, though not very often. He had thought of asking her for a haircut, but he did not want to trivialize these things. And maybe that wasn't appropriate for a bottle duster. But all he had to do was ask if she would like to have dinner in his splendid gingerbread mansion.

Faustin was nowhere in sight, and so he made the drinks himself. He knew that sooner or later, probably at breakfast time, he would have to pay for this transgression. But what was he to do? He wanted drinks. Nor did food arrive at the long table. He called Eva and she dutifully arrived and said several *"Oui, Mesié's,"* but the food still did not arrive. Palle went into the kitchen, which was easy to find, since it had the only lights in the darkened house. Why was this? he wondered. Everything was working in the kitchen.

"Generator, *Mesié,*" Eva explained.

In time, dinner arrived at the table, served by Eva and

Jean-Jean, somewhat grudgingly, Palle thought. Was a rebellion afoot in the house? He, too, had learned to look for intrigues.

In the morning, Palle took the bottle duster to her downtown home after a predictably scant breakfast. When he returned, Faustin was in the garden looking somber, which Palle recognized as his way of looking angry. Palle really was not going to stand for this scene. The staff did not like him bringing Haitian women here to sleep? That was not their business. He did not want a part of this very ordinary kind of thing.

"Faustin, you look unhappy."

"*Mais oui.*" The full octave slide.

"Why is that?"

"You were wrong, *Mesié*. You should not have done that last night."

"Well, Faustin . . ."

"We cannot wait on a girl like that. It is not right."

What! thought Palle. Haitians never disappoint. This is fantastic. Always a new rule. "Why is that?"

"She lives near La Saline. She is very low. Too low. It is not right to ask someone to serve someone lower than they are. You understand. You would not serve me."

"No, no, I see that. But it is not my job. If it were my job, I would serve you. You work for me. She is my guest."

"She should not be your guest."

"Listen, Faustin. There may be a woman coming to live here, to run the house."

"Lanuwobi is not a problem. She is a good-class black."
Palle wondered how he knew her name and how he knew her class and color.

When was Lanuwobi coming? He called her that night and told her that he was very unhappy about their relationship. "You should be with me. I am here."

"But you know I cannot come back with nothing. You could come to New York. You are an important filmmaker. New York would be good for you."

"New York is very expensive." He almost added that there he wouldn't be an important filmmaker. But he thought better of it. When Lanuwobi got off the telephone, she had to arrange herself so that she could do her rounds without anyone seeing that she had been crying. It was cold outside, and she was feeling very alone, and she missed the hot, redolent breath of teeming Port-au-Prince.

🐓

Sal Tenucci sipped San Pelligrino. It had no calories. Why should it? It was water. Tom Wilkins was talking. Tenucci hated having lunch with Tom Wilkins. He hated the way Wilkins could never just say something. There always had to be lunch. Then Tenucci had to figure out the calorie-free lunch or make himself pay for it at the gym. A half hour of hard labor for five hundred calories. He didn't even know Wilkins's title, but he knew he was corporate and he could not ignore him. Wilkins had an office with a view and would start thinking, and soon they had to have lunch.

While Wilkins talked—it was the warm-up talk—Tenucci allowed his mind to wander to the nurse. He kept thinking about the nurse. Just last night he had seen his aunt. She seemed fine, considering—considering she was dying. He didn't like to visit her. It made him feel guilty. When he didn't visit, he didn't feel guilty. He could not explain this odd reversal of conscience. But ever since he saw that nurse, he had been visiting his aunt more often.

All the way through the water and peppery arugula, Wilkins did not get to the point. Tenucci wondered what he could offer her. Production assistant? Something better. He could imagine her on camera—the eyes, the voice. No experience, though. Maybe a little spot. Weekend fill-in. Weather. Something like that. She was probably too black. They wouldn't buy it—Wilkins and all the Wilkinses in their offices would not take her. They would look at her and know why he wanted her and laugh. Nobody had anyone that color. They had coffee-colored, but not black. Skin like night. Soft looking. A luster. Like black velvet . . .

No. It would have to be something off camera. Too bad really, because she would look great on camera. Maybe she should do radio. Who did he know in radio?

He wondered what Wilkins had been talking about. Suddenly Tenucci heard him say, "Do you realize the whole news team is white men?" He had learned to sneer the right way when saying the word "men."

"I'm Italian."

"You're a producer. You're not on the air."

"Henry is Jewish. I think. Isn't Henry Jewish? 'Gross.' That's Jewish, isn't it?"

"Not good enough. It doesn't look good. It doesn't look—modern."

It is always like this, Tenucci thought. This pointless distrust of WASPs. WASP guilt and fear. It made them natural allies. They worry that we are thinking the worst of them. He liked them, liked Wilkins. "We have an opening on weekend weather," Tenucci suggested with disinterest.

Wilkins wasn't answering.

"We could find somebody for that. For weekend weather."

"Weekend weather. That's not much. It would have to be something really strong. A Spanish-speaking black-Chinese woman with a handicap."

"A woman. Yes. Say, a black woman." He tried to make "woman" sound as good as "man" sounded bad.

Wilkins was unimpressed.

"A Haitian woman."

"Now, that's something. Is she legal?"

"How do I know? She's beautiful. And she has a fantastic voice."

"How's her English?"

"Perfect. Just a little sexy accent. Somebody must have taught her English."

"Sexy?"

Tenucci thought so. But she would never go out with

him. He had tried everything. Big television producer. That seemed to impress her, but she wouldn't even let him show her around the studio. She said, "If you want to show me around the studio, you must offer me a job."

It was when he saw Eva hand two lightbulbs to Prosper that Palle began to rethink his position. He knew Prosper was off to La Saline. He had seen him selling everything from filets to laundry detergent. Palle did not want to argue about it. He did not want to spend his time negotiating the household budget. But the house was costing him much more than he thought it would. He was never going to be able to afford Lanuwobi's beautician school and beauty salon at this rate. He could save some money by going to Europe for a while. The staff did not like it when he went to Europe. It put them on a subsistence budget. Nothing extra to sell. No one to go to with a fresh order. It saved Palle a lot of money. Now he wandered the house and noticed that there were no lightbulbs. Bare sockets everywhere except in the kitchen. This was really too much. He would close up and go to Europe for a while and save up for Lanuwobi. It was getting hard with the embargo, anyway. Sometimes the house would not have water for days.

Palle did not yet know that Lanuwobi had become Lana Wobby. She did not know it at first either. They just did it. At a certain point in the broadcast the anchorman would turn to her and say "And how does the weather look, Lana?"

An excited letter from her mother insisted that she now realized that "Lana Wobby" was the name that had first come to her in the dream. She had failed to understand it. It had come from a box, which she now realized was a television.

These people at the television station lived at a faster speed than Lanuwobi had ever seen before. The men set their hair, and the women wore suits, and they all talked in loud, fast voices, and everything was possible. Whatever they did turned into money. They had the confidence of people with limitless futures. These were the Americans. This was the real America. It was exciting, but it was also frightening, because nobody was in control of it. Opportunity was riding people instead of the other way around.

The worst thing about the job was that often the news would be about Haitians. Dead Haitians. Murderous Haitians. Haitians flooded in hurricanes. Haitians in boats threatening America's coastline with unwanted immigration. Then, "And how does the weather look, Lana?" Poor Haiti. The *blans* could not be trusted. Uncle Edner was right. They would never understand the Haiti she missed.

Tenucci was not blind to this irony. He started keeping Haitian news off the weekend programs. It didn't look good. She still wouldn't go out with him. And it was hard again to visit his aunt.

Just like a Haitian, water was on Palle's mind. The air was hot. He couldn't shower. Every morning this week had been like this. He had to go to the hotel to use their water. Because water was on his mind, as he was leaving he noticed something he had never seen before. Running down the wide stone driveway, past the empty oval pool and the carefully gardened plots—slipping through a crack under the heavy black steel gate—was a garden hose. Palle started to walk down the driveway, and then he thought, no, this isn't the way to see. He, too, would use subterfuge. He turned onto the lawn behind the pool, past the gray trunks of royal palms with broad-leafed vines trained to climb them. At the outer wall of the property he found a thick, deep-green spreading tree and hoisted himself up onto one of the lower branches, and as he shimmied a bit to get a view over the wall, he noticed that this was—a mango tree. Not only was it a mango tree, but it was full of ripe mangoes.

But he did not have time to process this thought because he now saw something even more shocking. A long line went all the way down the street of people standing patiently in the hot sun holding buckets—green, turquoise, banana yellow, orange—glowing in the sunlight like a string of oversized Japanese lanterns. At the front of the line was Prosper with the garden hose, collecting money. He had a neat twist of the hose to cut off the water between buckets.

Palle thought about how far things had gone. How he used to drive his white car downtown, the white man coming for the poor black girl. And now here he was, the white man in the mango tree. He called all the staff together and told them that things were changing. "The water is for the house. There is no water to be sold. And I want a lightbulb in every socket. And there will be a budget for everything, and you will have to stay within that budget. I will start doing the shopping. I am going to go downtown today to buy rum." Even as he was saying these things, he was thinking how boring it was that he would have to spend his time on these things. But he wasn't a rich man. Not even in Haiti.

"And another thing, Eva. I like chicken. I want to have some chicken. I think Haitian chicken is very good."

Eva stared at the floor, her mouth covered with her long fingers, and said, "But, *Mesié,* the dog likes filet."

Oh, Palle admired these people, the way they always had an argument. You could never really corner them. The puppy stared up at Palle with a pleading face. "No. I think the dog can like chicken too."

In some ways Lanuwobi's job seemed perfect. Since it was only two days a week, she had time to take courses at City College. And the money was more than she had ever seen. Maybe more than Uncle Edner made with his medallion. And she was required to wear a new expensive dress each night. The job came with two dresses a week.

She was tired of taking the E train, and at one Sunday meeting suggested to Edner that she rent an apartment in Manhattan. From the edge of the room came the sound of women gasping.

Edner told her that it was foolish to pay Manhattan rent, that she should save her money and buy a house in Queens. Her father had a different idea. "You should help me to buy an apartment. Many years now I have been sending money to you and your mother. Now you have money. You should help me. I don't own anything. After I own something, I will save on rent and I can give the money to you, and then you can buy something. A father should own before a daughter."

Later, Lanuwobi's sister came up to her and said in a harsh whisper, "You give that Uncle Lionel money and I am never speaking to you."

"What can I do? He's our father."

"Not mine."

"He is. Besides, I have to answer him."

"Find something to say."

The following Sunday, Lanuwobi told her father, "I am sorry I cannot give you money. It isn't right."

"What do you mean? I gave you money when you were in Port-au-Prince."

"Exactly my point. You are not in Port-au-Prince. To send money to family in Haiti is one thing. But not to send money to Brooklyn. We don't do that. You have to be in Haiti."

Instead, Lanuwobi gave money to a cousin who wanted

to open a dress shop in Brooklyn. The shop did well, and Lanuwobi was paid a percentage. In only months, she had enough money for a down payment on a small apartment in Manhattan.

Palle sat at the end of the table in the dark. Faustin said they were out of candles. Palle had failed to put candles in the household budget. He poked at his Creole chicken with a fork. The best chicken in the world, he thought. In Europe they talked of "free-range chickens." But these tough little birds foraged in rural Haiti.

Things were going badly in New York. He had not foreseen all this. Weekend weather. Where but America would there be a job like that? She would irritate him in their phone conversations. "How are things there?" he would say.

"Cold," she would say. "Low of thirty degrees. With the wind chill it's twelve."

"I didn't call for the weather, Lanuwobi."

"I'm sorry."

Who called whom was also now an issue. She could call him for free at the station. At first he thought this was a very good idea because if there was one thing Palle enjoyed, it was getting free things from corporations. But Ernesto warned him that this was a very bad mistake. "The one who makes the phone calls controls the relationship." He could see that was true. He did not want to be pacing through his house wondering when she would call. He knew what kinds of things would be going on in New York. He knew about television producers and directors, fast New York men with huge incomes. She had probably already slept with a few of them. This filled him with a fury that he could only appease with waitresses from Petionville restaurants. They had to speak French to get these jobs, and so Palle was certain they were of a good enough class for his staff to serve them. He enjoyed himself on these nights, but in the morning he always wanted the girl out of the house as soon as possible. He didn't like the breakfast talk. He liked breakfast alone. He liked to be alone. So he could work.

He held out a piece of chicken in the dark, but the puppy showed no interest. It seemed as if the dog had not eaten anything since they stopped having filet. This made Palle laugh. They always won. Always. In the morning he would order some filet. Add it to the budget. Just a small amount for the puppy. He would be very strict about that. He could not let them win this point or he would completely lose control of the house.

Lanuwobi woke up at ten-thirty in her sunny bedroom in her good Manhattan building. Ten-thirty. The day was already half over in Haiti. It had not been easy to find an apartment she could afford in Manhattan. She was lucky. She only asked for two things, but they were hard to find— sunlight and closet space.

She had all week to study. Next semester she would take more courses. She could finish in three years. Then she would have a degree. And money in the bank. Would that be enough? Could she go back to Haiti? She could be with Palle. Why couldn't they buy a house? She did not want to be the *Madame* of a rented house. She didn't want to be a hairdresser anymore either. What would she do?

Sometimes she would fill in on weekday weather. She was paid well. They seemed to like her. They never forgot that she was Haitian. They joked about it and asked her about it. That was all right. She never forgot either. But she would rather have been speaking Haitian than about Haiti.

The only time she spoke Creole was on Sundays in Queens. And sometimes when she took a taxi, the driver would be just a few years out of Haiti—sometimes from her neighborhood—and they would speak the real Creole while the meter ticked.

🐓

Lanuwobi called Palle. He had told her not to, that he would call her, but she called anyway. Worse, she was calling from her apartment. Just paying for it herself. It was the same conversation. He wanted her to move back. She wanted him to move to New York. "Just until I get my education and save some money. Then we can move back."

"I don't know if you are ever moving back."

"Don't say that."

"It seems to me that you are very well set up in New York. You can find television producers and executives. Men with far more money than me. You don't need me in New York."

"I do."

"Why? What am I needed for?" He waited for her answer. He was sure it would be good.

"I love you. I want to be with you."

Palle was stunned. He hadn't expected this. No point of negotiation. Simply I love you? This was incredible. This was a different kind of offer. This was something he had to think about. For days he did nothing but wander the well-furnished rooms thinking about this. "I am not a romantic. I am not young enough for that anymore," he muttered. He looked at the floor. The puppy wasn't listening. He hadn't seen it in more than a day. He found Eva in the kitchen pulling stubborn feathers out of a chicken, the pull causing her sinewy arm to jerk each time.

"Where did the puppy go?"

"Prosper took it." No further explanation.

He went to Prosper's chair. Prosper pointed to the back of the lot. *"Se laba."*

Palle walked back to the kitchen with a confused expression. "Eva, what happened?"

Eva continued plucking. *"Mor."* Dead.

"Why? What happened?"

She looked straight into his eyes—something she had never done, maybe the first time she had ever really

looked into blue eyes. Were her eyes always angry? He
had never noticed before. Her face was full of menace.
But, her voice was gentle, like a voice coming from a different face. She said, "Sometimes you love a thing too
much and it dies."

"Let's have another sour."

Simpson was too limp to refuse. But Faustin announced
that there were no more limes. "It doesn't matter," said
Simpson, who had slowly melted into the wicker and
wanted to avoid seeing his friend once again embarrass
him with one of those colonialist outbursts. "I have to go."

Palle was relieved that he did not have to lecture Faustin
about the limes. "Well, what I wanted to ask you was—can
I get a green card?"

Simpson, slouched to almost horizontal in his wicker
chair, burst into an indecorous belly laugh; sounds roared
out and into the nearby fronds. He struggled for control.
"What on earth for?"

"It's just Lanuwobi, you see. If I were to go to New
York, I would keep this house. A lot cheaper while I am in
New York. But if I did spend some time there for a few
years—it's her family."

Another sizable noise wheezed out of Simpson. From
where Palle slouched he could not exactly see him but
could hear the chair squeaking as Simpson shook from
laughing. Palle started to smile. "The uncle says you have

to have a green card in America. I could argue, but I never win these arguments."

"The truth is—" Simpson started, but his shoulders began heaving uncontrollably, tears were running down his scarlet cheeks, and he could only wave his hand to indicate his inability to finish.

Palle was now doubled toward his knees and slapping the banister trying to gain enough control to speak. "You know, if I could get a green card"—he sucked in heavy air to form the remaining words—"I could drive a taxi," composure failing him, he squeaked out, "maybe even get a medallion." The two of them heaved with laughter.

After a few minutes' struggle, Simpson managed, "The truth is, Palle, your best chance for a card would be if you married her." And they both roared laughter that flew through the gingerbread up into the rusting tin-roofed turrets and to the tops of the royal palms.

It was the same day the mayor of New York gave her a public service award—a gesture toward Haitians or immigrants or blacks—three days before a commencement speech at a Harlem high school that had called her "a role model and an inspiration to African-American women" that she met with Tenucci.

"We are going to give you a new contract. Weekday." He said "weekday" the way Faustin said "butler." He put up his hands to stop her from speaking. "I know you're going to bargain hard for the money like you always do, and you will probably mostly win like you always do."

"No."

"What do you mean 'No'?"

"I'm going back to Haiti."

Tenucci slumped into his chair. "This is—it's a joke?"

She shook her head.

"You're going to give all this up and go back to Haiti? How are you going to go? They've canceled all flights. They'll probably invade. You can go in with the marines."

"Maybe."

"Hey, maybe that's an idea! Maybe we could . . ."

"No, I mean it."

"Why would you do that? I thought you wanted to finish your degree."

Lanuwobi turned her head away.

"What will you do? Will you do television in Haiti?"

"Too dangerous."

"My God, what are you doing? Why go back there?"

"You think I have a life here? You are all very nice. My job is very nice. But I don't have a home here."

"Lana, don't do this. You have everything here, Lana."

Lana, she thought.

On her way out, she passed a news executive coming in. He shrugged at Tenucci. "What?"

Tenucci shook his head. "Haitians," was his only reply.

Lionel told her once again that the family would be through with her if she went to live with Palle in Haiti. But she was ready to go. She would sublease her apartment to keep paying the mortgage and return as a partly educated property owner. She would come back better than she left, and she could work something out in Haiti. She knew Palle would never come to New York.

But Palle told her not to come. He had taught her English, taught her many things, taught her to drive, got her a visa. He could feel good about the experience. She was better off for having known him. She had gotten something. But he had thought about it a lot. He had talked it over with Ernesto. Everything had changed. What could he do for her? She didn't need him anymore. She just loved him. That is not the same thing. It would have been another European-style match. That was not what he had moved to Haiti for.

Tenucci had already replaced her. With a Japanese woman renamed to sound Chinese. But the new weekday position was waiting. There were always opportunities in New York. No manners, but opportunities. Maybe people with opportunities didn't need manners, didn't need to follow rules.

In a way, like Edner, she had gotten her medallion. Now she understood that Edner could never go home again *because* he had a medallion. She had nothing that she could take back with her. Palle had been her only way back to Haiti. If she went now, she would go as a woman thrown out by a white man.

Would Lionel really have rejected her? She believed he would have. He wasn't really a father. He and Edner were her family here. But they weren't her real family. Her real family, all the real things, were far away.

DEVALUATION

It was one of those December mornings when Rosita Pineda was about to emerge. Nelcida Martínez Menea gazed past her own weather-beaten shutters at Rosita's perfectly painted house—turquoise with red trim, just like their house. "The same paint, just fresher," her husband, Danilo, had pointed out in that annoying way of his.

Nelcida's husband, Danilo, was standing in the street talking to Alvarita, the witch. Alvarita was fat like someone who wanted to show off how much she had to eat. She smiled to show her gold teeth. You did not want to know how she got the money for all that gold. Why, Nelcida wondered, was Danilo consulting the witch? She hoped he was trying to get a little powder to put in Rosita Pineda's turquoise-and-red, freshly painted doorway. But she didn't think so. Rosita was their neighbor and their friend.

Danilo would not be wrong with a neighbor. He was a good man. Nelcida once again reflected on the fact that her husband was a good man, a better man than Rosita's husband, who had run off to George Washington Hikes and probably, no matter what Rosita said, had three women there and paid for them with cocaine. Everyone knew what went on.

Nelcida understood these things the same way she knew for certain that Rosita Pineda was about to come wiggling out of her freshly painted house. She would be wearing something new, and it would be very tight, not because she wanted everything to be tight, but because, according to Nelcida's theory, her husband in George Washington Hikes had not seen his wife in so long that he didn't know how fat she had become. This thought always made Nelcida laugh until Rosita came out and Nelcida was forced to admit that Rosita was one of those lucky women who only got fat in her bottom, which was exactly where men wanted you to be fat. Once Rosita was walking away from them in her New York clothing and Nelcida had noticed her good husband, Danilo, looking after her, his eyes clearly focused on the fattest parts, one eye on each.

Nelcida didn't have Rosita's luck. If she got fat, it would all be in her stomach. But Rosita didn't have a good man as she did.

And now Rosita did emerge as predicted, wearing something tight and new and bright blue that shined across her bottom. It was December and she had started to get the packages. Every December she would get packages from New York filled with clothes that were too small for her and more electronic games for their children—boxes and tubes and consoles and remote-controlled airplanes, cars, trucks, and boats. Their two-room house was furnished with these things. There was no table space left over. If Rosita wanted to put out a dish of mangoes, she had to put it on top of an electronic machine. When she laid out her New York clothes to decide what to wear, she had to lay them over electronic machines.

Nelcida and Danilo and the other neighbors didn't know exactly what any of these devices did. Most of them did nothing most of the time because usually there was no electricity. But everything was always kept plugged in, and sometimes at about ten in the evening the electricity would miraculously kick on. Everybody knew the exact moment more from sound than sight. Some lights would come on. There were three streetlights on their block, which, by the way, was a paved block. But the main thing that happened when the electricity came was that Rosita Pineda's house began heaving strange electronic beeps, bleeps, buzzes, and burps. And there was something that played the first three bars of "La Cucaracha."

The reason Nelcida had known that Rosita was about to emerge was that a package had come. Everyone had seen it delivered by a man on a motor scooter. Now she would have to come out and smile at everyone and talk about the weather before adding, "Oh, and I heard from Rafael!"

"Oh, well," Nelcida thought. "She has bad hair. She

probably had Haitians in her family." Nelcida took her position by the weather-beaten shutter, brushing her own smooth, Spanish hair so that Rosita, as she made her rounds, could see the difference.

Danilo had not wanted to talk to Alvarita at all, but because she was a witch, she could see his secrets. If someone like that wants to talk to you, you can't ignore her. Danilo had a bad tooth. He had felt it coming a few weeks ago. First his teeth all felt a little out of line, the way they do when you have been punched in the mouth. Then came the ache and sometimes a throb, and sometimes it would travel up the entire side of his face and jab in somewhere at the underpart of his brain so he could not think. He should get someone to pull it. Luis Manuel wanted one hundred fifty pesos to do it. That was the way everything was getting to be. One week's salary just for one tooth. If it had been in the front, he could have done it himself.

The tooth would have to wait until he had bought his family Christmas presents. He had to do that fast because everybody said they were going to devalue the peso again. If they devalued the peso, he would never be able to buy Christmas presents. Rosita would be next door with presents. Her children would have more gadgets, and Sonia on the other side would have presents for her children because her man was in Puerto Rico sending money, and Nelcida and their children would have nothing, or maybe worse,

Dominican things, because that was the best he could do.

His tooth felt like a metal bar wedged inside somewhere pressing against his face. All he wanted right now was to get out to the cane fields and get a cool glass of green cane juice. Danilo had been suckled on sugar, and it comforted him. The village he came from in the Cordilleras had no milk. All the babies were given sugar and water. It was as good as milk. When his own children had needed milk, he had been able to pay for it. But that was before the devaluations. If he had a baby now, he would probably give it sugar. Sugar soothed everything, even his tooth.

But first he had to talk to Alvarita. Since he could not get his tooth pulled, he did not tell anybody about it. But Alvarita could see it. He wanted her to give him some kind of leaf or powder to stop the pain, but Alvarita said that she could see that there was nothing wrong with the tooth. "It's a sign."

"A sign of what?"

And in a low, raspy voice she said, "A *curse.*" She always said it like that. She could never say the word "curse" normally. She liked to scare people. It was a way of controlling them. Danilo was a policeman, so he understood.

"You will never get rid of it by losing the tooth. You have to lose—the *curse.*" According to Alvarita, the only hope was to kill a cat, and she made a motion with her fat hands like opening a stiff jar lid, which was supposed to mean twisting a cat's head off, which, it seemed to Danilo, was probably impossible to do.

He passed Beni and his brother. Beni's brother was nineteen and muscular, with skin the color of good leather, and always had a stack of pesos that he counted in silence, as though daring someone to take it away from him. Beni was nine years old, small and cheerful. He always said, "Hey, Danilo, good luck today." Then he winked. Beni was a nice kid, but Danilo didn't like the wink. He knew Beni worked with the army, and though he knew Beni hated them for taking his money, you couldn't trust somebody who worked with the army.

He was the last to get to the post because he had to get cane juice, cool and grassy, which he swirled around his tooth and held in his cheek until he had only a vague ache. It was a good post, a broad traffic circle on the highway between Santo Domingo and San Pedro de Macorís. Everyone who went to the Free Zone, where the women sewed and connected wires for the American companies, had to go that way. The company owners, the bosses, men with money in their pockets, would come flying through that good, straight, flat road past the cane fields, looking like one of Alvarita's curses—with the yellowish smoke from the harvesting cane fields swirling furiously in the headlights, circling out of the way of the oncoming car— and then suddenly, with no warning, the car would reach the circle and the tires would moan as the driver downshifted to make the curve. Then, while he was slowing down into the curve, they had him.

Danilo or one of his two partners would go out onto the

road and motion for the car to stop. Sometimes the car kept going. Danilo and his partners were not about to waste their gasoline chasing after it. They would sit and wait in the circle, surrounded by the cane fires whose smoke smelled like vegetables roasting in caramel, and try to flag down the slow ones. At the end of the day they would siphon off the tank and sell the remaining gasoline. They would get more gas from the police garage. The whole beauty of this spot was that cars had to slow down, so it was easy to stop them without using up gasoline.

There had always been something not quite right about Danilo, his partners thought. He hadn't even wanted to do the speeding ticket business until after the second peso devaluation. He must have been the last one in the department. When Danilo's partners stopped someone, they would tell the driver he was speeding and tell him he had to pay a two-hundred peso fine. Sometimes the driver would pay it, but usually he would just hand over fifty or one hundred pesos. Sometimes the driver would argue, and it would get into bartering. "No more than fifty pesos."

"I'm sorry sir, the fine is two hundred pesos."

"Here, take one hundred."

They would always take it.

Danilo had a different way of operating. He would stop the car and say, "You were speeding. Let me see your license, please." He would stare very intensely at the driver's license, comparing the photo with the actual face, back and forth as though there were a checklist. Eyes, two. Check. Nose, one. This always softened them up. It reminded him of the way Alvarita said *"curse."*

Then he would say, "You have to pay a fine."

Up to this point, Danilo's partners admired his work, but then came the part that really provoked them. The driver would ask how much the fine was, and Danilo would always say, "It's Christmastime. I have three children. Give what you can." And they would give anything from a few coins to a few hundred pesos.

His partners did Danilo impressions. This little nasal voice pleading, "It's Christmastime; give what you can."

"Jesus Christ, Danilo," they would shout as the driver left. "We're suppose to be the fucking cops!"

But Danilo always argued that it was important not to get anybody angry. "They could make a complaint. If they make a complaint, the army hears about it. If the army hears about it, you know what happens."

They did know. If the army learns about a good spot, they take it away from the police and use it themselves. They had paid two thousand pesos to get this spot.

They got their spot at Christmastime, but only Danilo was trying to buy Christmas presents for his family. To his partners this was further evidence that Danilo was not quite right. It was normal for cops to grab a little extra in December for Christmas with their families, but a beautiful spot like this that cost the three of them a real investment—who would use that for Christmas presents? They were going to use the money to leave and get work in dollars and send it back. Danilo should do that too. "Next year, your family can have lots of presents," they would say. "And you won't have to worry about devaluations either. The lower they drop the peso, the richer you get. Think about that."

Danilo would say, "Listen, do what you want. You go somewhere else and you are as good as a Haitian. You have to stay in your country and work and give things to your family."

Danilo knew exactly what to buy with the money. First of all, Nelcida would get something blue. It had to be blue. He saw that this morning. And the boys would get battery-operated toys. Things that worked without electricity. Their house would buzz even during the blackouts. And the youngest boy would get an M-16 he had seen. If he could get it before the devaluation, it would only be two hundred forty pesos. It looked exactly like the real M-16s that the army sons of bitches had. And it came with three clips that you could put in and take out. His youngest boy had wanted an M-16 ever since Danilo had told him how the boy's grandfather had been shot in the foot with one by an American marine in 1964.

By Kings' Day, when Danilo would be giving his family presents, his partners would have to already be across the passage. In January, the sea got too rough to cross. Before then, they would have to raise enough money to pay for the *yola* and have enough left so their families would be all right if they didn't get anything to them for a while. They spent much of the day arguing about how to tell a good *yola* from a bad *yola* and what was a fair price. "Never make a deal with a green-eyed *yola* man. You will end up at the bottom of the sea," one said.

"Just make sure they don't have tar on their pants. It shows they have been patching the boat."

"You want someone who doesn't patch his boat?"

Another topic was whether to stay in Puerto Rico or go on to New York.

"You can make good money in Puerto Rico."

"You make better money in New York, asshole."

"You go to New York and you are spit on by Puerto Ricans."

"So, you think you aren't spit on by Puerto Ricans in Puerto Rico, you faggot?"

"So, dumb shit, why travel all the way to New York to earn dollars and get spit on by Puerto Ricans when you can do both just on the next island!"

The two would get so involved in these debates that they would seldom notice an oncoming car, and invariably Danilo would be left to flag down the car and go through his procedure. Then the others would hoot and start doing their Danilo impressions.

Sam Ellis was happy to be back. He loved this place. When people asked him, he could never explain it. Sometimes he thought it was just that he was the only one. No matter how squalid and miserable Haiti got, everybody loved it. Shouldn't someone cross over and love this place too? Sam Ellis did. He was first here as a Peace Corps volunteer and had since come as a human rights advocate, an adviser to an urban planning firm, an election observer. But it was getting harder every time. He hadn't been down in more than a year when he learned that a group of North American union leaders wanted a report on labor conditions in the Free Zones.

The union leaders had not given him much of a budget. The urban planners had been better. Now he had to stretch out a small stipend twice as far as intended. It would take time to find out what was really going on in these Free Zones. He wasn't going to do a quick job just because the budget was small.

For the moment, he was wandering on foot in the old colonial zone, enjoying being back. For lunch he would go down to the Malecon and have crabs and rice and beer for only fifty pesos. With the devaluation, it was less expensive than last year. That was one break in his favor, anyway.

Beni's brother walked up alongside Sam Ellis and whispered nervously, "You want to buy pesos?"

Ellis waved him away.

"I'll give you fifteen hundred."

Last time he went for crabs and rice on the Malecon, it was 30 pesos, which cost him about $7.25. Now it was 50 pesos, which would cost him about $6.25. But if he changed on the street, it would cost him about $3.30. And what did that mean about his hotel if he paid cash? Or even his car rental. He couldn't calculate right now because Beni's brother was whispering numbers in his ear. "For one hundred dollars you get fifteen hundred, or for two hundred dollars you get—I'll make it three thousand pesos. Maybe thirty-one hundred pesos. For three hundred I can—"

"How much for fifty dollars."

"Sorry, there is a one-hundred-dollar minimum."

Sam wanted to see how this worked before he put out too much money. But he liked this kid with his minimum. He made him laugh. "What are you? American Express?"

Beni's brother laughed. "Do it for three or four hundred," he said, patting Sam on the back. "You stay around here? How long are you staying?"

Sam loved these people. "Okay, I'll change two hundred for thirty-two hundred pesos."

"Thirty-one hundred!" Beni's brother protested.

"No, thirty-two or nothing," Sam insisted.

"Shit," said Beni's brother. "You guys. . . . Okay, let me see the two hundred dollars. How long are you staying?"

"Let's see the thirty-two hundred pesos," said Sam. Reluctantly, Beni's brother took out his thick stack of pesos and skillfully counted out thirty-two one-hundred-peso notes, folded them over with professional finesse, and handed them to Sam, who counted them again while Beni's brother tried one more time, "You staying here long?"

Sam Ellis took out four fifty-dollar U.S. bills and handed them to Beni's brother just as Beni came running down the quiet old colonial street rebuilt for tourists who had not come. "Mister. Mister!" shouted Beni almost out of breath. Then he turned to his brother. "You are so stupid. Are you crazy standing here changing money? The army is coming." Indeed, there were a number of bored soldiers in green, dragging weapons as if they were mops, drifting their way.

"Maybe this is not a good idea," said Sam. "We stood here too long."

"You are still standing here!" Beni whispered hoarsely. "This is stupid." Sam suddenly realized how foolish he would look criticizing Free Zone management if he were arrested for black-market money changing, so he slipped the pesos back to Beni's brother, and Beni's brother slipped the dollars back to Sam. "Maybe later," said Beni's brother as they both shoved their own money back into their pockets. "How long are you staying?"

"I don't know. Awhile."

"Come on!" said Beni, pointing at the soldiers. Beni's brother and Sam Ellis walked quickly in opposite directions, leaving Beni standing there.

By the time Beni and his brother met with the army to give them their twenty percent, Sam Ellis was back in his hotel examining the one-dollar bill with one-peso bills folded inside.

Beni's brother took out a fifty-dollar bill and a ten-dollar bill. He showed the lieutenant the fifty-dollar bill and handed him the ten-dollar bill, saying, "I got a fifty off of him." The lieutenant slapped him on the left ear. "You think I am stupid?" He grabbed Beni's brother by the right wrist, twisted it until the boy was kneeling, took both bills out of his hand, and walked away.

"Shit," said Beni's brother, rubbing his ear as he stood up. Beni reached up and patted his brother on the back. "That's the problem with the military. You know that. They're not honest, the fucking military. That's what's wrong with this fucked country. You know that."

There was a trumpet blowing one long suspended note in Beni's brother's left ear. He only heard Beni's voice as though in the distance, from the other side of his head.

It was dark and the electricity had not yet come on when Danilo got back to the neighborhood swishing fresh, cool green cane juice in his mouth from a thin plastic cup. A slight rustle in the trees, the hum of a few men's voices in the street, and the occasional clang of a pot, a baby's wail gathering force like a hand-cranked siren—these sounds stood out because it seemed so quiet in the dark.

It had not been a bad day. When they split everything three ways, including the gasoline they sold off—almost a full tank—they had so far brought in enough to earn back their investment. Tomorrow would be the day they would begin making a profit. Danilo's tooth made him feel as though his whole mouth were being crushed and distorted.

Profits. He felt almost certain that if he looked in a mirror, he would find his mouth completely askew. Tomorrow the profits would start. If only there would not be a devaluation, not just yet. He wondered if Alvarita knew how to stop a devaluation.

Nelcida was trying to cook dinner on a charcoal grill. The bottled gas they had been using had gotten too expensive for a policeman's salary. They were back to charcoal or even wood, just like in the mountain village where Danilo was born. He remembered his excitement when he had heard that in the capital, where they were going, people cooked with gas. He could not imagine what gas was. His mother had explained that it was something that burned but you couldn't see it. One of the wonders of the capital, now vanished, through devaluation.

Five minutes of rain at six o'clock had been just enough to find every loose seam in the tin roof, and the charcoal had somehow gotten wet and would not burn. "Maybe there is some wood in the neighborhood," Danilo suggested.

Nelcida looked over at Rosita Pineda's freshly painted house, so shiny that even in the dull moonlight of this cloudy evening there was no missing the fact that it was fresh paint. "Maybe Rosita has wood."

"Only plastic. Everything is plastic."

"She should tell her man in George Washington Hikes to send machines made out of wood next year. Then they could be used for something." She smiled triumphantly, but her joke was ruined by a glimpse of Rosita in her house. She was cooking on a gas burner.

Danilo went out to the paved street where the men leaned against the lampposts and passed the dark, quiet evening whispering. No one felt like talking in a full voice with the electricity out. It seemed as if they tried to go easy on their own energy until the power came back.

The reason that the street was paved and had three streetlights on tall metal posts was that the families on the street backed the government. No matter how bad things got in this government neighborhood, as the men stood in the dark and talked about the prices, the devaluations, the blackouts, the shortages (sometimes it was even hard to find sugar in the stores), sooner or later someone would scrape his shoe along the blacktop and say, "Well, he paved the road." It started as a serious point; then it became a joke; now it was just something you said, a meaningless traditional refrain. They had moved on to other jokes, like smacking the metal post of the unlit street-light and saying, "He gave us something to lean against, anyway."

Suddenly there was a whirring noise, and the throb of a distant merengue, and blops and beeps and "La Cucaracha" from the Pineda house, where purple and orange lights flashed and tiny little vehicles left their ports and zipped across the wooden floor and crashed into walls. Bare white lightbulbs illuminated the green interiors of the houses, and two of the three streetlights came on, and—most important of all—fans started moving the warm heavy air. The men returned to their homes to enjoy a few hours of electricity. Danilo had been thinking that if Christmas went all right and he could keep the good spot, perhaps he could buy a gasoline generator and run it off of the gas he siphoned instead of selling it at the end of the day.

The electricity lasted only thirty minutes that night, but the stab, blunt as a screwdriver, in Danilo's jaw lasted all night and would not let him sleep. In the morning he passed Alvarita without speaking. She puffed up one cheek, pointed to it, made a meowing noise, and then twisted her fist and clicked her tongue like the sound of something snapping.

Sam Ellis didn't even allow himself to think about the two hundred dollars he had stupidly lost. He would make it up in other ways. He rented the cheapest car he could find, a powder blue lightweight pickup truck from a local rental agency. The Dominican press had gotten interested in his project, and he was giving interviews, particularly bearing down on one shadowy figure named E. J. Tyler who had opened up three different assembly operations in the past sixth months. In one plant where they had demanded he lower the quota for overtime, he had fired all three hundred workers. He said he lost his contracts. A week later he announced new contracts and hired a different three hundred women.

E. J. Tyler did not like Sam Ellis, whom he had never met. He had read about him in newspapers. The articles had made him angry. He was bringing jobs to the Dominican Republic. He called some friends in government and arranged to deliver a speech entitled "Duty Free Zones, the Engine of Dominican Development." Then he got into the luxury car he rented when he came down to visit the plant, rolled up the windows, turned the air-conditioning up full, and sped off to San Pedro. The day before, he had been stopped for speeding. The cop had wanted two hundred pesos but seemed happy with one hundred. With all the devaluations, one hundred pesos was nothing, and it seemed he would be stopped no matter what speed he went. So he might as well go as fast as he wanted.

Danilo could not concentrate on his work. The cane juice wasn't working. The electricity had been off too long, and the juice vendor had no way to keep it cold. He buried it in the field by the side of the road and hoped the ground would keep it cool. The juice was siphoned up through a rubber hose, exactly as they did with the gasoline. Out of habit, he even spit out the first mouthful when he primed the tube. But the lukewarm cane juice did not help Danilo's tooth.

Normally, in Danilo's line of work, when you see a big waxed rental car like E. J. Tyler's rocketing toward you, you jump into action. These were the kinds of cars that paid. But something else caught Danilo's attention as he stood in the circle, his tooth feeling the bite of something prying into his jawbone, watching E. J. Tyler's big car push away the cane smoke and shoot toward him. From out of the cane field came—was it a mongoose?—no, a cat, a black cat running right out in the road in front of the fast-cruising rental car. The cat stopped a fraction of a moment to assess and then made the remarkably bad decision to try and make it across, reaching with its body in huge strides, then snapping together and reaching again, stretching its elastic stride right in front of the new thick-treaded tires.

"Would this count?" Danilo wondered, crossing himself and hoping for the worst.

But as if the cat were only made of air, it just kept going and disappeared into the field on the other side of the road as the car squealed around the circle, downshifted, and got back on the straightaway to San Pedro.

"Hey, Danilo, you sleeping?" said one of his partners. The two partners were lounging in the car slouched down, the doors open, debating unlucky numbers. "I'm just saying, if you don't want to end up on the bottom, don't get on a *yola* on the seventh, fourteenth, or twenty-first."

"Listen," said Danilo. "I have a problem with a bad tooth. Why don't one of you take the next one?"

"You take the next one. We will take the one after."

The next one was perfect. A good quality rental car driving slowly down the highway. The ideal candidate for a speeding ticket. Danilo signaled him to stop. But after he gave his Christmas speech, the driver looked at him angrily and said, "Give what I can? You mean you want a bribe!"

"No, sir," insisted Danilo, feeling threatened. "We are not allowed to take bribes. This is a speeding ticket."

"In cash."

"Yes, please."

"So it's a goddamn bribe. Here take a hundred pesos bribe. I don't care."

"No, sir, I cannot accept a bribe. Only a—"

And at that second the driver snapped the hundred peso bill out of sight and said, "Fine. Don't take a bribe," and put his car into gear and left.

Danilo's two partners started smacking their heads with their hats in comic frustration. "Danilo, Danilo, Christ almighty." And they went into Danilo impressions. "*OOHH!* No, I can't take a fucking bribe!"

Danilo explained that they had to be careful with people like that, but his partners weren't listening. They would take the next car. Only the next car didn't look very promising. It was traveling slowly enough, but it looked like a local truck, just some little powder blue pickup truck. They wouldn't have stopped it at all except that it was going so slowly that they had time to see that the driver was a Yanqui. They weren't going to take less than two hundred pesos. They had to show Danilo how to do it.

Sam Ellis thought, this is exactly the kind of thing that is rotting this country. It's everywhere, and people have to start saying no. So he refused to pay.

"If you don't pay, you will be arrested."

"Good, and you can go to the U.S. Embassy with your superior and explain all about the two hundred pesos. I wasn't even driving fast."

"I say you were."

"Fine, you tell your story, and I will tell mine." He crunched the stick shift until he found first gear and drove off.

"Those are exactly the kind of Yanquis you have to be careful about," said Danilo.

Three mornings later, Danilo was leaving for work, and Beni, instead of winking and wishing him good luck, reached up to tap Danilo's shoulder. "Hey, listen, I think I heard something. Some Yanqui complained. This one sounded really interesting to the sons of bitches in the army. I think they were talking about your spot."

So that was it. He had warned his partners. He knew exactly which Yanqui it was. Never stop a Yanqui with a bad car. Alvarita was probably right. He probably was cursed. The devaluation would probably come today too.

They worked hard that day, thinking it could be their last chance. At three in the afternoon they stopped one of those big expensive rentals. He was going fast, but now they were even stopping speeders. Danilo stuck to his proven technique. "It's Christmas; if you could just give whatever you can. I have four children." (He added the fourth for effect. He was desperate.)

"Is that right?" said E. J. Tyler. "And those two are your partners? Why don't you bring them over here." While Danilo was talking his two partners into getting out of the patrol car, E. J. Tyler fumbled underneath his new guayabera for his wallet. He handed two U.S. one-hundred-dollar bills to each of the three of them, wished them Merry Christmas, and then, as an afterthought, gave each of them one of his business cards. As he drove off he thought to himself, "No son of a bitch is going to go around this country—my fucking island—calling me a cheap bastard." The three policemen stood in the road, their eyes shifting from the bills to the card to the last shadows of the dark rental car vanishing in the opaque clouds of cane smoke.

A few days later, Danilo's partners were gone and Danilo was reassigned in the capital. He drove by the spot one day and saw the army was there. But it didn't matter. U.S. dollars were devaluation-proof. And Beni could get him a good price on pesos. He bought boxes of presents for his family. The one disappointment was that there were no more M-16s and he had to settle for one with curved clips. The salesman explained they were better. "The Cubans use them." But his father wasn't shot in the foot by a Cuban and he couldn't tell the boy that this was the same kind of gun with which they shot Grandpa in the foot.

Still, he had done it. He even got his tooth pulled by Luis Manuel for one hundred fifty pesos, which only cost him eight dollars. It was like being a Yanqui. And there he was a Dominican man, still living in the Dominican with his family, bringing home presents for Christmas. He felt like a man, the way his father must have felt in the days when he could grow crops.

Nelcida was trying to start the meal, fanning the charcoal. They weren't making the charcoal right anymore. It just didn't burn right. She could see Rosita, the frizzled nest of bad hair glowing blue in the light of the gas burner, where she was cooking her dinner. "Danilo, how much money do they make in George Washington Hikes?"

"Who knows."

"I wonder how much you could save if you went there for just maybe six months."

Danilo felt a sting like what he had felt when he was a boy and his mother slapped him. He walked over to her. "Would you want to be like these other women without your man here looking after things?"

Nelcida Martínez Menea gazed past her weather-beaten shutters at the perfectly painted house of Rosita Pineda. "No, Danilo. You are a good man," she said.

THE UNCLEAN

An odd and angry impulse periodically overtook him, to just once grab a handful of big pink shrimp and jam them into his mouth in front of everyone.

It was a beautiful place, Rabbi Ben Berman thought. Perhaps because it was more beautiful than his native Philadelphia, he was completely blind to the fact that the entire island was desert—nothing more than limestone sticking out from the sea. It rose only a few feet above the water at its highest hilltops and was covered with scrubby brush and tough trees that needed little water and could bend permanently in the wind, giving the island a sideways look like a sprayed hairdo that had been blown off center. Yet to Berman, it was beautiful.

He could ignore the oil refinery whose smoke was decaying the tombstones in the Jewish cemetery. He liked the old Dutch buildings, especially the synagogue. He liked being the rabbi of the oldest working synagogue in the Americas, and he appreciated the community's old traditions, the beauty of their Sephardic rite, which seemed more lyrical than the Ashkenazic ways with which he had grown up.

To Ben Berman, the only thing wrong with the island was that the food was all unclean. The island produced goats, but who ate goat? There were also pigs and chicken. Pork, of course, was out of the question. The chicken would have been all right if it had been killed according to the laws. When Berman first arrived, he talked to Emmanuel Gomes-Peres about this.

The Gomes-Pereses had been on the island for more than four hundred years. At least the Gomeses had. There were no more Pereses, and a Gomes had added his wife's name to keep the name on the island. The Gomes-Peres family owned the largest bank and were thought to be the island's wealthiest family. This may not have been the truth, but they were the wealthiest Jewish family and no one believed anyone could be richer than a Jew.

It was Manny Gomes-Peres who had first invited Berman to the island and offered him the position of rabbi. When the new rabbi arrived, Manny brought him to his air-conditioned, modern, one-level home outside of the city. It could have been a home in Philadelphia, with its thick carpeting and well-stuffed furniture. But the mezuzah on the doorway was eighteenth-century, as was the brass menorah in the glass case.

Manny mixed drinks, and Sarah led the rabbi to a squishy couch into which he sank so deeply that he felt helpless. The Gomes-Pereses were handsome, dark-eyed, olive-skinned people with expensive clothes and good, soft leather shoes, and Berman, who had nothing to wear but dark suits, suddenly realized that he never polished his shoes. Did these people polish their shoes, or did they throw them out when they got scuffed?

Sarah was explaining the pictures of their children on the table—which one was at MIT, which one at Harvard, and which at the University of Pennsylvania—but Berman kept thinking about the polished shoes. Suddenly, a young black man appeared with a tray, and Berman couldn't help wondering if that was who did the shoes. The man held the tray in front of him, and Berman, immobilized deep in the cushions of the couch, looked with horror at the offering.

Arranged in pink-and-white swirls, like the brush strokes on a Van Gogh painting, were large, peeled shrimp.

There was no compromise on this one. Deuteronomy: Chapter 14—"Whatsoever has no fins or scales, you may not eat; it is unclean to you."

"I'm sorry," said Berman. "I—I can't eat that."

Manny came toward him, his loafers squeaking as he stepped and his glass of scotch making friendly tinkling noises. "Allergic, huh," said Manny, as he handed Berman a scotch.

"No. It's not an allergy. It's *traif*. I can't eat shrimp. Actually, I'm very sorry, but I won't be able to eat anything here. I'm kosher. I assumed that you were."

Sarah and Manny smiled at each other.

"I'm sorry, I don't mean to offend you."

"You're not offending us at all," Manny said with a reassuring pat on Berman's shoulder. And, in fact, the Gomes-Pereses were not at all offended. They were charmed. They were pleased with their choice. The new rabbi was so quaint. So authentic. It was marvelous.

"I don't suppose you know where I can get my kosher food."

"This is not Philadelphia," said Manny, laughing. "There is nothing kosher here."

"Nothing? So no one in the entire community keeps kosher?"

They both smiled as they shook their heads in the negative. They were charmed by the rabbi's shock. Apparently he had really thought they would be kosher. He would see that there was nothing to eat but pork and shellfish. You could forgo the pork, but not the shrimp and lobster from Venezuela.

"What about chicken?"

"There's chicken everywhere."

"But not supervised slaughter."

The Gomes-Pereses laughed. Later, they told others in the community, the Mendes-Samuels, Dr. Gonsales-Levi. They all laughed with approval. How wonderful the new rabbi was, searching for kosher food on the island. And they all thought it would be great fun if the rabbi tried to talk one of the chicken farmers into kosher slaughter. Manny Gomes-Peres had the idea of John Blades.

Island chickens were lean and tough and not much in demand. John sold chickens to the Caribee Restaurant and to almost no one else. It was the only restaurant that specialized in island cooking, the only place left—the last eatery where locals could get a bowl of *giambo* and hot *coo-coo* with okra or a goat *stobá*. It was the kind of food that not many people knew how to cook anymore. But everybody's mother had cooked it, and people still remembered. Dozens of locals went there every day for lunch, crowding around the Formica tables, eating the day's special. The Tuesday special was John Blades's stringy chickens, which to Caribee customers seemed to have twice as much flavor as fat, off-island chickens.

Blades came on Thursdays for warm *coo-coo* and *giambo*, thick and peppery and not too slippery with okra, and he stayed around the table later joking with the others and with the owner, Maria Johns. Blades, after his second beer, would wonder what it would be like to live with a woman who cooked like Maria Johns, and after three beers wondered what it would be like to squeeze the soft parts of her fit-looking body, and sometimes he did. Pressing tightly against her, reaching into her dress hungrily, he would try to persuade her to go upstairs, where he knew she had a room. But she would gently push him away and rearrange herself and sternly declare, "I'm not taking anybody up for a fast trip above my own restaurant."

Maria Johns had clear ideas. She had raised two girls on her own. She had supported them by buying Venezuelan goods and selling them in Trinidad during the oil boom, when the Trinis had been crazy to buy everything. She made enough money to open the Caribee and become a businesswoman. John Blades had a nice hard farmer's look, but if he wanted to make love to a businesswoman, he was going to have to take her home.

His farm was a short trip out of town on a dusty square of land. He never took anyone there. The one-room, thick-walled house was the same type that slaves had lived in. He was not going to take Maria to see he lived in a slave house. But he had plans.

Blades had gone to the Gomes Bank asking for a two-thousand-dollar loan. He told the loan officer that his house was one of the original slave homes just like the one on the northern road, and with money he could take the tin roof down, make an old-time thatched roof, put every-thing right, and it could be a tourist sight just like the other one. "I could charge admission and pay back the loan quick," Blades suggested.

But there were problems. There was some question about the authenticity of his house, and the Island Historical Preservation Society had already turned him down. Manny sat on the board of the Island Historical Preservation Society, but Blades, in spite of his bad habit of often saying, "the Jews run everything," did not know this and assumed that Manny wouldn't know about the prob-lem with the Preservation Society.

Still, Manny felt bad about turning Blades down

because, though it wasn't much of a farm, it was one of the last working farms on the island and he would have liked to have kept it working. Soon Blades, too, would give up like everyone else and try to get a job in the oil refinery. Manny wondered if Rabbi Berman's quest for clean chicken could save Blades's little farm.

The new rabbi, forced into vegetarianism—expensive South American vegetables, since little grew on the island—was enthusiastic. But he had to find more kosher chicken customers. He wrote a letter notifying the entire Sephardic community that he was going to try to institute the kosher slaughter of chickens and he wanted to know how many customers there would be. No one responded. He wrote a second letter explaining the importance of being kosher but also that even if you were not kosher, it would be a mitzvah to order chickens to help the people who were kosher. There was one response.

James Holder, a young mulatto from the Health Ministry, had heard about the rabbi's plan from his wife, who was a teacher and sat on the same education commission as Manny Gomes-Peres and Dr. Gonsales-Levi and had overheard them joking about it. Holder wrote to Berman:

> I have listened with great interest to members of our community discussing your plans for clean kosher chicken. I have long been concerned with the quality of food for children on this island. All this okra and pork

and cornmeal and no good vegetables, and no one knows anything about what the animals we eat have been fed. I am delighted to hear you are setting up a system for clean Jewish meat. Everything the Jews have undertaken on this island has always been done first class, and it is good to know that at last we will all be able to enjoy clean Jewish chicken and pork.

Sincerely,
James Holder
Assistant Deputy Minister of Health

P.S. I wonder if you could also look into the local island beer. I have never trusted the brewery, and I think some Jewish supervision would make a far healthier product.

Berman had one hope left. There were some thirty Ashkenazic Jews who refused to pray at the synagogue because they claimed the practices were "too liberal." Instead, they prayed in a room in a house. They were all immigrants from Poland who had fled the Nazis, poorly educated lower-class newcomers with whom the Sephardim did not wish to socialize. If the Ashkenazim thought the Sefardim too liberal, surely they would want kosher chickens.

Their leader was a Polish Jew named Yakob Heigelmann, who spent most of his time at his discount store on the waterfront. Berman did not want to discuss this at the discount store. He waited until Sabbath, and then after the morning services he walked three miles to Heigelmann's home, which was where the Ashkenazim prayed on Saturdays.

Berman could feel the tropical sun soak into his dark suit. He had to find some lighter clothes. As soon as the matter was settled with the chickens, he resolved in his methodical way, he would do something about his clothes. When he arrived at the flat-roofed Heigelmann house, his charcoal suit was moistly draped on his slightly too-pudgy frame like leaves of steamed lettuce. Sweat was dripping from his face, and he had no way to make himself presentable before he rapped on the blue door, shunning the electric doorbell because it was the Sabbath.

The thickset sixtyish woman who answered the door looked at him with the disdain he was certain his appearance warranted, and said, "He's in the store."

"But, it's Sabbath," Berman gently protested while contemplating the walk back into town.

"So go to Israel."

"I'm sorry, I didn't mean to criticize, it is just that I thought he was Orthodox."

"Orthodox. He *is* Orthodox. But he is also retail. It's Saturday. You'll find him in the store."

It was a hard and hot walk, a few miles on the shoulder of the road back to town. A big black car that must have been German stopped. It was Manny Gomes-Peres offering him a ride, but of course it was Sabbath, and the rabbi politely thanked him and declined.

Once Berman reached town, off the desert and onto streets with pastel Dutch houses and a waterfront, it seemed cooler. The discount store was near the old port— three stories of inexpensive everything, chaotic with hungry customers, which was why Heigelmann stayed open on Saturdays. Worse, Berman found Heigelmann by the cash register, a balding gray-haired man with rolled up shirt-sleeves handling money on Sabbath.

"Berman, yes. What are you doing with the Sephardim?"

"They hired me."

"Yes, because their synagogue is so fancy. But we need a rabbi too."

"So come to the Mikve Israel."

"With all respect, Mr. Berman. The laws are not kept at the Mikve Israel."

"I'll admit, I have had to make a few compromises. But you make compromises too."

"Not with the Torah. There is no compromise with the law."

"Working on *Shabas?* That's the Torah."

"Yes, well, this is retail. You want to close on Saturday, go to Israel."

"I understand, but it is a compromise. I am sure that everyone at the Mikve Israel would agree with you."

"They would agree with me if I had a hyphen in my name."

"Do you keep kosher?"

"Yes. I keep kosher. We all keep kosher except for some of us."

"And where do you get your meat?"

"Frozen from Miami. But it's a big problem. I got it from Chicago, but they stopped because the order was not big enough. Miami charges more. Now he is getting impatient. If you wanted to add to the order, it would help. Maybe we could get a better rate."

Berman agreed to order some frozen meat. Then he told him about the idea of local kosher chicken.

"It will be *traif*. You can't get these fellows to take the trouble."

"I'll supervise. It will be rabbinically supervised. And we will pay extra for the care."

"Pay extra all you want. I'm a businessman. I know even if you pay top money, you are going to one day find something on your drumstick that looks a lot like a pork chop."

John Blades reasoned that the kosher business was not going to be as good as the historic-landmark trade, but for the time being it had its advantages. Chicken for the Jews. It would be a good business. Blades had always suspected that everyone in Willemstad was Jewish. The banks, the stores, everything. There must have been thousands of them in the town. And rich rich. Whew! That rabbi said they would pay more. Yeah, probably double or triple.

And he liked the knife. The rabbi had given him a special knife to slit the chickens' throats in one easy move. It was the sharpest knife Blades had ever seen. The rabbi had said that the chicken had to die painlessly. Jews were willing to pay double to eat a chicken that didn't hurt when it died! They were something!

And you could not dip them in hot water to pluck the feathers, and you had to be careful how you singed off the down, and they had to be cleaned more carefully than he had ever cleaned a chicken. It all took time, but they were going to pay.

The knife was the best carving tool Blades had ever found, and he was using it to make some "original slave carvings." With the money that would be coming in, he could fix the place, get a concrete floor that he could sweep, and buy good wood and build hand-carved furniture. He would be careful about the changes he made, because he still thought the historic landmark business would pay. But more important, he imagined Maria Johns in front of the stone hearth in the yard stirring an iron skillet of *coo-coo*. It would be hard to keep things authentic for the preservationists and still nice for Maria. She didn't want to live in an authentic slave house. He thought about her in his bed, not the small, rusty, iron cot that he was looking at but the large—king-size or maybe more—bed that he would build from South American mahogany and carve with the knife the rabbi gave him.

These thoughts were interrupted by the grumble of a polished car with government plates coming up his dirt road. He had to quickly toss his carving, knife and all, into the thornbush because it might be a preservation man come to talk about his landmark house.

James Holder carefully rebuttoned his gray pinstriped double-breasted suit as he got out of his car. Before he had a chance to explain anything to Blades, the farmer was leading him into his thick-walled, one-room house, showing him tools and other slave relics. "And this here," he said, proudly pointing at a framed gray photocopy on his wall, "is my great-grandfather's copy of the emancipation."

Holder looked more closely. "Well, maybe this is my grandfather's copy of my great-grand—"

"Blades—"

"I forget my—"

"I'm from the Health Ministry."

"The Health Ministry?"

"It's about the Jewish chickens."

"Oh, yeah, the Jewish chickens." His enthusiastic face melted sour. "How'd the government get in on that. That was looking like a good business without a government. Why do you want to mess with it?"

"Clean chickens—Ministry of Health. It's our business. How much they paying for these clean chickens?"

"Well, that rabbi says they'll pay something like double. I don't know. I think they don't care what they pay. Jews have money. But these chickens are not easy to do. They want more than clean. They want everything. They want the chicken to die sweet with a Jewish knife. Beautiful knife. Then they have this thing about chicken blood and all these things. And this rabbi has to watch me when I do it so he can put some obeah on the thing. And he puts some kind of little paper on each one with Bible writing. It takes time. He doesn't want that many, anyway. I was surprised. This island is full of Jews. They only want a few chickens. I'm surprised they don't just kill them in their own ceremonies."

"But you could make good money if you could sell enough chickens."

"Yeah, man, they pay like these were fine birds. They're just little island chickens."

"I think we can do good business with this. Even do some export trade. Maybe a few thousand a month. That would be some money."

"I don't think I can get the rabbi to do that many."

"Well, you let the rabbi do his, and we can do ours. Make some money. What do you think?"

"Maybe we could get them out somewhat faster when the rabbi wasn't here."

"Fifteen percent value-added tax of course."

"I've got to pay you?"

"For a thousand clean Jewish chickens a month. You will do fine. You just have to do them a little faster to make money."

The Oneg Shabbats were always irritating to Rabbi Berman. He did not expect the congregation to keep kosher. But the Oneg—every Friday night after the service they would all step into the side room by the synagogue and sip wine, even say a blessing on the wine, and then there would be those trays of Venezuelan shrimp. Shrimp in the synagogue for Shabbat. Rabbi Berman would shake his head at the incongruity of it. They didn't understand. It wasn't that it offended his religious sense. It offended his sense of logic.

He had not intended to start a crusade for kosher food. He thought the chicken was a good idea because it meant that he could eat fresh chicken and not just frozen gray beef from Miami. And maybe if good kosher food were available, a few more might join in. But the chickens had brought too much attention to his kosherness. Sarah Gomes-Peres was only one of the people who delighted in offering him shrimp, popping them into her mouth in front of him, rolling her eyes underneath her purple eye-shadow. "*Mmmm,* you don't know what you are missing. Don't you wish you could just try one? What do you think would happen if you just took a bite?"

"Did you ever think about sneaking a bite?" said Manny.

"God would know," said Dr. Gonsales-Levi with a mocking finger pointing toward the ceiling.

Many times Berman tried explaining, but they never understood. "Nothing would happen if I took a bite. It is not that I am afraid. It is that I am Jewish. It is an agreement. Something I do to be Jewish." They did not really listen.

The members seemed, nevertheless, open to the idea of kosher chicken. Many said they would try it. They all agreed it would be fun to have their own kosher chicken. They would order it for the Jewish holidays. Mrs. Mendes-Samuel said she would order it for Rosh Hashanah and Yom Kippur, but Rabbi Berman pointed out that Yom Kippur was a day of fasting.

Only Manny Gomes-Peres was more skeptical. He said that it didn't make economic sense. The chickens would cost more than lobster.

"I'm not doing it to make money," Berman protested.

Manny smiled. "Blades is doing it to make money. If he doesn't make money, he will stop doing it. That's the way things work."

Heigelmann was in the living room looking for something to watch on television when he heard his wife shriek, "These chickens are *traif!*"

The first chicken came with a label showing that Berman had supervised the slaughter. She could not remember the label from the second one, which they roasted Thursday night. But this one had a completely different label. It said, "An authentic kosher chicken—guaranteed clean by the Rabbi of the Netherlands Antilles," and it bore the seal of the Ministry of Health.

This was not a kosher label. Heigelmann took it to Berman, and Berman took it to Blades. Next to Blades's house stood a new, large chicken coop, and the once quiet spot was filled with a deafening chatter. The dirt yard was dusted with fluffy gray feathers. When Berman arrived, he noticed a bloodstained hatchet resting on a chopping block.

"Mr. Blades, I think you have been slaughtering chickens on your own."

"No, sir."

"And you are not using the *challef*."

"I am using the olives," Blades protested unconvincingly. "Of course I use them."

"The *challef*. It's the knife."

"I know that."

"It looks like you have been using this hatchet."

"This! This hatchet belonged to my great uncle who was born in the Congo and—"

Berman showed him the label.

"You see," said Blades. "That's a government seal. I'm not doing anything on my own. We are selling more than a thousand chickens a month. You work too slow for government. They are working toward independence. We have to move. Self-reliance."

"But it is not honest."

Blades's dark eyes began to shine at Berman. "Not honest! It's a damn chicken, isn't it? It's a good chicken. It tastes good. It's healthy and clean. My great-grandfather was brought here from Africa. He raised chickens here. These chickens have African blood. Okay, they don't have any blood when you're through with them. But who are you to come here and tell me what an honest chicken is? You don't like my chicken, don't buy it. It's government certified!"

Manny Gomes-Peres was right. The new chicken was more expensive than lobster. What he had not realized was that this made it a delicacy. An article in an American travel magazine identified it as "the most highly prized chicken in the world." James Holder asked the island tourism board to print brochures. They borrowed the phrase "most highly prized chickens in the world." The hotels began offering "island Jewish chicken" because most tourists had to try it.

Maria Johns recognized the opportunity, and that marked the end of the last restaurant for island cooking. She put tablecloths over the Formica tops and started opening for dinner. The new name was the Caribee Chicken, and reservations were needed. She was sometimes booked for more than a week in advance.

Blades was feeling more confident. He was making money now, and, thanks to him, Maria was doing even better than before. Now she had an upscale restaurant for tourists. But, when he invited her to his farm, she would not go . . . until the second time he asked, which happened to be her fortieth birthday. Her daughters were all gone to school in Miami. Thanks to Blades, she was now truly a businesswoman. The chicken was so easy to prepare and so profitable that she hired other people to do the cooking. Free from labor at last and it being her birthday, she wanted to do something special. She couldn't just spend the day in her restaurant. She reasoned that Blades's life had also changed. His farm would now be a prosperous working farm, a reasonable place for a businesswoman to go on her fortieth birthday.

They drove out in her car, which was better than his rusting little flatbed truck that he used to bring chickens to the restaurant—in the old days he would carry them, but now she ordered by the truckload.

He confidently led her onto his new concrete floor, freshly swept. Now that he had a floor that could be swept, he swept it whenever he could. It was a pleasure to sweep a concrete floor. The bed with the carved, dark wood headboard was in one corner, and there was a matching chair. Finely crafted "antique" tools decorated the walls. "This is it," he said with a faint smile.

Maria had not exactly heard him. It was hard to hear anything. They had upset the chickens by driving up, and the birds were all still protesting—a sound like a thousand squeaking wheels. Soft, curly, down underfeathers were levitating off the floor, the chair, the headboard. To Maria there was something repulsive about these little feathers. Blades reached for her, wrapped his arms around her, started searching with his strong hands.

She let him, but she was thinking about the chickens.

How she hated that noise. And those sickening little feathers. No, it wasn't that. It was the smell. The smell of chickens was everywhere—a bitter, sour, horrible smell.

"Do you have to keep the chickens so close to the house?"

"It's not an estate. I mean, it's an historic piece of property but not that big, you know."

"But they stink," she said, angrily pushing him away, even more decisively than when she used to shove him away in the restaurant. "They are not clean to have around."

"Not clean!"

"What's the matter with you? You can't smell? They're not clean."

"They happen to be the cleanest chickens in the world. I've got a rabbi to say they're clean. That's as clean as there is!"

"They still smell!"

Berman, not sure what to do and feeling his inadequacy as an outsider, went to the restored antique pink building with the modern air-conditioned office of Manny Gomes-Peres, whose family had been on the island for more than four centuries. But Manny was not bothered by Blades's chickens. "Look," he explained, "this man's farm was failing. Now it is making money. Everybody is buying these chickens. They think they can export them to Aruba.

Maybe even Venezuela. When was the last time we produced something for export to Venezuela? Since they bought the refinery, do you know what our balance of trade is with Venezuela?"

"But it's a fraud. These aren't kosher chickens."

"The five people around who are kosher look at the label and see that. It didn't fool Heigelmann. It's not a fraud. It's a concept. It's marketing. It is the sort of commercial idea that this island was built on."

"I think someone in the government is syphoning off profits."

"That's the kind of idea this island was built on too. If you make profits, someone always gets a piece." Manny had been lecturing government bureaucrats for years about using marketing ideas to promote island products. Holder had done it right, and although there did not seem to be any state revenue showing up yet, Manny was not going to stifle this kind of initiative. "The important thing is to make a profit. Somebody makes a profit. It doesn't matter who. It goes into the economy, and everyone gains. The idea is essentially brilliant. They have raised the price of chicken to more than lobster. Now people who would only eat lobster want a Curaçao clean chicken. Everybody wants our special clean chickens. I'm going to arrange some financing for exports. I think this thing will work. I know people who have never touched an island chicken who *have* to order it now."

As Berman started to walk out of the air-conditioned

office, Manny looked up from his glass desktop and said, "Oh, Ben?"

"Yes."

"I don't think you should eat the chicken here."

Leaving the office, Berman could hear Manny Gomes-Peres snickering, and for days afterward he thought he heard the people of his Sephardic community laughing at him.

That Friday night for the Oneg Shabbat, a tray of little fried chicken fritters, each artfully sprinkled with curry powder and green herbs, lay next to the tray of shrimp. It did not escape Berman how often well-tanned, jewelry-festooned arms pointed at the tray of chicken. Then he would hear suppressed guffaws or airy giggles. Oh, they thought it was all so funny. Being Jewish and the law and five millenniums of history would all become giggles on this funny little island. They had to learn what it was about. Not fear, but a love of the law.

"So," said Sarah Gomes-Peres, holding a perfect little chicken croquette in one hand and a pink shrimp in the other, "suppose you had to have one. Which would it be?"

Berman thought about reaching over and cramming the shrimp in his mouth and saying, "You see? It is nothing to do this!" Then he would spit it out. He lunged for the table with the trays and grabbed a fistfull of large shrimp, the tails sprouting out from between his thick fingers. He tilted his head back, opened his mouth, and stuffed in the shrimp.

The room was quickly hushed by gasps of shock and fear. Dr. Gonsales-Levi ran out for his bag as the rabbi sank to the floor, his bloated face turning berry-stain purple.

The first shock for Ben Berman was the softness of the texture. Not at all resilient and rubbery as he had imagined. And the taste was very mild, but rich—nauseatingly rich. Then his breathing stopped.

By the time Dr. Gonsales-Levi returned with his bag and readied a shot of adrenaline, Ben Berman was lying faceup, his tongue swollen too large for his mouth, his lips ballooned into two large floats, his swollen eyelids blocking his vision, and his rapidly swelling face glowing strawberry. He could feel himself inflating and being choked off.

Minutes after receiving the shot he was starting to feel better. "You seem to be allergic to crustaceans," said Gonsales-Levi. "It's very common."

"I never knew," said Berman. "I just never knew."

But now everybody knew about Rabbi Berman's allergy. It was said that the rabbi had to specially order food because he had allergies. That was why his chickens had to be specially prepared—because he had allergies. This completely changed the way Blades's island chickens were viewed. They were now something medicinal. Manny Gomes-Peres thought that would be the end of the entire chicken venture. Since other people did not have these allergies, they would not buy the more expensive, allergy-free chickens. There was no market for allergy-free chickens.

But word spread in the eastern Caribbean of the medicinal power of John Blades's chickens, and he started to sell them live to obeah men to sacrifice in African ceremonies. The obeah men, even more than the Jews, respected clean chicken. What's more, they paid better than Jews, and they did all the slaughtering themselves.

NAKED

Stripped naked, she lay with no more secrets, this island once discreetly draped in lush green velvet. And on this island, equally naked, lay Ministry Special Counsel Sarah Bellot, her hazelnut skin hot and lustrous, with a softly damp smell resembling the missing foliage. Her scent filled the hungry head of State Secretary Rolly Austin, who was naked on top of her. And after a week with affairs of state, he was lost in Special Counsel Bellot, his entire existence melting away, his eyes drifting shut, when he glimpsed something odd outside his familiar, rough-cut mahogany window frame. But the counsel was moaning softly, like an ancient siren calling from the rocks, and he growled into her until he collapsed. Barely conscious underneath, she heard his voice somewhere over her say, "I didn't know we had white people next door."

Suddenly the state secretary felt to the special counsel like an enormous weight upon her.

"Damn, look at that," said State Secretary Rolly Austin.

"What?" groaned the special counsel.

Austin got up, slipped past the stacks of blankets that filled one corner of the room, and leaning on flour sacks, looked out the window. "Isn't that—it's that Miss—you know, the development woman. Yeah. And that American—what they call him, crisis manager or something?"

"Disaster relief coordinator."

"Yeah. He's coordinating."

"Let me see." She also went to the window, stubbing her toe on a case of flashlights. "Look at that."

The development woman was all lace and flesh. White lace, a bra, and little panties that curved high on her waist and cut away on the sides to emphasize long pink legs. And the disaster relief coordinator? He was on the floor, naked, kissing. . . He was kissing her toes and moving up her foot—the development woman pushed him away. She was doing—well, it was like a dance. Rolly Austin thought she moved like a white person. Still, there was a certain—a certain élan. And she did have great feet.

Sarah Bellot was less impressed. Suddenly she realized that she was naked. She looked further down the side of the mountain, and there was the finance minister, equally naked, staring at her breasts. As she ran to the bed to wrap herself in a sheet, she thought about the fact that the governor general's spokeswoman was standing naked next to the finance minister. She had had no idea about that.

Amazing the things you could still get away with on a small island. He was supposed to be still pining for *her*. He would pay for this somehow.

The hurricane had been called Eunice, and its 185-mile-per-hour winds had swirled over the island for about one hour. Rolly Austin had heard a high-pitched squeak and a sucking noise like a huge kiss on the rooftop, then a dull thwack, and he knew there would be no more CNN or MTV. The satellite dish was gone. It would probably mean months of nothing but local island programming, the dreary island programs sponsored by his government for the good of its people.

Eunice took away television, but having stripped away all the thick tropical vegetation, there was something new to watch. The finance minister, the white people, all of them lived on different streets, but now it turned out they were all on the same mountain with nothing but a few naked branches between them in a dead winter landscape with hot summer light.

Rolly had never realized that the PM lived at the top of his hill. He could hike up there in three minutes now. He use to spend ten minutes in his Mercedes, winding up the curving lanes to the PM's home. Who was the PM sleeping with? Rolly wondered. The PM was always sleeping with someone. That was why people voted for him. Who was it now? Miss Beryls? Neat, trim Miss Beryls. What did she look like without clothes? He greedily turned his glance up the hill.

The PM was in a bathrobe, yellow terry cloth, watching

television in the dark—alone. He had managed to get his electricity and satellite dish back immediately by arguing that it was vital. Rolly was not sure why it was vital, but he did not want to question it because someday he would be prime minister and would be grateful that a larger figure who had come before him had established such precedents. The PM had said something about CNN, but now Rolly could see the colored screen flashing and was almost sure he was watching *Dynasty*.

The development woman was at last naked. The disaster coordinator was in horizontal pursuit across the floor, snakelike, clutching at her long dexterous toes . . . Rolly shook his head. He had had no idea they were like that.

He could see other houses on other hills, and he could see that there were people in those windows too, but he could not see if they were naked or not. Many of them seemed to be doing what he was doing—watching. Was he a voyeur, a Peeping Tom? He carefully stepped back to make sure he was out of the light and peered out from between boxes of portable gas burners to get a view.

The development woman was standing defiantly naked in the middle of the room, her hands on her hips, her right foot extended. He was still on the floor—he was licking her foot! Now he was—well, he seemed to be doing her toes again, one at a time. The more Rolly looked the more he worried that someone could see him watching. But he couldn't stop. Were others looking at them too? Or were they watching him looking?

A BBC correspondent had observed this phenomenon of islanders standing in front of windows in every house and had filed a dispatch saying, "You can see the trauma on the faces of the locals as they stare out the windows of their brightly painted wooden houses, their faces numb with shock."

Rolly Austin did not realize what had happened to him until the government emergency session the following morning. The first thing was that he couldn't look at the disaster relief coordinator in quite the same way. He had never known white people were like that. To avoid looking at him, Rolly kept his gaze down. In fact, they were well into the meeting before Rolly realized what was happening. He was comparing the surprising variety in women's feet.

He could see through an assortment of footwear—island made, since his government had defied the Americans and put back the tariff on footwear and apparel, which was the other reason why people voted for the PM—he could see through all this island leatherwork in various colors that some women had sexy feet and others didn't. Miss Beryl had kicked a shoe off, and he could see everything, but it did nothing for him. In spite of the other promising aspects of her anatomy, Miss Beryl had no arches at all. Special Counsel Sarah Bellot was remaining discreetly shod, but he already knew all her secrets and he seemed to recall rather stumpy toes. The more he thought about Sarah's feet the less pleased he was that she would be coming over to his house after the meeting.

The development woman, however, shifted her legs under a cotton dress. The feet, covered in small, black leather pumps—just a little slipper of a shoe, probably foreign made, foreign leather—moved restlessly. Her left shoe would sometimes touch her right shoe and it would look to Rolly as though she were about to flip a shoe off. But it didn't happen.

Even from the distance of his window, he had seen that she had exquisite feet, with long, pink, fingerlike toes slightly rounded on the end, the nails painted hibiscus red.

Then came a feeling of shame: Did he crave only white feet? Did he crave the feet of white women? This was against everything his government stood for, against the entire history of the Democratic Labour Movement. Here he was, probably the PM's anointed successor, the next Prime Minister, and yet he wanted to suck white women's toes. It wasn't fair. He was a free man. He only wanted what the disaster relief coordinator had. Yes, he wanted it very much.

And the more he recognized how politically wrong this was, how disastrous such a yearning could be for his career and his party, the more he wanted to drop to his knees, crawl under the table, and disgrace himself in front of the entire government by slowly removing a black leather foreign-made pump. . . .

"Rolly, what do you think?" asked the PM. They were all looking at him, including the development woman with her long, cream-colored legs and her long, pink toes. Maybe it had nothing to do with race. Maybe it was just that he knew these were feet that got licked. They were lickable. Ready to be licked—

This had to stop.

The government was trying to figure out how to get more relief money from the U.S., and the finance minister said they should put out some devastating figures on the millions of dollars of damage and the years it would take to recover. But the tourism minister pointed out that the season was only a few months away and they could not make it sound too bad. The PM pointed out that he had to call elections before the tourism season.

Rolly Austin made a mental note to try and see who the tourism minister slept with. The minister lived a bit away, but Rolly might be able to see a window over the eastern rise.

🐓

When the meeting ended, Rolly went home. Soon Sarah arrived. But he ignored her. He could see that the development woman and the coordinator were beginning again, but he didn't want Sarah to see him watching. He wanted to be alone to watch. Angrily, Sarah went about her work, stenciling names and pictures on sacks and cases. Making as much noise as she possibly could. Why was he suddenly ignoring her?

"Going to the crisis center. Be back," he said, casting one last wistful glance out the window before leaving. The crisis center had been set up in the PM's office, which was a small leaky concrete building designed to look contemporary—an architecture to which Eunice had not been kind. It still had its roof, except for one wing, but the carpets smelled of mold and were variegated with water marks from the flooding. The old gingerbread Finance Ministry had held up better, but the PM mistrusted the ambitions of the finance minister and he wanted it said that the crisis center was "in the Prime Minister's Office." A blue clothbound book with lined pages and the word "Records" embossed on the cover was waiting for government officials fresh from touring the island to request urgently needed materials for the next relief flight. Rolly Austin, having been on the west coast, where roofs had been blown off and people were sleeping in camps, requested in the book two hundred blankets. He hesitated a moment and then wrote, "one pair of binoculars." Then he thought how suspicious the word "one" looked and wanted to change it to "twenty." But he didn't want to cross out the "one." He contemplated "one hundred" but settled on "one dozen." Then he saw the word "binoculars" again. The finance minister had asked for one hundred folding cots and ten binoculars. The tourism minister had asked for two hundred flashlights, batteries, and fifteen binoculars.

The next day a flight came in from Miami with binoculars. They were not Rolly's order. He knew this because there were no blankets. But he took one of the pairs of binoculars, anyway. From his window he could see across the naked ravine to the tourism minister's house—the tourism minister and Miss Beryl. She looked better without her clothes than Rolly had imagined. But her feet would still be flat. Up his own hill, above the skeletal branches, the PM was in his bathrobe staring into his large-screen television. The development woman was in lace again. The disaster relief coordinator was stalking her, reptilelike, on hands and knees.

Rolly had to wonder about these people. They were not normal. He adjusted his binoculars. Yes, her toes were long. They looked long enough to grab on to something, almost like fingers, long, white fingers with round pink tips.

This mountainside was the only part of the island that had gotten back electricity. Linemen from America were working on the rest of the island, but the government and the development woman had agreed that in this critical period they had to have electricity to work into the night. The telephones were still out, and Rolly could leave his lights off and feel completely alone in his dark house. Rolly Austin had become an invisible nocturnal creature.

In the daytime, Sarah was there labeling. Once darkness came, Rolly would take his place by the window. At first he would try to resist and casually work his way over. Eat some dinner first. After a few nights, he even ate his dinner by the window.

The disaster relief coordinator was always naked. He surely started with his clothes on, but Rolly never saw his clothes come off. And he was always on the floor somewhere. Sometimes he was under their window and Rolly could not see him at all. Then suddenly two hands would grab at the flesh of the development woman or a head would lunge at her as though to devour her. The development woman danced slowly. Over the course of hours they would perform an endless variety of rituals. Later at night, he would always have her feet. It was like the satellite channel that you didn't have to watch much early in the evening because you knew it would be on long after the government channels had darkened.

The tourism minister and Miss Beryl were pure endurance—a kind of cinema verité, honest in its predictable unfolding, without drama or device. The light down the hill was Pastor Thomas, who failed to provide scandal. The pastor, in a T-shirt without sleeves and green shorts, shifted his weight from side to side, running in place with a rhythm and swing of the arms that suggested he was doing this to music. The finance minister's two young sons practiced death and resurrection, whacking each other with swordlike strips of wood like two very cloddish knights. Just the sight of Pearl Cartwright and her daughter spending the evenings together preparing food was worth watching. These were the ways people acted when no one was watching, and Rolly, undetected, could see it all. Surely some night George was going to leave his corner and put his big hands all over Pearl. But it hadn't happened yet.

Brownlie Harrison put his hands on Merle. Usually about eight-thirty their faces would turn ugly, their teeth sticking out, foreheads becoming taut and veiny. Then Brownlie would start hitting her, real blows that came from far out to the right and landed with the force to knock her down. Should he say something? Rolly wondered. Do something? What could he say? How could he admit that he was watching them, watching all of them?

Sooner or later he would start thinking about licking the development woman's feet. And he would shudder with fear. These people expected a lot of their leaders. The sexual exploits of the PM, who had had five wives and five divorces, were part of his popular lore. His predecessor, the independence leader, was said to have slept with most of the island. But the one thing that wouldn't go here was a Labour leader who liked to crawl at white women's feet. Is that really what he wanted to do? He picked up the binoculars, stumbling over some new shipments of canned beef.

The first few nights everyone else was watching too. He could see them at their windows. But after a week it was mostly him. Most everyone would have a look for a while, but only he kept watching. Rolly shuddered when he thought about any of them finding out.

He started noticing things during the daytime that he had never noticed before. Merle had bruises. Pastor Thomas was very fit-looking under his baggy clothes. Pearl Cartwright looked lonely.

But Rolly was growing accustomed to his own invisibility. He talked little in or out of meetings. He did not socialize at night anymore but noiselessly went to his window. One night, he woke up in the dark from a nightmare in the form of a banner headline on the *Island Record:* AUSTIN SUCKS WHITE TOES.

The *Record* was there. Glenis Laws had bought a home on the bottom of the hill. It was the worst house on the hill—an old Victorian with a high-pitched roof. Before Eunice arrived, it appeared to be listing ten degrees. But it looked no worse after she left.

Glenis Laws made little money as the star and really only reporter at the *Record,* and she was not fond of her neighbors, who built new houses and had not had to struggle their way up from Lower Allentown Road. Most of all she remembered that the DLM, in spite of their independence promises, had not helped her to go off island and get her degree, and the NPP had.

Glenis stared up the hill and wondered about her newspaper's polls. The party in power always profits from a disaster because people are afraid that if the ruling politicians were voted out, they would take the foreign relief money with them. Yet, the PM was steadily dropping in the polls. And with an election coming. Why wasn't he cashing in on the foreign relief? What was happening to all the relief they were bragging about?

She stared up hill at the old man—yes, for the first time he was looking like an old man, in his yellow bathrobe, collar up, in front of his television. Did people resent him having the only television? No, of course not. That was power. You couldn't turn against the only man on the island with foreign television programming.

She had asked the *Record's* pollster why the PM was doing so badly and he had said "a loss of mystique." Since the hurricane, everyone in the rum bars had been laughing about the PM in his bathrobe watching American soap operas. That had never been his image. She had talked to her source in the party, the finance minister, who said they were all aware of the problem. But no one had the courage to tell the PM that they were all watching him in his bathrobe at night. "I wouldn't want to be the one to tell him," said the finance minister with an affable smile. Glenis Laws did not trust the finance minister, but she could not understand why the PM didn't mobilize with elections coming up.

🐓

Night fell. The stripped branches became black claws against the slowly darkening hot coral sky. As the island faded, the lights on this one empowered hill came on. The development woman was home. But she seemed to be alone. The tourism minister and Miss Beryl were just talking and drinking beer. The finance minister wasn't home. His wife was at the window with binoculars looking at the far slope that Rolly couldn't see. She must have been looking over at Sarah Bellot's house. A flash of irritation rose in Rolly. Just a thought. What was she watching over at Sarah's house? What was Sarah doing tonight? Why was that the one house he couldn't see? Of course Sarah was at his house every day working and angrily glaring at him. So what did he care what the finance minister's wife was looking at?

Rolly was an ordinary man. Everyone in politics joked about how uninteresting Rolly Austin was. His accomplishment had been giving ordinariness standing in politics. The PM had picked him for his ordinariness. The PM did not like the ambitious finance minister, who made it too clear that he wanted to replace him. The PM had even said it. "The romance of independence is over, and it is time for the DLM to turn to ordinary people to solve the ordinary problems of daily life."

The PM was not ordinary, nor was his predecessor. Nor were the two opposition leaders the NPP had produced. They were great athletes, renowned lovers, stirring orators. The PM in his youth had been a bowler for the West Indies. The opposition leader sang so well he had cut some records with his third wife, a British reggae star he had met at a concert and swept away. These were all men who could sweep people away. And now, somehow, Rolly had positioned himself to take their place.

The PM thought Rolly could get on with the boring business of good government while people remembered his own flair with a little nostalgia. The PM, whatever his accomplishments, was a legend, and he did not want to be succeeded by another legend. He thought it would be a good thing for his country and his reputation if the best thing that was said about his successor was, "He was competent," a word rightly or wrongly never used in connection with the PM. Choosing the right successor was the key to securing the right place in history.

Rolly worried that after the PM was gone and he was on his own, no one would support him, because he was so ordinary. But now it seemed he was not ordinary at all. He was a pervert. A voyeur. A man who spied on naked white women and wanted to suck their pink toes. Was that really perverted? Wasn't it just a taste? An inclination?

And now a new degenerative phase of his disease had arrived. Degenerative. Exactly. A deepening of the perversion. Rolly found it hard to believe that it was he, Rolly Austin, in all this. If he was shocking himself, what would . . . It seemed to be someone else he was observing—someone else who had actually stolen the shoe.

He looked fearfully at the pile of blankets under which it was hidden. At least it had been hidden. What if someone found it? Sarah could find it there. He groped through the pile and it was still there—a black leather, foreign-made left shoe. Ever since he took it, he had lived in fear of discovery. He couldn't even enjoy it. Enjoy it? What was he talking about! There was nothing to enjoy. He would have put it back if he could. But that would be too dangerous. When she had come back up to the edge of the road, she could only find one. No doubt she had been wondering about it ever since. She probably couldn't imagine. What had possessed him? Why did he steal it?

No, he suddenly realized. She knew. This was a woman who had her feet made love to every night. No ordinary woman. Maybe that was what excited him. Maybe he was normal after all. Wouldn't it be normal for an ordinary man to want to do something out of the ordinary with an extraordinary woman?

While having these thoughts, he had gripped the shoe tightly and was holding it close enough to detect the scent of foreign leather as the supple skin pressed against his cheek. He wanted to drop it from his hand, throw it somewhere. He became frightened and searched his crowded house for a place to hide the shoe. Under the laundry? No. What would they think if they found it there? Who were *they*?

Someplace far out of his sight. Maybe he would bury it. No. He would put it under his bed. A man in his position should have a woman's shoe or two under his bed. Probably the PM had plenty of women's shoes under his bed. There was something vaguely stimulating about that thought.

The development woman had probably thought the relief coordinator had stolen the shoe. But suppose he had been with her? Besides, a woman like that could see things. She would know. She would have seen him looking at her feet and she would know. He clutched his binoculars and turned anxiously to his window.

The development woman was still alone, wearing a large T-shirt, her hair wrapped in a towel, huddled in a corner reading a book, her feet tucked under her. It was a blue book. It was the requisition book. She was studying the requisitions—examining who had ordered binoculars. Rolly flattened himself against the dark wall.

No, lots of them had ordered binoculars. He looked out again. The PM was in his house. He was not watching television. Perhaps there were no soap operas on Thursday. Instead, he was waving his hands and whirling as though to invoke spirits. Rolly saw that the finance minister was there. So he was not with Sarah after all. Then he saw that Sarah was there also. They were having some kind of meeting behind his back. Was it about him? Had they somehow found out something? It was Sarah. She knew. Maybe she had found the shoe.

Someone else was there too. Rolly tried adjusting his binoculars. Suddenly, the PM impatiently picked up his own binoculars and scanned down the hill, stopping at Rolly's window. Rolly realized that they were staring at each other. Had the PM always watched him?

At the same instant, both Rolly and the PM put down their binoculars. Rolly had not realized that, standing in his window, he was glowing, exposed in the pale light of a big white moon. He wanted to look at the PM, but he didn't dare pick up the binoculars again. Even in the distance, he could see the PM's impatient twitch. With an exaggerated sweep of his arm, he was summoning Rolly up the hill.

Rolly drove the long way around to the PM's house. Were they going to actually say it? Were they going to ask him to explain himself? He hoped for a quiet demotion. The old English way, where nothing was ever said but you knew your career was blocked. Still, it would get around the island to every rum bar. It would be in songs and there would be an outbreak of toe jokes. . . .

The PM's house was built low, and until Eunice, nobody could even see it. The grounds were still covered with stacks of construction material. A smiling prime minister greeted him with a glass of champagne, saying, "Imported champagne, Rolly?" Everybody always talked like that on the island: "Imported champagne." "Have some imported whiskey." "Nice imported car." As though there were domestic cars or island champagne.

The champagne was not a good sign. The PM had cultivated an image for high living, and the more cornered he felt the more he tried to show it off. The finance minister, tall and thin, chewing his nails, stared down the naked hill. Rolly could see his own darkened window. What kind of PM would the finance minister make, biting his nails?

Special Counsel Sarah Bellot was avoiding Rolly's gaze. Or was he avoiding hers?

The PM put a paternal arm around Rolly Austin's shoulders and walked him away from the others. "Let me put this very simply. Rolly, boy, you've been found."

Rolly felt ill. "Sir, I . . ."

"Listen, Rolly, no time for this. Somehow Glenis Laws found out what you've got stashed in your house. It is going to be in next week's *Record*. So there is only one thing to do. Get rid of it. Do it tonight."

"Yes, sir. What about the . . ."

The PM smacked his palm on Rolly's back. "Just do it, man." The PM smiled warmly. "When the hell are the god-damn leaves going to grow back?" He suddenly leaped toward the terrace. "We've got paper to cover. Where the hell is Miss Beryl!"

"She's still with the tourism minister, sir, " said Sarah Bellot.

"When they going to be done with all that!" said the impatient prime minister.

"I'll check, sir," said the finance minister, and, picking up the binoculars, he stepped out onto the terrace.

Rolly drove down to the bottom of the hill, turned right, and then climbed halfway up again to his house. Without switching on a light, he groped under his bed until he found the black shoe, which he quickly shoved into his shirt. He drove along the south coast road, thinking he would throw it in the ocean. The currents in the south moved away from the island. If the shoe didn't sink, it would end up in Miami.

But there was no longer a quiet spot on the south coast. The entire shoreline had become a refugee camp of mostly homemade lean-tos and campfires. So he circled over to the north coast. He would put the shoe back where he found it by Caiman Bay, where people bathed in the calm water, which is what the development woman had been doing when he found her shoes.

He parked his car and got out, looking for a spot by the roadside to drop the shoe. But he realized that the narrow cove along the moonlit beach was filled with bathers. It was a tinseled moon-glowing night. A couple was coming toward him as he hesitated with the shoe still in his hand.

In a backhand flip, the shoe cartwheeled over the reeds. That was the end of it, and he leaped back into his car and drove off—not even hearing the startled grunt of the disaster relief coordinator, who was sitting on the beach, considering an evening swim, enjoying the warm island evening.

The coordinator immediately and fondly recognized the shoe. He gripped it passionately, this splendid artifact of secret moments, holding it against his cheek, remembering many things, like the times they had spent together at this very spot. He would be leaving soon, going back to his wife in Maryland. This was where she had lost the other shoe that wonderful afternoon. She had been angry, had said they were good shoes and you couldn't trust people on the island anymore, the tourism had made them all that way. She said things she should not have said, but she was angry about the shoe.

He rubbed the shoe tenderly and smiled, thinking of this bad-tempered woman who had driven out here to throw her useless other shoe at him. One night away and she already missed him. He should give it back, though. In case the other one turned up.

Rolly Austin slept well. He realized that having the shoe in his house had been troubling his sleep. Now he could sleep with the quietude of innocence.

Until *The Record* came out.

There was nothing about shoes or feet, but there was a full front-page story about how State Secretary Rolly Austin had been warehousing relief supplies in his home, printing the prime minister's picture and party logo on the items. The plan, as the *Record* revealed, had been to hold on to the supplies and then distribute them with the new labeling as soon as the elections were announced. The prime minister denied the story. "In this hour of national calamity, while our people are still homeless and huddled in blankets at the south coast, the NPP are using the people's tragedy to make low politics."

The PM was good. Everyone had to admire him. But

then, amazingly, an inspection of Rolly Austin's home showed that the supplies were still there with the logo and picture stenciled on. The prime minister, a man of great character who was always loyal to his friends, stood by Rolly Austin as he explained to the press that "we have all been a little traumatized by the hurricane. Austin is a dedicated public servant but just has not been thinking clearly in the wake of Eunice. It is human to make mistakes." He then, from a suddenly widened far corner of his eye, shot a split-second glance of homicide in Rolly's direction and gave him a warm hand on the back. Rolly could see the backslap coming behind him like a huge hand swatting away his political future. Still, he felt relieved. At least he had not been exposed and humiliated. Instead, he only stood accused of misdirecting foreign aid, a respectable political crime, the kind of flesh-and-blood thing his people would understand in time.

The PM was forced to call elections, and the NPP carried three out of five parishes. Even the PM lost his seat.

The DLM party conference named the former finance minister as party leader. The new party leader made Sarah Bellot a party secretary, and she was thought to be in line for a ministry if the DLM got back in, which seemed likely, since *Record* polls showed that the public was already disappointed that disaster relief had not improved under NPP leadership.

The leaves grew back.

Rolly Austin became director of the Manufacturers' Association.

The disaster relief coordinator returned to Maryland. His wife eagerly met him at the airport. "What an exciting time you must have had. Tell me everything." He put his arm around her as they walked to the car. "I will," he said warmly, with the seamless rhythm of a man who had been in political arenas.

The development woman never found her missing shoe.

BEAUTIFUL MAYAGÜEZ WOMEN

Dolores Del Valle was the most beautiful woman in the Barrio Albizu, which was remarkable because her sister was very ugly.

That Dolores was beautiful was considered normal. Barrio Albizu was a fetid marsh near the industrial port in Mayagüez, and it is often said that Mayagüez has the most beautiful women in Puerto Rico, which, to many, means in all the world. But even before Dolores was gassed and her sister taken over by the devil, things had never been completely normal in the barrio.

The women all worked and the men collected welfare. That much was normal. The beautiful Dolores, her ugly sister, Mercedes, and most of the people in the barrio had come from the mountains. They had moved to Mayagüez to sew in the assembly plants in the Free Zone. They were paid by the piece, and many of the beautiful women had such nimble fingers that in a ten-hour day they could earn one of the best factory wages in the Caribbean, which was still cheap enough for foreign companies to bring pieces there to be sewn together. They sewed all kinds of clothes, but mainly women's, and especially undergarments. Mayagüez women sat together sewing brassieres, and maybe just the thought of that made everyone want to insist that they were all beautiful.

In the mountains there had been coffee, a little farming, and welfare. But here there was only sewing and welfare. In the Barrio Albizu, while the beautiful women sewed in the Free Zone, their men planted chairs and tables in the mud by their houses and played dominoes or strummed the five double strings of beaten-up *cuatro* guitars to the tunes of old *montañas,* the country ballads most Puerto Ricans had forgotten. They liked this music, especially the recordings of Ramito, the now-dead singer, and his *cuatro* player, Masso. They liked dominoes too, pursuing the placement of matching dots with unwarranted intensity and a few shots of rum. But they were used to hard work, and they were getting restless.

The children, both the boys and girls, learned sewing from their mothers and sometimes earned extra money doing piecework. But the men, having never learned to sew and in search of activities, became accomplished cooks, preparing the old-time country dishes—*mofongo,* mashed green bananas with pork and lots of garlic, *sancocho* with every kind of vegetable, and *gandules,* pigeon peas cooked slowly with fat ham hocks and mountain herbs. Nobody had time to cook like that anymore, but the men, missing their life in the mountains—the days when they had farmed and their women had cooked dishes that took time—set up in front of their little block houses and fried *bacalaitos* in the evening before the women came home. They served them in the old way, with yams.

The men did not laugh when they cooked but were grimly competitive, each determined to develop the best recipe and prepare the best version of every dish in a narrow and well-established repertoire. The undefeated champion at *mofongo* was appropriately called Mofongo. He made it Mayagüez style with crab. Mofongo was an individualist, a small balding man who rejected the *cuatro* and played a Cuban *tres,* his fingers working the six triple strings with a speed no one could explain.

The most contested title was for best pepper sauce. The best would not only be the hottest but would have to burn in certain ways on certain parts of the mouth. Someone would come out to the street with a concoction in an old Coca-Cola bottle, and each of them would carefully dab it on the back of their hand and lick it, and, if it was good, shout and stamp their feet from the pain. The maker would hold the pepper sauce title until someone else emerged with a new formula.

While the men argued about food, they agreed about women. Dolores Del Valle was the most beautiful. It made them nervous to have her in the same barrio, turning up without warning, with skin that was smooth and cream-colored like the face on a porcelain doll from France and thick, straight, black Spanish hair—hair that flowed like cane syrup off her shoulders. And if the men loved her hair, clearly Dolores loved it more. She spent hours brushing it in the evening while sitting in a chair in front of her house, her back to the barrio—or was she facing that way to show the barrio her hair? The men couldn't decide. But after an hour of brushing, her mane flowed to the middle of her back, shining soft and satiny in the evening light.

Mercedes, the sister, was as ugly as her sister was beautiful. Her lanky body was too tall, even her hands and feet too large, and her voice high and squeaky.

Dolores was a mystery. The men all sensed that she had secrets. She seemed to have no interest in men, seldom looked at them with her large caramel eyes, and always kept close to her sister. It was said that Dolores had a husband in New York, but a number of people from the barrio had moved there and no one had ever seen him. The one thing that was known about Dolores was that she had a temper. She seemed angry. She was especially angry about her work. "It is a plot," she would say. "They give all the work to the women to destroy the men. Destroy the men and destroy Puerto Rico." Most of the men agreed that a wonderful fire burned in Dolores del Valle's eyes when she was angry like this.

Around Christmastime, Dolores was working on buttonholes, which took a lot of speed because there were more than a hundred stitches to a hole and many holes to a day's wage. Women on buttonholes didn't look up very much, and that is why Dolores never saw it coming.

She woke up on the floor and looked at the women next to her. Several women were on the floor. Then she saw it— a green cloud, such a loud green that for a moment she thought it had something to do with Christmas. But that didn't explain why they were all on the floor or why something was roaring inside her head, like an electronic scream, or why she tasted blood in her mouth. She spit on the back of her hand to see if she was bleeding. She wasn't, but her lips felt bloated and itchy. After stumbling and stepping around other women, she got to the mirror in the washroom. Her lips looked normal. Maybe a little swollen. She felt as if she was going to be sick.

Her sister, Mercedes, helped her get home. On the way home, Dolores picked up several chocolate bars. The bitter sweetness seemed to help the nausea. When they got to the barrio, Dolores quickly ate another chocolate bar to try to counteract the sickening smell of frying *bacalaitos*. A man at a fryer waved happily, thinking that he would like to walk that way—with Dolores Del Valle leaning on his shoulder. Then he realized that Dolores, appreciated for her fair skin, was looking too fair and was being held up by the larger Mercedes as they made their way to their house. He asked what had happened, and the only answer from Dolores was a weak but angry, "Fumes."

He pointed defensively under his large frying pan. "I'm cooking with charcoal."

"No," said Mercedes. "At the zone."

"Fumes? What kind of fumes?" questioned one of the domino players as he slapped a tile hard on the table.

"They didn't say. Poisonous fumes," Dolores said, unwrapping another chocolate bar and furiously feeding it to herself. She retreated to her room and stayed there for the next twenty days. Mercedes went to work alone.

Dolores was not ignored in a barrio of men with too much free time. Since she lived without a man, the men all reasoned to their wives, she had no one to cook for her. So the men of the barrio began taking turns cooking their competing specialties and bringing them to the beautiful Dolores, who rewarded them with a faint smile and a glance from her large, soft eyes.

But Dolores ate very little, except chocolate, and Mercedes wanted the men to stop bringing the food, as though it were their fault that she was ill.

Mercedes started buying chocolate bars for her sister, because she said it helped the nausea. Sometimes Dolores would just let the wrappers drift to the floor, which was not like her. Mercedes would pick them up without saying anything.

The mysterious Dolores kept to herself and her chocolate bars. Occasionally she would be seen leaving the barrio for a few hours, but she never explained where she went. After twenty days the company said that if she did not return to work, she would be replaced. Someone had to talk to the management. Mercedes was too awkward and strange

looking and didn't talk much with anyone but her sister. So
Felícita, Mofongo's wife, decided she would go.

Felícita, Dolores's supervisor, was one of the original
seamstresses who had brought women and their families
to this swamp to be near the zone. She had named the
barrio after her favorite Independentista hero. Although
everyone insisted that she, too, had once been very beautiful, Felícita had a bloated look and her skin had turned to
coarse leather. Her voice was raspy and harsh, and children, and maybe some adults, were afraid of Felícita. Her
fingers had been sewing for so long that they worked
without a brain. They were always moving in rapid cen-
timeters. Children told jokes about Felícita's fingers. They
would say that Felícita's fingers sewed even when she was
"doing it." They supposed that she did it quite often,
since she had six children from six different men, all of
whom had moved to the mainland. The rumor was that
Felícita's men could be identified in the Bronx because
they all had buttons sewn to their "things." And now,
number seven just cooked *mofongo* and looked after the
children.

Felícita was the one to send to the management. All the
women in the barrio thought so. Even Mofongo thought
so. He grinned at the idea of some white factory owner
having to face her.

The head of the company was a mainlander, a white
man named Mr. Hall. Mr. Hall had never noticed that
Dolores was beautiful or that Mercedes was ugly. He had

noticed that Dolores had fast fingers, and Mercedes did not. When he had first come to Mayagüez to set up his plant, the zone manager, a Cuban named Fernandez, had told him that the women in Mayagüez were beautiful. But Mr. Hall did not see it. He did not even see that Puerto Rican women were beautiful. He noticed only the speed of their fingers. Fernandez decided that Mr. Hall must be a little *maricón*—he didn't like women.

Mr. Hall's only friend seemed to be Mr. Tchin, who ran a plant for a company from Taiwan. Mr. Tchin's company and Mr. Hall's, the two newest arrivals, were next to each other at the far end of the zone—the end with the poisonous gas. The Puerto Ricans all called Mr. Tchin *Chino,* which meant "Chinaman," and Mr. Hall suspected it might be an insult. But Mr. Tchin did not mind. He didn't tell Mr. Hall what the Puerto Ricans called him. Mr. Tchin did think the women of Mayagüez were very beautiful. He looked at his employees with great appreciation, sometimes singling one out for a smile and a polite nod, but his admiration went unnoticed because he was Chinese and who knew what they liked.

When Mercedes was carrying Dolores out of the plant, Mr. Tchin had been standing next to Mr. Hall, watching the evacuation, and Mr. Tchin commented on what a beautiful woman she was. The zone manager, Fernandez, had agreed. "Which one?" Mr. Hall had asked as the two women passed. Tchin and Hall saw many things differently.

When Felícita entered Mr. Hall's office, he sat motionless behind his desk. Felícita wondered if there was any woman for whom he would have stood up.

"Dolores del Valle isn't ready to work."

"Then she can't work. What do you want me to do? I am laying people off here. You want me to pay her not to work and lay people off who want to work?"

"She wants to work, but she's sick," Felícita said in a tough voice intended to feel like a slap. But Mr. Hall felt nothing until she added, "You gassed her."

Then his face changed as if she had just gassed him. His eyes, which were small and dark behind the thick lenses of his glasses, got even smaller and darker like hard little beans. "Who told you to say that?"

"Say what?" she said, not really trying to sound innocent. "You didn't gas her?"

"There was an accident. We don't know the cause. Something came in from another plant or up from the sewer system. The other ten women who were hospitalized have all come back to work. If you and Señora Del Valle want to make trouble instead of working, that is your decision. There is no labor shortage. Don't come back here. Go tell your friend that the same will happen to her if she makes trouble. You are not working here anymore."

"I have been here longer than you have," she said defiantly.

"You are not here anymore," he said, dismissing her with a calm manner. He had been expecting this encounter. Neither he nor Mr. Tchin had believed that the gassing was an accident. It was part of a larger plot, and they were braced for the next move. He knew this Dolores wasn't really sick for twenty days. He thought he handled their little trap fairly well. He would tell Mr. Tchin about what had happened and see if anyone in his plant had tried the same thing.

Felícita walked alone along the trail by the sulfurous green-scummed canal, tall grass slow-dancing all around her. It was the route she had walked hundreds—no, thousands of times between the industrial zone at the port and the Barrio Albizu. "Señora." Why was that the Spanish word they could always master? Her eyes, dry from the ache of not crying, stared straight ahead, her fingers still flailing like the legs of a working crab. What would she do now? Mr. Hall would tell all the plants. She would be branded "a troublemaker." What about the children? Then she pictured Mofongo feeding them stews with special *sofritos*. What would poor Mofongo do? He wasn't good for much of anything, but she loved him more than all the others.

She would have to turn to the Independentistas. They would know what to do. Mofongo always argued that if the Independentistas knew what they were doing, Puerto Rico would be independent by now. But Felícita believed that they would know what she should do. They were smart and had been educated on the mainland, at Yale University, and knew the gringos.

She did not want to go home and tell Mofongo. Instead

she walked over to the mango-colored concrete box where Dolores and Mercedes lived.

Mercedes opened the door. Felícita saw the beautiful Dolores looking noticeably less beautiful, sitting on the couch in her pink housecoat, her hair unbrushed, even dirty, like washed-up seaweed. Mercedes was her usual homely. Felícita explained that Mr. Hall would not listen and Dolores would have to go back to work. "It was just a little accident," she said, wrinkling up her nose and holding her finger and thumb still for a half second to emphasize the idea of little. "You are not really sick. It is too much sitting around the house. You will feel fine when you go back."

Dolores agreed to go back to work, and then Mercedes helped her to the back room to lie down. When Mercedes came back out, Felícita confessed everything—how she was fired, how Dolores, too, would be marked as a troublemaker if she didn't work. She stared at her working fingers and began to cry. Mercedes held her and stroked her shoulders with surprisingly strong and sure fingers. The fingers surprised Felícita because Mercedes worked in her group and was never a particularly fast or skilled sewer.

"What am I going to do? What am I going to tell Mofongo?"

Mercedes, still holding Felícita, looked down into her eyes. A strange deep voice came out of Mercedes's mouth and it said to Felícita, "Tell him to get a job sewing."

What was this? As a girl Felícita had left the countryside, which was full of spirits and healers, so she had not encountered the devil in a long time. But that must have been his voice!

Mercedes angrily grabbed at her own breasts and then began to undo the buttons on the front of her blouse. Panic-stricken, Felícita realized that the devil must have taken over Mercedes and was now trying to seduce her. Or was she going to force herself on her? In spite of her terror, Felícita could not help but marvel at the clumsiness of Mercedes's long thin fingers as she undid her blouse. Then Mercedes pulled at her brassiere and lifted it up—breasts and all.

Underneath—hairy, angular, lumpy, muscular, a bit bony, without softness—was a man's chest. Mercedes smiled. "I'm sorry." He apologized, but he felt emancipated. "How else could I show you? The hair is real. Dolores does it for me. I'm her husband."

"Really," said Felícita, inspecting Mercedes's swirls and bangs with genuine admiration (though the style was all wrong for the shape of Mercedes face, of course). "She's really good."

Mercedes explained how a man in their village, who had been good at sewing and bad at farming, went to the Free Zone for work and no one would hire him. That was what gave Mercedes the idea to be Mercedes. He would not have come to Mayagüez for Dolores to work with him unemployed. He would have lost her. Everyone in the village had wanted Dolores, and he had won her, because the good-looking men were not as smart as he. Dolores's father had approved of him. "He will take care of you," her father had said.

"My little Mofongo could be a beautiful woman," Felícita said, thinking out loud. "Except he has no hair on the top of his head."

"Get a wig."

"Yes. Dolores could set it for him."

"Yes. He would be a better looker than me," Mercedes suggested courteously.

Felícita smiled, avoiding the obvious response.

"Can he sew?"

"Did you ever watch his hands when he cooks? Do you watch him play the *tres?*" said Felícita.

She was right. He had good hands, and she was able to teach him very quickly. With undergarments stolen from the zone and her skilled fingers, she soon made him a suitable woman's body.

Mr. Hall, to no one's surprise, had been lying. He was not laying off. He was hiring. And soon an attractive new woman was walking along the canal with the others each morning. Also among the women, purse stuffed with chocolate bars, was Dolores, walking with her husband, Mercedes. All of the barrio now knew Mercedes's secret, but they still called him Mercedes. Dolores worked without ever complaining of nausea, stitching buttonholes while unwrapping candy and slipping chocolate in her mouth, never slowing down on the holes. Dolores was good at her work.

And then, as though a curse hung over the doorway, it happened again. This time Dolores saw the cloud coming because she had been reaching for chocolate. A strangeness to the air, a blurring of edges, then a definite greenness, a green cloud moving through the assembly room and women withering and sliding to the floor as it approached them. Others started running, not to escape but to find a place to vomit. Dolores made it to a sink. When she was through, her body aching, tears wetting her cheeks, humiliation in her heart, she looked up and saw firemen with gas masks, dark hulks with huge bulging insect faces moving through the room, scooping up women and carrying them away on their shoulders as though it were a harvest. Dolores did not want to be harvested and steadily tried to make her way to the door. But when a giant with a green hose running out of his nose grabbed her, she did not have the strength to resist and she, too, was a bundle carried out of the zone. Mofongo was also carried out. Mercedes insisted on walking.

This time more than one hundred women fell ill. It was in all the papers, and journalists, lawyers, chemists, environmentalists, union organizers, and politicians rushed across the island to fill the quiet, prosaic little restaurants of Mayagüez, each shouting his own different version of truth over hamburgers and beer, maybe a pork sandwich and french fries, or buckets of Kentucky Fried—the kind of food from which the men of Barrio Albizu had rescued their people. The unions, with the help of their lawyers, had determined that the gas came up from the sewers and that management was responsible and could be sued because Mr. Hall had not put valves on the sewers. The women adopted appropriately indignant tones when talking about the lack of valves, as though they had only taken the jobs because they assumed the sewers had valves. "He didn't even stop to put valves on the sewers," they would say, shaking their heads and clicking tongues.

Immediately, Mr. Hall installed sewer valves. The women went back to work, not so much because there were now valves on the sewers as because there was no other work. Dolores wrapped up more chocolate bars and went also.

It happened again. Exactly the same. This time Dolores got out without being carried and did not go to the hospital but straight home to vomit in her own toilet. The roar had returned inside the back of her head and was accompanied by a rhythmic bass thud. She stuck out her lips in the mirror to see why they were pulsating. Her chest hurt. Right in the middle. Was it her heart? It seemed to hurt only when she breathed deeply. Was it her lungs?

The case of the sewer valves was ruined, and without it, gone was the promise of a money settlement for the woman. Even the chemists and doctors and environmentalists could not say what was causing the gas. Fernandez knew. So did Mr. Tchin and Mr. Hall. But they did not agree. Mr. Hall was certain it was the Independentista, but Fernandez and Tchin suspected it was the Communists. It was Fernandez who found the compromise. "Well," he said, "the Independentistas are probably Communists." They could all agree on that. They could also agree that these gas attacks were reducing the productivity of their plants, though they did not believe the women were really sick.

Mr. Hall invited journalists into his office three and four at a time to discuss his own theories. "It is pretty clear who is behind this. You only have to ask yourself who wants to destroy the Free Zone. *Hmh?*" His eyes would get big and inquisitive, feigning a search of the journalists for the answer. But the journalists would sit silently and wait to be fed. Then he would whisper, in a voice too proud to really be a whisper, "The Independentistas!"

Mr. Tchin, insisting on his own point of view, would always add, "The Independentista are Communists!" Mr. Hall could see from the way the press reacted that Mr. Tchin was making them seem less credible, but he could not stop him.

Felícita warned the women not to talk to union organizers. "If you talk to any union people, you will never work here again. Ever. You know that. Maybe you can go up to the mountains and pick coffee like an illegal Dominican. Is that how you want to end up?"

Felícita knew that she wasn't far from that fate now. Only the Independentistas could help them. No one else would really care about the people of Barrio Albizu.

Certain of the women from Barrio Albizu avoided talking to the press. Since Mercedes had revealed himself, he had been urging other men to put on dresses and go to work. "The first duty of a man is to feed his family," Mercedes would say, repeating a favorite line of his father's. When his father left the banana farm to get a job in one of the new hotels in San Juan, that was what he told his son. Later, when he came back on visits from New York and Mercedes would ask him why he didn't live with them anymore, he repeated the line. Then his father retired and moved back to the farm just as Mercedes and Dolores were leaving for the Free Zone, and the son repeated the line to his father.

The men in the barrio thought Mercedes a little strange. It was a habit. They had thought he was a strange woman, so he was probably also a strange man. But, after the third gassing, they started listening to him. The men started thinking of sewing in the zone as dangerous work, more appropriate for men. Some men refused to let their wives go there anymore. Dolores did the men's hair, sometimes their own and sometimes wigs. She worked on her customers at the same chair in front of her house where she used to stroke her own hair. The men liked getting their hair done by Dolores, being fussed over by the beautiful woman who, until now, had never talked to them. Their wives didn't mind. Dolores was not beautiful anymore, though it seemed the women noticed that more than the men. The men were slow to change their thinking and still saw beautiful Dolores and ugly Mercedes. The women so admired their husbands' hair that they went to Dolores also. She liked doing hair at home, where she was not in danger of another gassing. Soon she was earning almost as much as she had made sewing. And for the first time since they had come to the Barrio Albizu, she was happy.

Another woman had left the zone to open a waxing salon in the barrio. The entire barrio heard the shouts of the men as she yanked strips off. She waxed legs, arms, upper lips, chests. Anything. Ruben Alvarez, current pepper sauce champion, had to have his fingers waxed.

One woman was able to quit the zone and work as a manicurist. Many of the men thought a good manicure made their fingers look more feminine. Between the men and the women, whose nails were in constant need of repair from sewing, manicuring was a good business in Albizu.

Felícita was sewing again, but at home. During the gas attacks Mofongo would scoop up undergarments, panels, straps, and parts, and Felícita gave the men appropriate women's bodies. There were some men that even Felícita couldn't help. The people of the barrio decided that they dared not produce women any uglier than Mercedes.

Now at least some of the men were going to work and some of the women were at home helping them, and a lot of the men and women thought life was now getting more normal—except that everyone was wearing dresses and getting their hair done.

About a third of the women walking to work along the

green and scummy canal were husbands. All they had ever seen before of the zone was a gate and a fence where women lined up. Most men admitted to being a little frightened the first time they were led through the gate in their dresses. What a strange planet was inside. They walked on a blacktop that was exactly black, into flawlessly white buildings. The cleanliness of everything was terrifying, bespeaking some dark power that had banned dirt.

Neither Mr. Hall nor Mr. Tchin noticed that some of the Mayagüez women were not very beautiful. Many still were, and Mr. Tchin one day even pointed out Mofongo as an example of a pleasant looking "local girl." He smiled and nodded at Mofongo, who uneasily smiled back. Mr. Hall, tired of arguing the point, agreed. And, in truth, Mofongo had nice eyes and a good figure. Also he sewed well.

Fear was spreading among the workers. It was pointed out that the river was an unnatural tint of bright blue, and it was widely agreed that it had never been that color before, and then women reported the ocean turning pink and that green mists had been sighted in the early morning. The managers of the plants were growing concerned. These gasses seemed to be having an effect on the workers. Mr. Hall, in particular, noticed that many of the women in his plant were not very good. Productivity was down, even when he was offering overtime. Someone was out to destroy the zone. He knew who it was. Finally agreeing to talk to people from the unions and the political parties, he still refused to talk to Independentistas.

One quiet morning when Dolores had no other customers, Felícita came to her to have her hair done. "You know," Dolores whispered, "I've never been so happy."

"*Shhh!*" said Felícita, with a look of panic. "Happy! You look terrible."

Dolores smiled. "I know," she whispered, absentmindedly unwrapping a chocolate bar and beginning to eat it. "But I am starting to feel better. The headaches have stopped. As long as I don't go back. I know I don't look good. But I have a good, hardworking husband who takes care of me. It is so much easier not to look good."

Felícita understood. "Listen, Dolores . . ." she said with a deep sigh.

Dolores took her hand and smiled. "Don't worry about me," she said with the fire that the men loved returning to her soft eyes. "I know what they are doing, those bastards. I want to get them too. Get them before they poison my husband!" and as though to demonstrate her sincerity, she shoved the chocolate bar in her mouth.

"So why are you still eating chocolate?"

"I love chocolate. I used to worry about it being fattening."

Felícita laughed and held out her hand for a piece of chocolate. Dolores saw that her friend understood, and so she decided to share her other secret. That afternoon Dolores took Felícita to El Burger Paradiso, a bright Mayagüez restaurant, decorated in yellow and orange. Dolores showed her the best burger, "el gordo," with its multilayers and voluptuous orange melted cheese food, the lettuce, the onions, the special pink sauce. And she showed her the trick, lifting off the middle layer and sprinkling hot red pepper sauce. The women struggled to get their mouths around their *gordos* and bite in. They both moaned with pleasure.

Then, dropping her voice from ecstasy to conspiracy, Dolores whispered, "I'm no statehooder, but I love burgers."

Felícita smiled in agreement and said, "But, Dolorita, never tell the boys." Then she ordered some fries.

And so began numerous pleasant afternoons at El Burger Paradiso.

Just before the sun rose over the coffee and plantain mountains, when a glow behind the violet crests showed the day already beginning, Mayagüez was a cool crystalline blue. People in the Barrio Albizu got up in the blue part of the morning, led by the screams of overtrained fighting cocks waiting for their Sundays. Somewhere a tape was playing of Ramito's tough voice with Masso's *cuatro* strumming.

The children were running through the muddy streets, wearing off their first burst of the day. Since their parents had told them that costumes were fun—in fact, their parents wore costumes—the children played in home-designed outfits that they sewed themselves. One girl was

a knight with a gauzelike nylon skirt from the waist down
and armorlike silver denim from the waist up. A boy wore
a scarlet dress with a matching headband and slung
crossed toy cartridge belts over his shoulders, Mexican
bandito style. He insisted he was Zapatito, the Puerto
Rican independence fighter.

The adults were having a meeting, because Felícita had
invited the most famous man in Mayagüez to the barrio.

The most famous man in Mayagüez was famous because
he had shot an American politician—shot him in the ass, it
was always said. The man was firing wildly, and the politician—some said it was a representative, others a senator, or
a governor; a few in Mayagüez insisted it must have been
the U.S. president, though they couldn't say which one, and
maybe it was just a bank manager—was trying to flee, duck
for cover. The hero of Mayagüez shot at what target he had
and spent thirty years in U.S. federal prisons for having hit
it. Then he returned to Mayagüez as a legend.

All of the people of the barrio wanted to meet him. But
the men did not want to meet the great man in their work
dresses. Felícita agreed that the men could all be men. All
except one, who insisted on keeping his hair appointment
early that morning even though Dolores warned him that
it would still be setting. And Mercedes.

Mercedes had dreamed of meeting this man for many
years, talking to him about his own ideas about freedom
and the future of Puerto Rico. Now the great man was
coming to their house. Dolores was the showcase victim.

To the people of the barrio she was still the beautiful Dolores, their most beautiful woman, and anyone would be moved to see what was happening to this beautiful woman. But Felícita warned Mercedes that if Dolores's sister turned out to be a man, they would both end their days "picking coffee."

Mercedes, who had started his days picking coffee, understood her point. But maybe picking coffee was better than dying slowly in a factory. His wife was ill. In recent weeks she had been spending less time in bed and more time cutting hair, but they could not tell the great man about her hairdressing business, so they would say that she spent the entire day in bed. Even the men were starting to notice her good looks disappearing. She was becoming very heavy—from the chocolate bars, they all supposed. For the occasion, Dolores cut her hair short, which horrified most of the men, including Mercedes. It was so much easier, she explained. The men resolved to show the great man what was happening to their most beautiful woman. "It is a plot," Dolores agreed. "Tell them it is a plot."

By the time the first flesh-colored rays climbed over the mountain to light up the barrio in silly hot pastels, the great man had arrived. He was tall and confident with the air of a man who never lost his balance. He walked up to the door, a head taller than the crowd that had followed him, and just touched the iron gate as a courtesy, not really a knock. He smiled at Dolores as he entered the small, dark concrete room with its red couch and color TV, and took her hand warmly and leaned down and kissed her on the cheek. His was the smile of a man who was giving a gift that he knew was something wonderful.

Mercedes, in his green nylon shirtwaist—he had an idea that he looked best in green—pushed through the crowd that had entered his house and then cringed as Felícita introduced the great man to Dolores's sister, Mercedes. Once again, the great man leaned down, put his hands tenderly on Mercedes shoulders, and softly kissed him somewhere between a cheek and the lips.

When Felícita told the lawyers at the Independence Party that the great man had visited Barrio Albizu, they were upset. Their leader flew in from San Juan, an affable blond-haired lawyer who had gone to Yale, and he, too, went to the barrio and kissed Dolores and Mercedes. He told them that if Puerto Rico were an independent country, they would not be poisoned by Yanqui factories.

When Mr. Hall learned that the Independentistas had visited workers in their barrio, he became furious. He called his friend, a financier from the statehood party. Mercedes had known about this man for as long as he had known of the great man. This statehooder, who came from his region, was known to him as the richest man in Puerto Rico. And though Mercedes had a low opinion of statehooders, he was astonished that the richest man in Puerto

Rico was going to visit his dark little house. He wanted to paint the house before the rich man came, but there was no time.

The statehooder—a lean octogenarian, with eyes the color of aluminum, in a silk suit of a color to match his eyes—arrived in the barrio, Italian shoes refusing to sink into the mud. Mercedes was kissed by the richest man in Puerto Rico, who explained that they were suffering from a "status of inferiority" and that once Puerto Rico became a state, somehow—no one in the barrio could remember if he actually explained why—they would not have to breathe poisonous gasses anymore.

Over and over Dolores told her story, and the more she repeated it, the more polish it had. What was at first described as "a weird smell" was now "a scent of roasted almonds and coffee grounds and then something sour like a green mango." And the cloud, originally "greenish and then kind of faded" became "parrot green, then it turned pink like the breast of flamingos and then gray and oily like pigeons." But Mr. Hall and Mr. Tchin did not believe that the woman was really sick at all. It was just part of a conspiracy.

By the time they were informed that the governor of Puerto Rico was coming to their house, neither Dolores nor Mercedes was surprised. Dolores would tell her story again, and they would both be kissed by the governor of Puerto Rico, and nothing would change. Mercedes wanted to ask him which system of government would relieve his wife's headache. But it was very hard for a man like Mercedes to speak out while he was wearing a dress.

And so he stood by in silence, and got kissed, and listened to the governor of Puerto Rico, in his blue suit and red tie—was he trying to dress like the flag?—explain that because of the unique blessings of commonwealth, a solution would be found. Dolores was nodding her head with her brow knit into five deep furrows. Mercedes suddenly interrupted and in a full male voice shouted, "Can't you see she's sick?" The governor stared at him. Mercedes cleared his throat and continued meekly in his falsetto, "I just think she needs a doctor."

Like Mr. Hall and Mr. Tchin, Dolores became increasingly convinced that the poisonings were part of a broadening conspiracy. Conspiracy theories were an island-wide preoccupation. Everything was being connected to what the press dubbed "green gas attacks." A lake near Juncos turned green, the ocean off Ponce was reddish, a village came down with cancer—these things happened in Puerto Rico—now it was always theorized that there might be a connection to the green gas attacks. Dolores carefully followed all of these theories, reading every tabloid, magazine, and newspaper. The papers were stacked against a wall in the living room, a few stray candy wrappers mixed in. She would not allow any newspapers to be thrown out, as though they were all important evidence for an upcoming trial.

As her headaches became less frequent, her body was

overtaken by the painful throbbing of regrets. She could not bear to see her husband go off to the zone in the morning. She had done that to him, she and her father, who thought she was owed everything because she was beautiful. Wasn't she as bad as the ones behind the gas plot? Or was she working for *them*—wasn't sending her husband off to be gassed just what *they* wanted? She clutched Mercedes and talked about an outbreak of brain tumors in Caguas and begged him not to go to work anymore.

"Find something else," she pleaded.

"There isn't anything else. Besides," he said, "I like working."

With tears in her already red eyes Dolores said, "Yes, yes! I wanted you to work. But, it's not worth it. Don't you see what they are doing? This isn't by chance. It is all connected."

Mercedes shook his well-brushed head of hair and said, "Easy, Dolorita, it's just Puerto Rico. You know. A man sleeps with a woman in Bayamón and across the island a baby is born in Ponce and everybody says, 'Aha!'"

"And twenty years later the child grows up and finds out it was true!" she insisted.

There were no more gas attacks. And only Dolores and Felícita and the other women who stayed behind in the barrio ever talked about it. A few women were let into their secret rendezvous at El Burger Paradiso, and often, over *gordos* and hot sauce, they would trade conspiracy theories that no one else would ever hear. What about the

Chinese, who were opening more and more shops in the zone? Or the owners of the coffee plantations? Or people in Miami? But which? Or in Venezuela? Or the companies that owned the burger restaurants? Or the farmers who didn't? Or the Dominicans!

Most of the journalists and unionist and environmentalists had left. Even the lawyers were losing interest.

Then the gas appeared again, and this time Mofongo stumbled and fell just as Mr. Tchin was coming out. Mofongo stood up and straightened his dress. It was when he tried to arrange his hair that he realized his wig was still on the ground. He was standing there, in his bald head with the stringy black fringes, in front of a trembling Mr. Tchin, who was at first horrified by the sight and then, triumphant—at last face-to-face with the primordial enemy, a Communist agent. Mofongo, almost caught, grabbed at his few remaining hairs and held out his fist as though a clump of hair had come with it. "Look what you people have done. I am losing my hair! We are all going to end up in wigs!"

The incident was reported in the paper—"Balding Woman Gets Mad." Environmentalists reported that women were losing their hair from toxic waste. The Independence Party angrily denounced the managers, demanding that these women get immediate medical attention. The company doctors responded by warning the workers about taking too much aspirin for headaches, saying that it "could result in hair loss."

Meanwhile productivity was lower than ever at the

plants. Mr. Hall was having trouble filling his contracts even though he had an unusually high number of women on his payroll. He told Fernandez and Mr. Tchin that he was ready to talk to the Independentistas and find out what they wanted.

They met with the Independence leaders, who would not admit knowing anything about the gas or having any ideas about how to stop it. "That is because they are Communists!" Mr. Tchin triumphantly concluded.

But then the great man contacted the Independence Party and grandly asserted that he knew "what has to be done."

Felícita had been waiting for news to give the barrio. They were beginning to laugh at the Independentistas the same way they laughed at the others. They didn't even respect the great man anymore. Felícita heard Mercedes say to Mofongo, "He hasn't shot a gringo in the ass for thirty years."

When the Independentistas finally acted, when word came of the great man's idea, Mr. Hall was much happier about it than the people in the barrio. Felícita explained while sewing buttons onto the air with her nervous fingers, "The Puerto Rican Independence Party believes in social programs." The curious people of the Barrio Albizu looked at her hopefully. "They at last have gotten the zone to listen to our demands."

"Which demands?" the women asked one another, their voices tinted with dread.

Felícita had been speaking so slowly that it seemed several imaginary buttons had already been attached to the air. "They have gotten us a guaranteed medical program for every worker in the Mayagüez Free Zone."

Silence, heavier than mud, covered the barrio. It seemed they were to have their health carefully monitored. Several of the men uneasily tugged at their dressers. "Is it voluntary?"

"No," Felícita answered frankly, as though she had missed their point.

The management had agreed to the plan, but, sensing a left wing conspiracy, they were not going to allow the workers or the Independentistas to choose the doctors. They would try to fill the place with Independentista doctors. They might as well have union organizers. But the Independentistas knew that the management would get statehooders for doctors. In the end, it was agreed that the new health service would have equal numbers of pro-statehood, pro-commonwealth, and pro-independence doctors, which meant that the workers could be examined by a considerable number of doctors.

Mr. Hall had to admit it. The Independentistas had solved the problem. He didn't mind the cost of the health service because, after it was established, productivity immediately went back to normal levels. He was convinced that the key was making the health service mandatory. He had always known that these *señoras* were just using these gas incidents as an excuse. He was amazed that the Independentistas had given him the idea of the doctors. The Independentistas were sly. Turned against their own people. He must have been right. The Independistas must have been gassing their own workers.

There would be no more work for Mercedes, Mofongo, or the other men of Barrio Albizu. Most of the men had never become fast enough to earn a good wage, anyway— except for Mofongo, who was very good. Julio Colon, a dowdy, matronly woman who could barely sew the strap to a brassiere, was now back home making his excellent *guisado de bacalao*. The woman who had the waxing salon and the manicurist both closed down and went back to working in the zone. Even Felícita got a job. There were no more pleasant afternoons of conspiracies and cheeseburgers with pepper sauce. Mr. Hall was so pleased with the Independentistas that he decided "even the troublemakers," meaning Felícita and Dolores, could come back. There was a lot of work. Orders were coming in, and with less workers from Albizu, there were a few openings to be filled.

With Mercedes out of work, Dolores had to go back. At least, she could have her health carefully monitored by all three kinds of doctors. That was what she told Mercedes, but she knew she would be sitting, trying to sew as fast as she could, and waiting for the next green cloud. Who was gassing them? She was determined that someday she would find out.

But, of course, the ugly sister could not come back. Mofongo had set up their domino table by the canal to wait for their wives to come home. Mercedes sat down to reflect on his defeat. Dominoes was the perfect game for reflections on defeat, the one all the unemployed played, a game that was nothing more than luck and performance— you were supposed to *act* as if it was decided by skill. He hoped that at least the new doctors could help Dolores.

Mofongo could see that the *bacalaito* he brought to cheer up Mercedes was not working. Perhaps it needed more garlic. Mercedes ate it in silence.

"At least we don't have to wear those fucking brassieres anymore," Mofongo offered.

Mercedes nodded.

"How do you suppose women stand it all the time?"

"I think it's different for them."

"Everything's different for them," said Mofongo as he picked his *tres*—delicate, bouncy, and sad. Better than *cuatro*, though the others didn't know, just as they didn't know how good his pepper sauce was because it was not as hot as some of the others. "Did you ever think about going back to coffee?" he said to Mercedes.

"No. It didn't pay."

"That's what Felícita thinks too. But I don't know. Wasn't that bad. The land was good. We didn't need dresses to work. We were all healthy."

"Dolores reads the paper. She says it's poisoned everywhere now."

"Maybe," said Mofongo. "But who is behind it all?"

The sun was setting; the tangerine sky was losing its

glow, and the palms and tall grass were blurring into an indistinct purple shadow. Mercedes triumphantly slapped down a tile, the sound echoing over the once green canal water that in recent days had started shining pink—a loud, electric, flamingo rose color, gaily crowned with the pinkish petals of the hyacinths that were clogging the waterway.

Mofongo hoped the women weren't working too many hours tonight. He had made a pot of *mondongo,* stewing the rum-soaked tripe in a thick, spicy, clay-red sauce with pieces of *yucca.* He didn't like to cook it too long because the yucca started to fall apart.

VERTICAL ADMINISTRATION

The French make a virtue out of lucidity, which is really nothing more than a vice: an ideal vision of life which is in reality confused.

—*Three Trapped Tigers,*
Guillermo Cabrera Infante

Jean-Claude Aubaille was approaching his fiftieth birthday and it could have been said that not much was going on in his life until Deputy Führer Martin Bormann was dropped into his lap. Aubaille's parents had worked with the Resistance and raised their son with tales not only of their adventures but of the tragedy of deported and murdered aunts and uncles, and constant judgments about the good and the bad Frenchmen. Aubaille grew up with a strong sense of which were which.

As a teenager, Jean-Claude with his parents thrilled to

the Israeli capture of Adolf Eichmann. But Eichmann was not enough. They should all be hunted down, made to feel hunted. By the time Jean-Claude reached adulthood, there were no Eichmanns for him. He occasionally exposed a minor functionary or discovered who the hermit was who lived outside of the village. Soon they would all be dead. After almost twenty years of Nazi hunting the best he could claim was that he had made a few people a little less comfortable.

Then something happened.

He ran into a childhood friend coming out of the rue Cadet metro stop in Paris. Charlie Lemercier was a tall man in a permanently merry state of mind, as though he had always just received some wonderfully good news. His lips curled up in a smile at the least provocation, but the real mouth underneath was shaped in a frown. The frown was as unexplainable as the smile. No one would ever have expected Charlie to do anything exotic with his life, but he had somehow become the editor of a newspaper in French Guiana and was living in Cayenne. He told Jean-Claude about his paper and how humorously incompetent the reporters were and about his gingerbread Creole home near Cayenne and about the prehistoric fish they ate and the jungle and the heat and finally, remembering the manners of metropolitan life, he asked Jean Claude about himself.

"But what have you been doing in Paris?" he asked.

It was a difficult question for a forty-eight-year-old Nazi

hunter with only unknown Nazis to his credit. But Charlie lived in French Guiana, where no one asked for results. And so when Jean-Claude explained that he was a Nazi hunter, Charlie accepted that appreciatively. Whether or not he actually caught Nazis was an uninteresting detail in the same way that no one would ever ask Charlie how many people read his newspaper.

Charlie smiled merrily, as though Nazi hunting were one of the really fun pastimes, and said, "Well, I may have something for you."

"What kind of something?" Jean-Claude was cautious after three decades of tips.

"A Nazi." He put his fingers over his mouth in a token attempt to cover his smile at the great joke of knowing a Nazi.

Meanwhile, Jean-Claude's Nazi-hunting mind was at work. Charlie was the editor of *Guyane Matin,* which was owned by Charles Hernan, the biggest press baron in France. The name Hernan, once mentioned in his parents' home, had met with a torrent of angry history. He was the kind of man Jean-Claude exposed, except that he had already been thoroughly exposed. No one seemed to care. What kind of a Nazi would the editor of an Hernan paper be offering up? Why didn't Charlie go after this Nazi himself? Maybe he couldn't. Maybe this was his revenge. A way to settle scores and still keep his job with the bright-colored, gingerbread-garnished house. A different type of collaborator. You didn't meet people by chance in the rue

Cadet metro. It wasn't a busy stop. Why would Charlie be in this neighborhood, anyway?

Charlie leaned forward and whispered, "Martin Bormann lives in French Guiana." He nodded for emphasis and then began giggling like an adolescent who had just confessed a crush.

"But Bormann"—Jean-Claude calculated as he spoke— "would be ninety—more than ninety years old."

Charlie nodded. "Yes, and this man looks more like seventy-five. Furthermore, some say he is too short. He lives on the Oyapok. If things get too difficult, he crosses the river and he is in Brazil. It only takes a few minutes and a few francs, and nobody goes looking in the interior, anyway. People don't ask questions in the interior. It is too dangerous, too many accidents, no one to find you. Everyone minds their own business. It's perfect."

Charlie sounded giddy, but Jean-Claude was barely listening. Martin Bormann, the number two man. Known above all for his slyness. "The Machiavelli behind the office desk." Short, chunky, receding hairline, widow's peak. The file raced through his head as he bought the Air France ticket for Cayenne. When the Russians were a block away from Hitler's bunker and the Führer was preparing his suicide, Bormann was still giving orders. Still threatening. He made a last-minute attempt to negotiate safe passage from the Soviets. But this time the wily manipulator miscalculated. The Soviets turned him down. Or did they?

Brazil. Charlie had said that he stayed close to the

Brazilian border. Hedging his bets. Leaving room to maneuver. That was what got Aubaille interested. It was like Bormann to find a way to live in France, in Europe, and still be three minutes from Brazil. Bormann watched Hitler and Eva Braun go up in flames, gave them their last salute. He was seen a block away fleeing behind a tank that received a direct hit, and eyewitnesses said Bormann was killed.

Just across the river from Brazil, Charlie had said. One foot in France and one in Brazil. A good move. Another eyewitness said that he had killed himself with poison. His body had been seen under a bridge on Invalidenstrasse. Both witnesses couldn't have been right. But they could both have been wrong. Bormann was sentenced to death in absentia in 1946. Then someone thought he saw him as a monk in Italy. Later, Bormann was identified as a businessman in South America, several times in several countries. In 1973 the West German government produced a skeleton and officially pronounced Bormann dead. The same year he was spotted in Argentina. But the German court had ordered that all sightings be ignored. Bormann, the wily "brown eminence," was free.

Free and dangerous. The main thing was to identify him. Let the Israelis do the rest. If the French tried to extradite him, he would slip into Brazil. Let him go into Brazil. The Brazilian officials would probably be easier to fix. Just kidnap him. French officials would be too hard to get to. French officials, Aubaille reasoned, could be tough.

The main thing at any Guianese gathering, the simple, all-important detail, was the table set up by the entrance on which officers could place their hats. There were the blue hats of the gendarmerie, preferably a few with golden captain's braids and maybe one with the gilded sparkling cap of the colonel. There were the white caps of the legionnaires, including one with immaculate red, blue, and gold, if the colonel of the Third Regiment was there. A red cap of a visiting airborne was always welcome. And the fine gold hat of the two-star general of the Guianese Armed Forces was a good sign.

But the most sought after hat was the simple white hat (with blue visor and gold braid) of the *préfet. Préfets* are not in the military and have not worn uniforms since the days when they governed France's far-flung colonies, a symbol of power, Western civilization, culture, and meticulous laundering. Nowadays, French Guiana was a *département,* and all the *départements* of France had *préfets,* but they wore suits and ties. Even in former colonies such as Guadeloupe and Martinique the *préfets* wore suits and ties. The last four or five *préfets* of French Guiana had also worn civilian clothes. But this *préfet,* appointed six months before, decided in the name of tradition to revive the *préfet's* uniform, which was entirely white, including shoes. Only the visor and braid on the cap, which looked more like yachting wear than the stiff military headgear, had color.

The préfet, was a tall, broad-shouldered, round-chested man with a tremendous belly, all of which looked enormous in white. But he earned the admiration of the locals, which was what he had intended, as he strolled through this untamed country, head to toe in white, casually puffing on a pipe, looking immaculate and unperturbed. The equatorial tropics, he seemed to be saying, were beneath the dignity of France. The most impressive part was the white shoes, because French Guiana, the fabled Eldorado, is a land of mud. In the rainy season there is almost nothing but mud. In the dry season the wrong step will still result in sinking above the knees in muck. The only person who could walk around French Guiana in spotless white shoes was the *préfet*. The commandos at the Legionnaires Equatorial Forest Combat Training Center, generally half-naked and mud covered, still laugh about the time the *préfet* turned up wearing his whites for inspection in their jungle swamp.

The most impressive table of hats to be found in the *département* was in the town of Kourou, by the entrance to the reception at the Hôtel des Roches, a large modern hotel next to the radio tower that was built to receive messages from Captain Dreyfus's jailers on nearby Devil's Island. The old radio tower, built by the slave labor of prisoners, was rich in masonry details, whereas the hotel, built with good French wages, had squared corners and no details at all. The reception was held in its most splendid venue, a plain but large concrete terrace by the largest swimming pool in the *département*.

There were always two hats missing at the table. The two-star general avoided functions at which the *préfet* was present. He was a democrat and did not mind being out-ranked by a civilian, but not a civilian who wore a uniform, was fat and out of shape, and didn't know how to hold his shoulders. The other missing hat was the *préfet*'s. He liked to wear it in the reception.

The reception was held once a month after the launching of a satellite by the European Space Center, which used to be a major event. The international press and European VIPs would come. The guest list was chosen by Zelemé, a poor Creole from Cayenne who had succeeded in the French world and was displayed by the French as an example of how locals were benefiting from the space program. He was thought to wield tremendous power because he chose the guest list. His power had somewhat dwindled since launchings had become an almost monthly event and few reporters covered them and the only European space officials to attend were those whose wives wanted a week in the tropics. The local farmers working the sandy soil east of Kourou, because their good land had been confiscated "for security reasons," barely bothered to look up and curse at the monthly flash in the sky anymore. To most people, the only possibility of excitement was if the rocket blew up, which happened from time to time, but not recently.

But in a way, Zelemé felt even more powerful. When the launchings had seemed important, bureaucrats, politicians, generals, and businessmen were standing over him as he made up his guest list. But now that the list had become less important, he was freer to chose by himself. And locals who used to be ignored, grand Creoles from Cayenne, needed him if they wanted to be seen there.

For the military that was there to guard the space center and for the *préfet,* who was there to look after the president's interests, which included the space center, and for those who wanted to be seen with such people, the reception after a launching was the major event in the cyclical social life of coastal French Guiana. Unlike the launchings themselves, the receptions were a dependable event. Anything could happen at a rocket launching, but at the reception there was always endless champagne served in long, stately flutes that fit well in the hand when one was making an important point, and the same little pastries and little salt-fish beignets and those little Asian rolls the Hmong made ("Glad we let them in," the colonel of the Third Regiment always thought as he popped the little delicacies in his mouth).

Captain Longchamp commanded the gendarmerie in Kourou, which was an important post for a captain. He was tall, and his short blond hair had bleached golden in the sun. The most relaxed man at the reception, he looked like someone just out enjoying himself for the evening, a man who could depend on his handsome smile with its ingratiating laugh lines. But, in truth, he had too many things to worry about. For a forty percent bonus on his paycheck, he had volunteered for *outre-mer* duty, service among the remaining rocks, swamps, and beaches of the vanishing empire. But it was making his wife bitter. She longed to drive her car in a French town that had more than one paved road and to shop in a fish market that had something besides snapper and shrimp. And in order for her to get to do these things, Captain Longchamp was going to have to earn a good posting somewhere like Toulouse, and so he could not let the army outdo him and he especially could not let the legionnaires, "real military trash," ever show him up when he stood around the Hôtel des Roches sipping champagne.

He strolled up to Zelemé, the small Creole man with beads of sweat on his dark forehead. Zelemé often noted that the French, Longchamp in particular, did not sweat the way he did, and that made him sweat even more. But the French, who thought the Creoles notoriously duplicitous, appreciated the beads of sweat on Zelemé's forehead. You could trust a Creole who sweated.

Zelemé's problem was similar to that of Longchamp's. He also had to make good at these receptions—find a little something to pass on to DST, the government intelligence service, or maybe even a little something to slip through that haze of pipe smoke to the *préfet* himself.

Longchamp's wife was chatting with Zelemé and that giggly idiot from *Guyane Matin*. "Charlie actually got him to come here," Longchamp's wife said incredulously.

"Well, there are probably many Nazis here," said Zelemé, who agreed with most things as a matter of policy.

"Yes, I am a Nazi," said Dieter Lamdorff bitterly. Zelemé and Longchamp's wife smiled politely. Charlie giggled.

"I am a German, and so I am a Nazi," said Dieter. Dieter always said this. He was Zelemé's competition, because he did public relations for the European Space Agency and Zelemé did it for the European Space Center. But Zelemé didn't worry about Lamdorff. He was too morbid and he was German and the French didn't like Germans.

Lamdorff was not a Nazi. His father had been an important Nazi, convicted for war crimes. But no one remembered the name. In the 1950s, Dieter had immigrated to the U.S., where his father was soon forgotten. But whenever the subject of Nazis came up, he would make this strange confession, which was always taken for a heavy Germanic sense of humor.

When Captain Longchamp heard that someone was coming to Guiana, he eased over. It was always good to write the first report on someone new. Leblond, the army undercover security man, was, as usual, close behind, and Longchamp had to look relaxed enough not to alert Leblond, or the army would have a matching report.

"Who is your friend looking for?" he asked Charlie.

"I don't understand," asked Zelemé. "What exactly does he do?"

Too late. That nervous way of Zelemé's, leaning into the question, and all that sweating. Leblond couldn't miss it.

"He is a Nazi hunter," said Charlie, smiling.

"But what does a Nazi hunter do?"

"You know, like that Jewish fellow who brought Klaus Barbie back. And those people who kidnaped Eichmann."

"Wasn't Eichmann captured by Israeli intelligence?" asked Longchamp, hoping Leblond would bite.

Longchamp went home that night and wrote out a report that a Jewish associate of the *Guyane Matin* editor was coming incognito to do an exposé on the Nazi past of an as-yet-unknown military officer. The army report written by Leblond stated that the Israeli secret service was planning to infiltrate French Guiana, no doubt seeking to steal technical secrets from the space center. The report slipped to DST the following morning by Zelemé warned of the possible arrival of a "Jewish kidnapping ring."

But the *préfet* did not choose any of these reports for his midday reading. It was Wednesday, and on Wednesdays when he closed his door to read intelligence reports and not be disturbed, he let Zinnie, the soft and comfortable Creole woman who worked at the hotel on Place de Palmiste, in the other door. Not only was Zinnie's dark flesh a great pleasure to squeeze, but, the *préfet* was firmly convinced, she had the best intelligence reports.

As he reached under her skirt, she told him the most disturbing news possible. It was about the new guest at the hotel—an anthropologist. The *préfet's* hands dropped limp to his sides. "An anthropologist? You are sure?"

"That's what he said. Said he wanted to study the Brazilian border."

"*Hmm,*" said the *préfet,* thoughtfully fondling one of

Zinnie's breasts the way he sometimes fondled the bowl of his pipe when he was thinking. "He is going to try to go up the Oyapok! It is an unauthorized zone! He is going to try to sneak upriver without my permission!"

About a third of French Guiana was a zone that could not be visited without permission from the *préfet*. The reason was said to be a desire to protect the Amazonian Indians from disease, alcoholism, and other problems carried by the white man. But to the *préfet*, it was much more serious than that. The zone was his entire source of power. No one could enter without his permission. Some people were granted permission. Others were not. Only he knew who would get the permission. But there were always those who thought they could go without permission. That is when he had to mobilize the gendarmerie. And anthropologists! They were worse than journalists. They always acted as if they had a right to go. The more the *préfet* thought about this, the angrier he became. He told Zinnie she had to leave. Then he took the reports on his desk, shoved them to one side, called in his assistant with a list of people he wanted to call, and began to mobilize. No one was going up the Oyapok without his permission.

The twin-engine ten-seater bumped and squished into the reddish mud of the airstrip. The three passengers who stepped out squinting in the sunlight saw five people waiting in the shade.

Madame Dufort embraced her cousin, back from a visit to the *métropole* with jars of pears so they didn't have to eat mangoes for a while.

The man standing nearby, short and thickset with one tuft of white hair left on the top of his head, the stubborn remnant of a widow's peak, was at the airport for his shipment of sausages from Paris via Cayenne. The owner of the only restaurant in St. Georges, he was always called the German although he was Alsatian, not German. Perhaps it was just the sausages.

Also waiting by the airstrip was Filosoof, a Suriname N'Djuka tribesman four rivers away from home, but a better boatman than any on the Oyapok, which was an easy river by his standards, and he made good money taking people up. He didn't care whether or not they had a letter from the *préfet*. No one on the Oyapok could keep up with Filosoof. Even if they had bigger engines, he could slip into marshes and tributaries that no gendarme could navigate. Filosoof was named for his calm, quiet manner, the way he always looked as if he would come forth with an astounding observation if the world would only be quiet; but he never did, or perhaps the world never was quiet.

The sturdy, khaki-clad, mustached Brazilian who had been studying geological surveys in Cayenne was the passenger for whom Filosoof had come. They were going far up the river, touching on the Brazilian side but looking for gold past Camopi in Emirillon Indian country on the French side, doing it without permission from the *préfet*.

No one seemed to notice or care about the Brazilian. The main thing was the white man. They were always the ones to watch. A white man didn't show up without a reason. This one said he was an anthropologist. That was never the real reason.

Ronier from the gendarmerie who met the flights made a mental note, "Three passengers—one white," hopped back into his jeep, and sped the three-minute drive back to town, where the two other gendarmes were comfortably dozing in the shuttered gendarmerie. As Jean-Claude Aubaille made his way down the muddy road to St. Georges, Ronier passed by especially close so he could get a look before making his report.

The German, his jeep loaded with his goods, also passed by awkwardly on the right side of the road to get a good look at the new white man. The German was barely tall enough to see over the dashboard and had to lunge out the window to steal a look at Aubaille.

Aubaille kept walking, letting the others lead the way. Madame Dufort was busily chatting with her cousin pulling the little cart loaded with cartons of jarred pears. Aubaille couldn't help thinking that sometimes when this plump, green-eyed Creole with skin the color of smooth muddy water turned around to look at her cousin, she stole an extra glance at him. Past her best years and certainly beyond the dress size she was wearing, the dress's thin cotton straining at the buttons, Aubaille nevertheless found something appealing about her— a nicely aging, fleshy mulatto in a small dress on a muddy tropical road. He liked the way she kept looking at him.

Less appealing was the gaze of Filosoof, his eyelids drooping lazily over dark, penetrating eyes, his mouth in what was almost a smile. It was as though he could see a banana peel that Aubaille was about to slip on.

And so, locked in stares, half stares, and glances, they were making their way into St. Georges along the French bank of the Oyapok. There are only about a dozen towns in the interior of French Guiana, all but one on rivers. They are all similar, surrounded by voracious jungle that would swallow up a town in a season if it were not for regular slashing-and-burning. To assert its Frenchness, the center always had a little World War I monument and a French flag. There was always a *mairie,* which was usually the town's one contemporary building, ill-suited for the tropics with its unyielding concrete architecture that would soon mold, then crack, then crumble, and its low roofs that did not circulate the steamy air. Next to it would be the little tin-roofed church that would outlast it. And rising above them was the radio tower. Every town had to have a radio tower for communications, standing with the church and *mairie* in the center, looking like a miniature Eiffel Tower in the miniature French town surrounded by an impassable and threatening green jungle.

By the time Aubaille could see the little Eiffel Tower, Ronier was already using it, radioing in to Captain Longchamp to tell him that Aubaille had arrived.

"Who has he tried to talk to?"

"Nobody yet, he just walked into town. I think he looked like he wanted to talk to Madame Dufort."

"Dufort, that's interesting," said Captain Longchamp, who had become an expert on exactly to what office everyone in the *département* reported. "You know what that means."

Ronier thought everybody in St. Georges must know what that meant. He had had the same thoughts about her soft, generous form, always squeezed into those thin dresses—but why was this interesting? This was all annoying. Nobody else in the gendarmerie had to work today. It was always bad when you got involved with these coastal officers.

"Listen, Ronier, find some excuse to question him. Ask some questions."

"What kind of questions?"

"Questions. So I can make out a report. When this thing breaks, I want to show that I had been reporting on it all along."

"All right, sir." But in truth it was too late in the day to ask questions. It was too hot. He would go over to Madame Dufort's and drink for a while like the other gendarmes, and if Aubaille turned up, he would ask him some questions. Yes, Ronier thought, questions like, "Do you want a beer?" Ronier laughed, tucked his hair under his cap, and left to join the other gendarmes at the bar at Madame Dufort's.

Aubaille got his room and board—the only place to get

a room, and then walked past the bar, past the three rum-drinking gendarmes, and out the open doorway, across the muddy street to the German's restaurant. As he was about to step into the dark restaurant, he felt someone's eyes on him and, looking back across the street, saw the voluptuous hot-afternoon gaze of Madame Dufort.

While Aubaille sat eating sausages, making small talk with the German, Filosoof had already relayed his message back to Leblond at the army garrison. The message was simply, "Lone Israeli arrived on morning plane." Things were moving. Leblond was pleased.

"But I have already told you, I'm not German. It's just a nickname," said the German in a flawless French with some unplaceable regionalism to it. It might have been an Alsatian accent. Aubaille had never been to Alsace. He looked at the German across the table, so small a man that the tabletop came up to his chest, his chunky elbow forced skyward as he poured them another white rum. While each mixed in the sugar and squeezed limes in his own drink, they stared at each other, each so intent on his study that he didn't notice the other staring. Walking by noiselessly and unobserved, Filosoof looked into the dark room.

Filosoof wanted to keep the army happy, but he did not really care what their interest was in this Israeli. He knew that when a white man showed up in the interior without a good reason, he was looking for gold. So if the army wanted this white man followed, he was happy to do it.

"What year were you born?" asked Aubaille, hoping to sound casual about the question. But it didn't work.

"Why?" asked the German.

"If you were born in Alsace before the First World War, you were born in Germany."

"Ah, you surprise me, Mr. Aubaille. That's thinking like a German. Alsace was always French. It had just been occupied."

That was a good answer. Aubaille had to admit that. "What year were you born?"

He could have been lying about his age, the great papery folds under his chin and the crisscrossed drying surfaces of his cheeks, the bony, spotted hands all looked considerably older than mid-seventies. But he was not lying about his height. This man was less than five feet tall. He was almost a midget. There were not many photographs of Bormann. He didn't like being photographed. But Aubaille had one picture of Hitler with Bormann on the left-hand edge of the photo, and he looked slightly shorter than Hitler. That was short. But not this short, even allowing for shrinking with age.

The German smiled as though laughing at something Aubaille had just thought. "I look older, don't I? You try living in this cursed country."

"Why do you stay?" Could this man see other people's thoughts?

"Ah," he said, taking a large gulp of rum. "You learn to

live in this country, and you're not fit for anyplace else. Negroes and Indians. They can live here and it's all right. Like that N'Djuka, Filosoof. You saw him at the airport. I've never seen the expression on his face change. He can do anything, endure anything, and when he is my age, he'll look like he looks now. But for Europeans it's different. See, Filosoof doesn't expect anything but what is here. We all come here for miracles—the gold, the rockets to space, the adventure, all of that. Filosoof doesn't know what adventure is. He just calls it life. And a rocket is a flash in the sky, and gold—oh, he likes gold all right. Never stops by a sandy bank that he doesn't do a little panning. But he doesn't think it will make him rich or change his life. He likes his life now. He doesn't want to get rich and get out of here. He just likes gold."

The German's eyes were very watery, and Aubaille was not sure, but he may have been crying. "*Ahhh,*" he said, waving his hand in disgust. "We just stay here and get eaten up. Just like the wood. You see the wood?" He smacked the table and stood up. He was getting very drunk. Aubaille was feeling a little rubbery, but the German seemed worse.

"See, you've got to make everything of mahogany or harder. Otherwise it gets eaten up. You can't drive a nail into the damn stuff. So they use this softer wood, and look." He pointed to perfect round holes that looked as though they had been drilled into the wood. You have to be harder than this to survive here," he said, smacking a countertop. "You know, most of the wood here is so hard, it won't even float." He stumbled around his dark, softwood restaurant, throwing open cabinet doors, slapping walls, pointing out holes.

"Come on, take a look at what this place is like," he commanded in such a gruff voice that Aubaille had no choice but to stand up and begin inspecting, looking behind doors, opening cabinets, while the German shouted. But as Aubaille started to open one cabinet, he felt the German's spotted hand, hard as bone, clamp to his wrist with some mechanical force. Aubaille was suddenly looking into a hot, pale, blue-eyed stare. The German tossed a nod toward the cabinet. "You don't want to look in there," he said in carefully enunciated syllables.

By the time Aubaille stumbled across the street to Dufort's, Madame had already sent her report to the *préfet*. "The anthropologist is here, passing his time with the German, apparently looking for upriver contacts."

"I knew it," said an angry *préfet*. "He is going to try to go into the zone!" He told Madame Dufort to watch closely and report back.

Aubaille could see how Madame Dufort was looking at him. And Ronier saw these glances as he and the other gendarmes sleepily shuffled back to the gendarmerie for their afternoon rest. He had enough for another report. Longchamp would be pleased. "Suspect conferring with the German. Also, secret connection between suspect and Madame Dufort."

Longchamp was pleased. This was good. He could elaborate, give more details, in his report. It was becoming clear. This man had arrived to expose a Nazi in the military. He only talks to two people, Madame Dufort, who works for the *préfet,* and the German, who was DST. So it was obvious that Paris wanted to disgrace the military. It came right from the government. The Socialists. Not that Longchamp wanted to get in the middle of this. It didn't matter how it turned out; only that he knew about it. Just file good reports and get back to Toulouse.

In the evening when the gendarmes were back at Madame Dufort's, drinking under the pale fluorescent light, Aubaille would sit on a bench on the riverfront, a short village block away, and watch the smugglers tie up in wondrous antique Amazon riverboats with ornate wooden balustrades. They quietly unloaded their goods. Aubaille certainly didn't care what they were unloading. He just wanted to look in that one cabinet of the German's. What was in there? Was it documents? Souvenirs of the old days? Political tracts? Hate literature?

Madame Dufort, realizing that Aubaille had gone to the riverfront by himself, panicked, left the bottles out on the bar for the gendarmes, and awkwardly pranced over in a stiff-legged run that was supposed to resemble walking. If he made it up the river from her town, she would lose the *préfet's* confidence and then she would have no standing with the French at all.

But he was just sitting there. Far from being perturbed by her spying, he seemed almost pleased and asked her to join him on the bench. He was more cunning than he looked. These French usually were.

While they were talking, Filosoof buzzed his canoe across from Brazil and walked over to the German's. Without saying anything to each other, Madame Dufort and Aubaille both strolled over to where the canoe was tied, making a great effort to look uninterested, the legs sauntering easily but the necks straining just a bit too much.

Down in the canoe were two young white men with shaved heads. They looked like legionnaires, but they did not wear uniforms. Several long crates rested along the rails of the canoe. As Aubaille stared down, he wondered where Filosoof had gone. He had probably gone to that cabinet. What would he take?

Soon Filosoof walked back to the waterfront without carrying anything in his hands, smiled vaguely at Aubaille, and got back in his canoe. He started up the river with the two mercenaries and the heavy-caliber machine guns that he would deliver to Cayenne, where they would be driven to St. Laurent and taken down another river to fight with the Surinamese guerrillas.

In her report, Madame Dufort pointed out the strange-looking foreigners and the long crates and the fact that Aubaille seemed very interested. The *préfet* studied the report with enough interest to let his pipe die out while he fondled it absentmindedly. The report raised a question that it failed to answer. Was the canoe going upriver or down? A small investigation revealed that it was smuggling arms to Suriname. This meant that it was only going downriver after all. He was a little annoyed that he had wasted his Wednesday afternoon on this matter when the canoe was not even heading upriver.

After Filosoof was through with the mercenaries, he stopped off in his village on the Maroni, took time to talk to the elders, be with his family, hunt and fish at night, remember who he was, and then he went back, stopping on the way in Cayenne to talk to army intelligence.

In Cayenne no one cared how well he handled a dugout canoe or hunted in the dark. He had to go to the slum by the river to meet the army intelligence officer, a lieutenant under Leblond who always went there to meet his contacts because he believed that the river slum was their neighborhood. Filosoof reported to the army that "The Israeli was working with Madame Dufort," and then he left for St. Georges. He didn't like the smell of the slum.

Army intelligence reasoned that the DST must have something to do with this plan and told Filosoof to watch the German.

Aubaille, after spending his days under shaded indoor ceiling fans, trying to hide from the heat, had grown accustomed to spending his evenings along the waterfront. There was no place else to go. The jungle surrounded the little town, and at night he could hear it roar and feel it straining, wanting to eat up this little enclave and reclaim its riverbank. The gendarmes at Madame Dufort's laughed uncontrollably as they drank away the night, but their stories were not very funny and it was a chore to always pretend they were. Here there was an evening breeze, starlight reflected off the river and gave a glow, there were the boats to watch, and the German's empty restaurant was right behind him. How and why would someone run a restaurant that was always empty? What, wondered Aubaille, was Filosoof's relationship with the German? Was Filosoof his getaway to Brazil, if he ever needed it quickly?

Then there was Madame Dufort. He only had to come sit on this bench by the river and she would soon show up. Pausing to change her pace as she came into view, thinking he could not see her eagerness. She was there now. He could feel her presence, her eyes looking amber at night. He could almost pick up a scent of her. He turned confidently.

Two pale blue eyes shone in the starlight, and he realized that he was looking at the German standing in the dark.

"It's nice here in the evening," Aubaille offered uncertainly.

"Yes," said the German. "A nice view of the river."

"Yes, in the starlight. Have you traveled on the river much?"

"You know," said the German, stepping closer to him and the light of the two street lanterns—the kind found on bridges in Paris—that marked the town's waterfront. Aubaille could see him smiling, though his smile looked like a threat, "I like it here, in general. Hear that. Don't talk a minute."

The German stood next to where Aubaille was seated on the bench, so that their eyes met at the same level, and they listened to the jungle—thousands of insects screeching at once, the swishing of a million thorned branches, and hundreds of screaming birds, howling monkeys, rampaging wild pigs, and foraging rodents in the night—the blended noise came into St. Georges as one continuous throbbing explosion, as loud and much bigger than the rockets that took off from Kourou. That was why the gendarmes laughed so much, to try not to hear it.

After a few minutes of listening, the German said, "Yes, it's right out there. That's why people don't ask many questions here."

"What?"

"You never find anybody when they are lost out there. They just found the wreck of a plane that crashed ten years ago with a big-name French engineer. He was missing for a decade. The wreck was only two kilometers outside of Régina. That is the way it is. Walk five minutes past this town and see what happens. A white man can stay alive for a maximum of three days. Now, Filosoof, it's his home. That's why he is so confident. Nothing can happen to a man who can live there. But you and I, three days at the most. So you don't ask too many questions because you don't know who you are dealing with and you don't want to find yourself out there. No one would even stumble across the body. That's why white people get along here. We know how to act toward each other. It is not like the city. Out here no one would be foolish enough to get into someone else's business. That's why we like each other. For example, you told me you were an anthropologist. I didn't ask what kind of anthropologist. That's why we get along. Jungle rules for white men."

Aubaille felt a strong, hard finger tap him on the collarbone—and then he was alone.

The German's report to the DST stated that the Jewish kidnapper so far appeared mainly to be interested in Madame Dufort. Obviously, DST reasoned, since Dufort was with the *préfet,* someone was trying to compromise the president of the republic.

The DST was pleased with the German's report, but it was not good enough for the German himself. Reports to DST were one thing, but eventually he would have to find out what this "anthropologist" was really doing.

Zelemé received separate requests, which he understood to be orders, from the *préfecture,* the gendarmerie, and the two-star general to invite Jean-Claude Aubaille to the next launching. In addition, he received a message from DST that Aubaille was already on the list. This was annoying, because everyone already on the list was a mistress, relative, business associate, potential business associate, or potential mistress of a French official. Zelemé's entire standing was based on his ability to produce these invitations. Odile, that delicious Creole woman whom he intended to seduce at the Hôtel des Roches after the launching, was the only possible name he could eliminate to make room for this Aubaille.

An invitation to the post-launch party at the Hôtel des Roches could be many things, including the most polite and correct way to bring someone in for questioning. Some came all the way from France for the event, and certainly no one would turn down an invitation, except, of course, for the general, who sent his intelligence man, Leblond.

Aubaille was not going to pass up the invitation. It was an excuse to get back to the coast, eat something besides river fish, game, cassava meal at Madame Dufort's, or sausages at the German's, check into a hotel with air-conditioning, take a bath in a long tub in an antiseptic tiled room, drink champagne, or even walk on a different street. He dreamed of all these things as he waited in the little room at the airfield for his ten A.M. Air Guyane flight. But by ten A.M. the ten-seater had not come in from Cayenne nor did it by eleven. After noon, other passengers began to notice. Aubaille stared futilely at the hot plastic-blue sky and tried to hear the twin engines.

"Going to Cayenne?"

It was the German.

"I'm trying to get there."

"I can take you. Air Guyane won't show up now."

"How are you going?"

He pointed to a small, white single-engine plane at the end of the mud-red airstrip. "Come on." He motioned at Aubaille, and then his sturdy compact body started walking toward the plane.

Aubaille could think of a number of reasons not to go. Single engine. Elderly pilot. Alone over the jungle canopy with a suspected Nazi. But he wasn't left an opportunity to say no and found himself walking behind the German to the little white two-seater.

Aubaille took the blocks from the wheels and pushed the plane by its tail onto the runway while the German shouted his orders. Once they were seated in the plane, the German instructed him to hold his door open. "It's too hot," shouted the German as he started up the engine. "Wait until we get up a few hundred feet."

Aubaille checked the straps of his seat belt and wondered what the German's plan was and by what act of passive madness he was sitting in this airplane as it scrambled down the bumpy runway. He kept a hand on the door handle as the little plane climbed. He looked down and saw a solid floor of treetops, nothing but bright mottled green with no break, except a distant ribbon of café au lait, the Approuague River, which led to Régina, where the ten-year-old plane wreck had just been found.

The altimeter was showing more than a thousand feet, and the air in the little cabin was cooling off, but the German said nothing about closing the door. Instead, he regularly gave an angry smack to the instrument panel, causing all the needles to momentarily jiggle. "Ah, zut," he shouted over the deafening buzz of the engine. Once Aubaille thought that instead of "ah" he might have said, "ach." He might have accidentally cursed in German. But the engine was too loud and he could not be sure.

Suddenly, the plane banked sharply to the German's side and dipped down and swung around while the German held his own door handle so that the door would not drop wide open. Aubaille clutched the edges of the seat and hoped the German didn't see his fear. The bumpy green floor below was rushing toward them with horrifying detail. Then they started regaining altitude. It was probably a rehearsal. Next he would bank the other way and give a good hard shove. Aubaille remembered the grip of the German's bony fingers and wondered how strong this small elderly man could be. He checked his straps again and closed his door. "I think it's cool enough now." They were at fifteen hundred feet and climbing.

The German only nodded and shut his own door. Then he smacked the instruments again, banked the plane the other way, and did another dip.

"What are you doing?" Aubaille shouted at the onrushing green, and could barely be heard over the engine buzz.

"I'm trying to take a look!" the German shouted back,

and Aubaille then realized that his pilot was too short to see over the instrument panel.

"What are you looking for?"

"Cayenne!"

When a European starts living in the interior, hotel rooms become one of the great late-night dreams. Aubaille was disappointed in his room at the Hôtel des Roches in Kourou. He dreamed better rooms than this. But the shower was a real shower and there was a bar with wine and Pernod and Air France flight attendants in sundresses. He skipped the launching. He hadn't been invited to the viewing platform, an intentional oversight by Zelemé, who was angry about having to invite this man at all. Later, Aubaille left the hotel bar and went to the swimming pool terrace for the reception.

The *préfet* had decided that he would not personally talk to Aubaille. When he saw him coming toward him, fearing a breach in the protocol he had decided on, he panicked and backed away awkwardly, knocking a beignet out of the hand of a Creole who had gotten on Zelemé's list. The wiry and fit colonel of the Third Regiment laughed to himself at the oafish, overweight *préfet,* but the Creole, who worked in the Kourou municipal government, feared having gotten a grease spot on the *préfet's* white uniform.

Longchamp moved in. Leblond was right behind: the

others gathered as best they could. Zelemé stood behind Aubaille. Longchamp's wife was with him. Dieter Lamdorff was way in the back, straining to hear. They all smiled and sipped from their champagne flutes and between sips asked casual questions.

"So, where have you been?" asked Longchamp.

"St. Georges."

"St. Georges! Why would you go there?" asked Leblond, and Longchamp smiled in his tall, blond, handsome way, trying not to show his irritation.

"How long are you staying there?" asked someone Aubaille had not met.

Aubaille, who had now been drinking for several hours, felt like being rude, like not playing the game, breaking the rules, being a man of the interior who did not take to questions. "Look," he said to Longchamp, "why don't I just talk to you. You can write up your report and pass it around to them."

He thought that perhaps he had gone too far. But Longchamp did not look upset. "Oh, no," said Longchamp earnestly. "French administration is vertical." He demonstrated with a stiff hand. "We each have to write our own reports."

Then Aubaille recognized behind him the giggle of Charlie Lemercier. How had he let this fool get him involved in this whole thing? What was he doing? Who was this German? What real evidence did Lemercier have? Was he somehow being set up for something? You don't run into people by chance in the Rue Cadet metro. He tried to pull Charlie aside. "It's no good, is it?"

"What? Your Nazi?" Charlie started to giggle and put his fingers to his lips as though he had burped.

"He's too short."

"Yes. I told you he was too short."

"So?"

"So," he started to whisper. "The story is that he had an operation to shorten his legs."

"Not really?"

"That's what I keep hearing. I've got to circulate. I find out everything at these cocktails. Listen, Jean-Claude, I think he is your Nazi."

Aubaille was despondent. Did Lemercier really believe that the German was Martin Bormann with his legs sawed shorter? He must have heard that at a cocktail reception just like this one. There was nothing but three tufts of hair that once may have been a widow's peak to connect the German to Martin Bormann. Except maybe his nickname. The only thing left was finding out what was in that cabinet. But the idea that Martin Bormann would saw his legs off in the middle so that he could run a restaurant in St. Georges . . .

Dieter Lamdorff was even more despondent. He had overheard just enough to confirm that Aubaille was a Nazi hunter, and he was certain Charlie Lemercier had told him about Lamdorff's father. In the morning he would write his resignation from the European Space Agency. And then he would leave. Find someplace else and start again. He should have changed his name years ago, but then he would have truly felt as if he was hiding.

While he was in Kourou, where they had dependable electricity in the wall sockets because they launched satellites into outer space from there, he charged up his laptop computer and studied his Bormann file, looking for something that would tell him what might be locked in that wooden cabinet if the German was Martin Bormann.

Like Zelemé, Bormann had made himself important by keeping the system inefficient. All orders had to be passed through him. But hidden behind this was his own secret passion for efficiency, such as the white cards on which he noted Hitler's comments. He didn't wear an SS uniform. He did not like things like that. What he liked was money. He was good at raising, stealing, using it to buy influence. But a cabinet full of money would prove nothing. Then Aubaille realized—it wasn't the money, it was the white cards. That would be like Bormann. After all these years still hanging on to those notes, keeping something on everyone. If he found a stack of cards with Bormann's notes, then he had him! Bormann would never have thrown those cards away!

Aubaille took an Air Guyane flight back to St. Georges. The German had offered him a return trip in a few days, but an Air Guyane ten-seater suddenly seemed luxurious.

And he could look around the restaurant and try to get into the cabinet while the German was away. But since the German had his own airplane for which there was no schedule, Aubaille could never be sure when he might suddenly return. Was that why he had the plane?

Aubaille's return, on the other hand, was carefully monitored by Ronier. He was relieved to see Aubaille because he had not seen the suspect leave. He watched only scheduled commercial flights. When he no longer saw Aubaille around St. Georges, he continued to file routine reports sighting the suspect at Madame Dufort's, at the waterfront, describing whom he had talked to—the same reports he had been filing all along. Longchamp did not respond, and Ronier, becoming nervous about his small deception, had decided that if Aubaille did not turn up in one more day, he would have to admit that he had lost him. Seeing Aubaille step off the morning Air Guyane flight, Ronier had to struggle with himself to repress his excitement. He ran up to him and shook his hand and welcomed him back.

"How was Cayenne?"

"Fine," said Aubaille, trying not to look perplexed.

"Did you just stay in Cayenne?"

"Oh, you know, the usual, back at the coast, ice cubes and air conditioning."

"You didn't run into my old friend Captain Longchamp, did you?"

Aubaille stopped to look at Ronier. "Who?"

"Longchamp? The cap—ah, never mind." He didn't know Longchamp. That was good.

Filosoof was waiting in the one-room building where the tickets were sold, just smiling at Aubaille cryptically. Madame Dufort seemed happy to see him, even as happy as Ronier, and they walked into town together.

At night he went back to his routine, strolling the waterfront looking for his opportunity. The German's was deserted, but he had no pretext to go in. He would be seen. Filosoof seemed to be watching, and the gendarmes were always across the street at the bar until late. Shortly after the gendarmes stumbled home, the next day's foot traffic started up in the dark, cool premorning light.

Madame Dufort often followed him to the waterfront. He was pleased with her company. One night when the day's high temperature had lingered after dark and steam was rising from the river, swirling around the smugglers as they unloaded Brazilian goods, Aubaille could feel the heat radiating from Madame Dufort's fleshy body and he pulled her to him. They embraced wordlessly and went back to the hotel to make love under a thumping ceiling fan in a dark shuttered room.

That was how he started spending his evenings. As she reported to the *préfet,* "I am keeping him away from the riverfront at night."

One night he was looking out through the shutters and saw the German's stubby body making its way to the waterfront. Aubaille had wasted his time, and now the

German was back. Then the buzz of the sixty-horsepower engine on Filosoof's canoe startled him. This was his chance—maybe his last chance. Simply telling Madame Dufort that he had to go, he ran downstairs past the drinking gendarmes and over to the German's, while she squinted anxiously through her shutters.

The restaurant was empty with only one light on. The German had gone somewhere with Filosoof. Aubaille feared he had fled to Brazil. What could have alerted him? Someone on the coast. The *préfet?* Or Charlie Lemercier?

The cabinet door was shut. It was locked. He found a stainless steel butter knife and pried at the wooden door, trying not to leave any marks. But he couldn't open it. Then a large, old-fashioned iron key appeared in front of his eyes. It was dangling from the pale, delicate hand of Ronier.

"Try it. We're lucky. He usually carries it."

It would be foolish to stop now. He tried the key and the wooden door opened.

"What are you looking for?" asked Ronier, leaning against the bar, not even watching Aubaille. Asking questions was his job, not looking in cabinets.

Aubaille did not answer him. Inside was a canvas bag that might have held packets of yellowed index cards but instead contained small, clear, cellophane bags full of a finely ground white powder. Aubaille supposed it was cocaine. Probably Colombian. Moved on the Amazon, down the Oyapok tributary, where it could be landed anywhere on the left-hand coast, and it was in France, in Europe, inside the European Union. But that was all. No white cards full of notes. No documents. Nothing Nazi at all—nothing pointing to the German being anything other than what he said he was, another Frenchman whose life ended up stranded in French Guiana. There was really no reason to be here anymore, other than those warm jungle nights with Madame Dufort.

"Find it?" asked Ronier.

Aubaille had almost forgotten the gendarme was there. He closed and locked the cabinet and handed back the key.

"No."

Ronier reported that Aubaille had searched the German's but failed to find anything. It would make an interesting entry on the final report showing that the suspect had been closely watched. Longchamp was pleased. Wanting the record to show his report was in first, he now had enough to hand it in to the colonel. The colonel discussed it with his Creole mistress, who told the DST agent in Cayenne, who discussed it with his mistress, who was a close friend of Zinnie, which meant that the following Wednesday all of the reports came together over a desktop squeeze at the *préfet's* office.

A decision was made. The power of the *préfet* was being compromised as well as the honor of the army and the security of the Space Center. A joint action had to be taken, which meant cooperation among the vertical administrations. Madame Dufort suggested to Aubaille a weekend journey to the Emirillon territory. Filosoof provided the transportation at the request of the army. Once in the unauthorized territory, Aubaille was arrested by the gendarmes and deported, placed on an Air France flight by Captain Longchamp, who said good-bye with a smile and touched his right hand to the visor of his hat in a friendly little salute.

Dieter Lamdorff saw that salute. He was leaving on the same flight, sitting three rows ahead across the aisle, pretending to read *Guyane Matin* and trying not to look back. There was no doubt in his mind that Aubaille was following him, working with the gendarmerie. He would have no peace. He noticed how Aubaille took his seat and pretended not to notice him.

Aubaille strapped on his seat belt, looked through the small window, and thought sadly of the soft brown flesh of Madame Dufort.

Filosoof casually sauntered into the German's restaurant, smiled, and held out his left hand. The German uneasily handed him the iron key. "Did they get rid of him?"

Filosoof nodded as he gathered up the small plastic bags.

"And the money?"

Filosoof looked at him with amusement. "You always get it."

"And they deported him?"

Filosoof nodded and walked away across the riverfront with the bags in the sack, tall, broad-shouldered, and self-assured. He noticed something large and white, glowing in the light on the dock. It was the *préfet* in his uniform talking to Madame Dufort, puffing on his pipe with great satisfaction. Filosoof gave his smile as he walked past them, and the *préfet* nodded and puffed a billowing cloud.

From the restaurant, the German shook his head. *"Ach, die lächerlichen Franzosen,"* he muttered. The silly French.

PACKETS AND PAPERSCRAPS

To be honest, race did have something to do with it. The blackness of his skin, smooth like the dark membrane on hot chocolate, his broad shoulders, a sinewy feel to his body, a smell that she imagined was unlike that of any other man she had known, the thickness of his lips, the surprising stiffness of his hair, the touch of taboo. She did not want to think that way. It wasn't thinking, anyway. It was just what she felt. Excited.

To him, whiteness was interesting, but what he liked was women who had been places and done things and fought more than small island battles. Women who had some money and power and walked into anywhere and weren't afraid of anything. And he loved the way they liked his blackness. Oh, yes, he could feel it. And they could sleep with men they did not know, whose families they had never heard of, and they didn't care as long as they liked the feel of him. And she did.

Afterward, she lay quietly, a rich, tranquil, bodiless spirit for a dreamy, unmeasurable few moments. And then . . .

It was always like this: she wanted to light a cigarette, and she wanted to explain something. There was always something to explain, something to clarify. Sex is not such a simple thing—this two hours of wrestling, of groping and probing and licking and tasting each other. It seems there was always something to clarify afterward. How could you do all that if you didn't feel you would have the opportunity to explain? She supposed it was true, as one annoyed lover had told her, that it was a French vice. In France, there is always the film and then the debate. But foreigners hated it, and every foreign lover had complained about it. One had said, "The French have sex for one hour, and then they spend three hours smoking cigarettes and talking about it." The man she thought she had wanted most had walked out on her, saying, just before he slammed the door, "You talk too much!"

It was true. She was trying not to talk too much after sex. But there always seemed to be something that needed to be said afterward, even though she was trying to learn not to say it. In this case, there was certainly something to be said. Something that had to be said. But maybe not right away.

She looked over at him, at Paperscraps, formerly The Mighty Paperscraps, at one time The Mighty Green Paperscraps. He had even tried to be The Mighty Green. But only Paperscraps stuck. Kitchner himself, visiting the island, had named him after the green paper on which he scribbled calypso lyrics. And now he was Calypso King, had been for three years, and no one could touch him.

She looked at him, the island king lying next to her. It was not like being king in Trinidad. She hadn't even known they had Calypso here. But it was wonderful that he was king and everyone knew his name. Or at least knew him as Paperscraps.

But she had to talk to him. Maybe she would just light a cigarette and relax a little. The cigarettes were in her purse. She looked around the room, cool in its darkness, with blue-edged stripes of hot light burning in from the cracks in the shutters. Her clothes were in wilted little piles where they had slid. Her purse was by the door, where she had dropped it. To smoke a cigarette she would have to get up. If she got up, he would prop himself up and look at her. Then she would have to talk. Maybe she shouldn't have the cigarette. He was lying there with the peacefulness of a man whose life is perfect. Look at the way his chest hairs curled up against his skin in a spotty dark outline. She wanted to touch them.

But she had to talk to him. She didn't even know what to call him. He had introduced himself as "Paperscraps." He had said it proudly, with no embarrassment, more as though he was expecting the word to have some spellbinding effect. Everything about him was proud. The way he stood. The way he loved the sound of his own voice. You had to agree.

Should she call him Paper? She had heard that his real name was Saint-Benoit Higgins. He must have hated it a lot to call himself Paperscraps. Maybe not. But then does she say, "Oh, Saint-Benoit?" Maybe just "Saint" or just "Benoit." She shouldn't disturb him at all.

He lay cooling as the late afternoon breeze evaporated the thin layer of sweat off his body in long minty licks. That was the best thing about afternoon sex, he thought, the way you sweat together in the midday heat and then when you are done, it is late enough for that gentle breeze to just cool it all away, like the vapor from a cold beer bottle, which he wouldn't mind having just now. The other thing about afternoon sex was that it was easy to get home and make something up, and everything would be okay for the evening.

She had wanted him so. It made him feel like what he was, the king. He would feel good going home too. Words were coming to him.

"The white woman fire/ Make me a liar"—What then? He could do this the old way. Four rhymed couplets and a chorus. "The off-island nooky/ Dat me hide from me stooky." No, that's not good.

"Scraps?"

"Huh?" The voice came from nowhere, so startling that he flinched, and it instantly drained him of his good ideas. "You calling me 'Scraps'?"

"No, sorry, Paper, ah, Saint-Ben—Wait. I have to go get a cigarette, okay?" she said, stroking his chest.

"You got a beer?" he called after her, watching her walk away with those long, fine, slender legs. Maybe a little bow-legged. There was a space there. But they were nice, anyway.

"No. You want a cigarette?"

"You should keep some beer here." He noticed that she seemed to press her legs together when she bent over to get the bag. He thought she must be self-conscious about being bowlegged. Then he noticed as she bent over that her backside, small and rounded, was even whiter than the rest of her. It was the whitest skin he had ever seen. It almost glowed with whiteness. He could write something about it.

"You know we could die from this," he thought he heard her say.

He turned over on his side away from her, not as a statement but just to get away. She had come back to the bed with an American cigarette in her mouth, the kind that cost more than fifteen E.C. dollars—it was like lying naked in bed burning money. The idea started to stimulate him, and he turned toward her, but she was sucking hard on the American cigarette and still talking about death. He knew what she was talking about. You shouldn't talk about that stuff, he thought. But he wouldn't say it to her because the conversation would end that much faster if he just kept quiet.

"It's not worth dying for," she was saying. "I did ask for a preservative. Remember."

She had. It was true. He had held her tightly, his hips

pressing hers, and she looked up and asked if he had a "preservative." He had smiled with his kingly confidence and reached inside her blouse and held both her breasts, and the smile and grabbing at the same time, the self-assurance of it, had been enough to make her stop wanting to think about "safe sex" and "the times we live in"—maybe she was even supposed to think it was worth dying for— and soon it was done, what epidemiologists were calling "an exchange of fluids."

What he was definitely not going to tell her was that he had just the day before given away dozens of preservatives, given them to fine island women. Not that he had given any thought to safe sex or AIDS or any of those things with which they were trying to ruin island life. He just gave them out because they were given to him. It was at the cricket match. Just a little small-island match, a chance to show the local boys who don't play on the West Indies team. Just as he was going into the stands, he saw Merle Welton. She wore her hair tied close on her head and glasses with clear plastic frames, and dull, down-to-business clothes that he always wanted to tear off her because he could see, hard and muscular as it might be, there was a real woman's body all enclosed in that seriousness and he would have liked to have known what King Paperscraps could do with it.

Merle Welton was distributing condoms, and she didn't see any humor in it, which were two of the reasons why people liked to call her Merle Wilt'em. She had grown up on the island, and she knew what people did after the cricket match, and she didn't want anyone else dying from it. Seven men were dead already, that she knew of. The first six had all gone off island so that no one would know why they died. Then one was stubborn enough to die at home. He had never left the island, so the person he slept with could still be sleeping with people, and it wasn't going to take much on an island this size. It made her angry. She got American money and started a program, calling it The Committee to Control Island Disease, which was a mistake because everybody called it The Committee to Control Island Dicks, but she had already ordered all the printed materials and they would probably have come up with something like that no matter what she called it.

What she regarded as her greatest accomplishment was a hot line people could call anonymously with questions about AIDS. She had gotten money to hire a second person to help her, Felicia Worrell, who had gone off island with her to study at St. Augustine.

Standing by the entrance to the cricket field with boxes of condoms, Merle handed them to everyone, men and women, who went in. People seemed a little shocked by that, especially handing them to women, but everyone joked about it, and that made it all right for most people to take one. Paperscraps entered, recognized by everybody, leisurely strolling toward the stand, maximizing his entrance to the public arena, shaking hands. Merle had to push through the crowd to come up behind him and tap his shoulder.

"Paperscraps, you're so bad, I better give you a supply," and she handed him a long strip of the little cellophane packets while all his admirers laughed and hooted and cheered. With so much attention he had to do something, so he tore them off one at a time and started giving them out to women like special prizes. The women grabbed them eagerly because that was part of the game.

No one, except maybe Miss Wilt'em, was thinking about anything nasty. It was all in fun. But now this foreign woman was making Paperscraps feel sick and in his favorite part of the day.

"It only takes one time, you know," she said, pulling hard on her third cigarette, growing more nervous and upset by the minute. "You don't know who I've been with, and I don't know who you've been with, and then we just pass it on to the next person. You go to sleep with someone you love and you kill them."

She wanted to stop, but she couldn't. He was smiling at her again, that same beautiful smile. He had to be made to understand. She lit another cigarette.

It wasn't working. The smile wasn't making her stop. Fear, like a snap in the solar plexus, slightly sickened him. She had to stop talking like this. This was not what making foreign women was supposed to be like.

Finally, he said, "All right. I got it. No need to talk a thing until it wilts and dies."

That made her suddenly self-conscious. "Am I smoking too much?" she asked with a worried look.

"What?"

He was starting to get dressed.

"Paperscraps?" she said softly, wanting to ask him if she would see him again. But instead she started laughing. "I can't do it; I can't call you that. What do your friends call you?"

"My friends all call me Paperscraps," he said with his smile, kissed her, and walked out the door.

On the way up the lane to the rum shop, people waved and greeted him. They seemed to almost wink, and with satisfaction he supposed that the word was already around the island that he had gotten the Frenchwomen. What a lot of work she was. It was a good thing he was at least getting credit for it.

He ducked his head and stepped into the cool darkness of the rum shop. His friend Mongoose was already there smoking weed and drinking beer.

"Hey, Benny," said Mongoose with the toothy little grin that got him his nickname.

Paperscraps reached behind the stack of crates that was the bar and into the cooler and pulled out a local beer. "Shit, Tatman, don't you have a cold Heineken?"

"Sure, Benny," said Tatman. "I know how you like that off-island stuff." Mongoose whooped approvingly and smacked Paperscraps on the nearest shoulder.

After the first few beers, when they were not tasting perfect anymore and the bad feeling the woman had given him in his stomach had gone away, Paperscraps was ready to go home. At home there was Dany. She could smell the beer and see that slight looseness to his walk, a little blood in the corner of the eye. Paperscraps counted on these signs, reasoning that she would see he had been in the rum shop all afternoon.

The evening breeze was now in full force, the sky going to orchid purple and the island losing all detail and blurring into mysterious silhouettes. He took his shirt off and lay on the bed.

"Want something to eat, Benny?"

He took her hand and led her down onto the bed next to him. She felt soft and familiar, like coming home to a cozy place, and he opened a button and reached for her breast, and it felt the way he knew it would, and he ran a hand on the soft skin inside her thighs, and he was starting to feel very good again.

She was thinking about the afternoon. It had been so hot, and she had heard there was free cold beer at the Dick Center, and so she went and drank a beer and talked and started getting scared. They gave her some packets and she wanted Benny to wear them, but she knew she couldn't just take one out. She knew what he did, but she couldn't talk about it. She always knew if she started talking about his women, he would leave her. Asking him to wear this thing was like accusing him of sleeping with other women. It would be the end, and that scared her out of talking. She kept the packets hidden close by in case she found a way to say it.

He could tell how excited she was as he put his mouth over the tip of her breast and in spite of himself remembered the words of the Frenchwoman, "You go to sleep with someone you love and you kill them." He tried not to think about any of that. He could feel her tensing up under him, and he just wanted to have her and not think of anything else. Only . . .

All the feeling was there, but it was as though somehow he had gone numb. It just wasn't with him. This had never happened . . . rarely happened. What was wrong? He wanted to make love. He didn't want to kill her. Why was he even thinking about that? The passion was everywhere but between his legs, as though the important piece was missing.

Dany understood. It was that white woman using him up so he had nothing left. That's the way Frenchwomen were.

It must be something about Dany, he reasoned. He was working fine. Or was he? Maybe it was gone. He had to try someone else. Just as he had that idea, he saw Bamsy Thomas walking toward him, a little plump and ripe-looking, all bouncy and jiggling, and smiling that gummy, big-toothed smile that always looked a little hungry. He put on his smile and started talking and was about to suggest they go back to her place and listen to a cassette of new songs he had just made in Barbados.

She still had the condom he had given her at the cricket match and wondered if, when it came to it, she should try to get him to use it. But before it got any further Paperscraps had a bad thought. He could not be messing with island women. Suppose he failed again? Just one of them and everyone on the island would know. Just thinking about that made him numb down there. He told her it was nice liming and walked away, leaving her to wonder what had gone wrong.

He could only try on off-island women. Someone unconnected. It was the hot rainy season, though a dry one this year, and no tourists were showing up. It would have to be the Frenchwoman, this Annette. But he was not going to go back to her as though he needed her. Not after the way she had treated him. She hadn't even given him a beer. Nothing but cigarettes, that girl. He would wait. She would come to him. He could see that in her face when he left her. That was why he had left her that way.

He was right. The letter came a day later—local letter with off-island penmanship. He spotted it immediately. So had Faustin Johns, the mailman. One look at the handwriting and Faustin surmised, "Must be that Frenchwoman," and shook his head in wonder at the Mighty Paperscraps.

Paperscraps opened the envelope and immediately saw the words "Dear Paperscraps." He rolled his eyes ironically. This was going to be like a fan letter. Then he noticed a second sheet of paper. At the top it said something about a laboratory. He quickly grabbed the phrase "Serodiagnosis HIV," and he realized that the unbelievable was happening to him. This was it. Thoughts of slow death and humiliation raced through his head as he sat down, then suddenly he caught the word "negative." The word "negative" appeared four times on the paper. He inhaled deeply, anger growing with relief. He looked at the letter.

Dear Paperscraps,

I had a test and as you can see it was negative. So as of meeting you I was perfectly healthy. Now, if you will get a test, we will know that everything is all right. Otherwise, I will have to get another test in three months. You should be careful with the women you love.

Je t'embrasse,
Annette

Who said love? This was definitely not what sleeping with foreign women was supposed to be like. He was enraged. Indignant. But he had to get out of this thing, had to get himself working again, and she was his only chance. He decided that he would act as though this had been a love letter. Strangely, she acted the same way.

"I got your letter."

"Yes," she purred.

"Can we get together?"

"How about tonight?"

"How about Tuesday afternoon."

Just like that! White women were really crazy. That was the only explanation. She seemed to think her charm had seduced him. He was glad he didn't live in their world.

Putting it off to Tuesday was so that he would have gone a full week with no sex. When had he ever done that? Surely by Tuesday he would be ready to explode. Dany noticed that Benny was not touching her and blamed it on the Frenchwoman.

When the afternoon came, he was feeling good. Like a calypsonian. Like a king.

"De ting in de afternoon/it cannot be there too soon."

The verses were forming. And he liked the way she was wearing expensive lacy little things that only foreigners wore, and he liked removing these things from her pale and eager body. He was feeling good. Everything was going to be fine.

Then she reached over to the night table and grabbed what was becoming familiar-looking cellophane packets.

He was going to lose it. No, it would be all right. He smiled and slowly moved his right hand up her thigh. But this time she insisted. "Look!" she said with playful enthusiasm. "They are from France!" and started opening the packets. The transparent circles were pink and green and blue and orange, with that bright look of something awful in a hospital that they were trying to make more cheerful.

He knew he was finished for now. She tried a little, but it was useless, and they lay there in silence. She wanted a cigarette, but she knew that would be a mistake. Don't talk and don't smoke. But wasn't this different? It wasn't really *after,* and shouldn't something be said? Her mind drifted, and for no apparent reason she remembered a leaflet that the tour packager had included with her plane ticket and bungalow reservation. It was called "Advice to Travelers" and had five or six numbered items under the word "Remember." One of them said, "This is a poor country, and things do not always work as well as they should. Be patient."

An involuntary gust of laughter pushed past her lips, vibrating them into a noisy burst.

The Might Paperscraps felt dark horror. It was the worst thing that had ever happened to him. A white woman was laughing at him in bed. He silently put his clothes on and left without saying another word. Annette, the muscles pulled tight on the sides of her mouth to try to stop the tears she could feel in her reddening eyes, had ruined things again. She would never learn. And she had really liked him. There must be something she could say.

Paperscraps sauntered up the lane to the rum shop. People waved and greeted him and still looked at him in that winking way. He loved these people. Why had he ever thought he needed foreign women, pale and cold?

He ducked his head and stepped into the cool darkness of the rum shop. His friend Mongoose was already there, smoking weed and drinking beer.

"Hey, Benny," said Mongoose with the toothy little grin.

"Still on the imported stuff," said Tatman with a big knowing smile, and handed him a cold Heineken. The three of them laughed.

"You know," said Paperscraps with his best sly smile, "the island product taste good, but it loses its bubbles." And they all laughed again.

"You mean—" said Mongoose, so enraptured with his newly formed joke that he could barely spit it out. "You mean, it doesn't keep a good head!" They all laughed again. Paperscraps smacked the wooden-crate bar. Then he noticed a basket next to his hand—a neat little off-island green basket. In it were the little square cellophane packets and a stack of cards.

"Tatman, man, what is this?"

Tatman looked ashamed and mumbled, "Just don't look at them. You know that Miss Wilt'em. She told me she would buy a case of beer from me every week if I let her put those things there. She's been buying it too. For the Dick Center."

Paperscraps started thinking. He wondered if impotence was a sign of AIDS. She had said she was tested, but maybe it hadn't shown up yet. He kept thinking about how free white women were. How they traveled around and could do it with anyone they wanted. A lot of people had been saying that white people had brought the thing to the island. How else could it have gotten here?

Paperscraps morosely picked up one of the purple cards. It said, "AIDS Hot Line—have a question? Call 65329. Strictly anonymous. Talk freely. No one will ever ask your name."

Then the card said, "Safe things you can do."

"Hey, look at this thing, Mongoose. You know what kind of sex they are telling us would be safe? Look—" He read from the card, "'Hugging, being naked, masturbating.'"

"Come on," said Tatman. "Don't read that stuff."

"Look at this," said Paperscraps. "'Unsafe things you should not do: Sperm or urine in the mouth.'"

"Shut up, Benny," said Mongoose.

"Or this is another one. 'Sharing of sex toys.'" He gave a big open laugh, but no one laughed with him. They didn't even look at him.

"But really, Mongoose, did you ever worry about, you know, about getting it?"

Mongoose didn't answer.

🐔

What Paperscraps had to know was whether AIDS could make you impotent. He wandered the upper town, where the bananas grew and people didn't talk much. From time to time he looked at the purple card. "AIDS Hot Line— have a question? Call 65329. Strictly anonymous. Talk freely. No one will ever ask your name." It was like one of those dirty phone calls. You could say anything. He went to the telephone booth that had been put in before election time and dialed the number.

"AIDS Hot Line," said the voice in the phone. It was that goofy Felicia Worrell. You could always recognize her squeaky voice.

Paperscraps lowered his voice to be more anonymous. "I had a question I wanted to ask."

Felicia covered the phone with her hand and, wide-eyed, said to Merle Welton in what was supposed to be a whisper but was more of a raspy scream, "It's Paperscraps!"

Merle took the telephone. "AIDS Hot Line."

Ah, thought the Mighty Paperscraps, the tight but promising Miss Wilt'em. It was anonymous, he could say anything, and there were some things he had been wanting to say to Miss Wilt'em. Questions about impotence were not among those things. But why not if she didn't know who he was?

"How can I help you?" said Merle. Felicia thought she noticed an odd eager glow on Merle's face.

"I was wondering—" began Paperscraps.

"Yes."

"—if you would be interested in doing some things you should not do."

"Well, I might if you had a blood test and used condoms."

Oh, God, he thought. No wonder they call her Wilt'em.

"Is there anything else?"

"No. I don't think so."

"Okay. Just remember you have to be careful with foreign women too."

Paperscraps slammed down the phone as though it had
suddenly burned his hand.

Merle hoped her disappointment did not show on her
face, but she could tell by the way Felicia was looking at her
that it probably did. "Felicia, it doesn't help me much if
every time someone calls, you hand me the phone. You studied all those booklets so you could answer the questions."

"I'm sorry," said Felicia, but she understood why Merle
was so irritable.

Paperscraps spent that night at home with Dany. She felt
soft and made him feel safe and strong and unafraid, and
they made love for hours.

Dany thought that now everything was right again. But
she was also worried. She wished she could talk to him
about it. Sleeping with a white off-island woman. That is
exactly how that thing got on the island in the first place.
Still, it was good to see him lying there all content again.
He was probably composing some rhymed lyrics. That's
what he did in these times.

But Paperscraps couldn't compose. A terrible thought
had just come to him. If he couldn't sleep with island
women and risk failing and having it get all over the
island—and if he did not want any more of these foreign
women, which he definitely did not—then he was going to
be sleeping with only Dany. It was wrong what was hap-

pening to island life. Not at all as it should be anymore. One afternoon with that Frenchwoman and now he was saddled with this fidelity thing.

Annette, with a purple card in her hand, strolled back to the bungalow, walking alongside the *cas-cas* that grew by the edge of the road. The sky was turning the color of blacktop; leaves were showing their silvery backsides, the palm fronds and the *cas-cas* blades starting to thrash and make a noise like a muted scream. It looked as if the rains were finally coming. It was not going to be much of a time here in the rain. And it could have been so nice—rainy season in the tropics the way it should be. How could she have done it differently? Still, there was nothing more stupid than sleeping with men in the Caribbean without any protection. But there must be a different way to say it. You don't have to make him impotent. It's a different culture. She should get some anonymous local expertise.

The number rang twice before Felicia answered, " AIDS Hot Line."

"Hello. I would like to ask some advice."

Quickly, Felicia clamped her hand over the receiver and, wide-eyed, turned to Merle and with exaggerated lip movements whispered, "It's the Frenchwoman!" as she handed Merle the telephone.

THE DEERNESS OF LIFE

The preoccupying question was what to do with the corpse. It couldn't just be left somewhere in a gruesome state, hanging in a macabre posture or with a hole in the head or lying in a pool of blood or, at the very least, with a pale contorted face—can you control your face when you die?—and someone would find it, have to deal with it, no doubt someone close. It is an ugly thing to stick somebody with a corpse, and you can be sure they will end up hating the thing.

On a quiet Saturday summer morning, a perfect seventy-five degrees in the Atlantic sea air of Fire Island, safe from the hot city, while her husband Billy was spreading Caribbean travel brochures on the rough pine table that was on the deck at the back of their house, Lena was planning her death.

Billy was worried about Lena. He was disappointed too, but for her it was something else, and the one thing she didn't need was another long, gray winter on the island.

Instead they would winter in the Caribbean. That was a sonorous phrase, but the decision was a bit of a defeat. They were proud of being among the few year-round residents, with one of the few winterized homes. They always bragged of enjoying the solitude. But not this winter. Not the way she was.

Lena was half studying the brochures. Very difficult to decide. Similar-looking hotels and tall drinks in bright colors and the same palm trees and smiling blond women everywhere. She wasn't blond; Caribbeans weren't blond. Where did these blond people come from? Billy loved projects like this. Studying brochures. She could see that this Caribbean idea was making him happy.

"I don't even want to go to the beach. Golf, drinking, shopping. Things like that," he said.

She smiled vaguely. She was still thinking about the body. She almost felt that she would do it if she could figure out what to do about the body. She didn't want it found. It was not that she was being morbid. Just the opposite. Leaving a corpse around for family and friends— that was morbid. If you could leap into some kind of inferno, instantly disintegrating all physical trace, nothing to be found, nothing to be identified—God, her legs itched. It just spread if she scratched them, but . . . "Do any of those islands have volcanoes?"

"Volcanoes?" He reshuffled the brochures with one hand while sipping his coffee with the other. "Arnold gets in today. We can ask him." Arnold was the editor of a popular travel magazine.

Several deer, two does and a three-point buck trotted over to the deck and stared at Billy, looking as though they wished they could help.

"Wait until Arnold gets in. He'll know," said Lena.

Billy took a deep sip of his coffee. Lena shrieked, "Don't move!" And she wound her arm far back and came swinging around with an open-handed right cross, which landed on Billy's collar, knocking him, the brochures, and the coffee across the table. Lena reached over as coffee-drenched Billy stood up. She picked a small bug off his collar.

"I'm sorry," she said.

"Look at these brochures."

"I thought it was a deer tick."

"Really?"

"No, it's okay, it was just a bug." He turned to the deck railing but the deer were gone.

On the windswept, sunny top deck of the ferry, all the way over, for twenty-five minutes, Arnold was muttering to himself about his life. Not a bad life, but there was one thing he truly hated—his summer weekend home in the island village of Saltaire. He hated the *e* on the end of the name. The ferry always stopped first in Kismet. Kismet was not as expensive and therefore had no final *e*. They could increase the taxes and become exclusive, call themselves Kismette and be just like Saltaire, but they didn't seem to want to. It was the same island. He would walk guests over to Kismet and show them how seedy it was, noisy with loud music late into the night. Not for him. Still, he had a secret thought he never uttered. Every time they took the ferry and all the people got off in Kismet, he would always say to himself, "There go the people who are going to have fun this weekend."

He had come with his wife and two sons, who wanted to come out every weekend when the weather was good. They always took Polly and Esther, the goddamn family weasels, another thing about his life that he hated. He wasn't supposed to call them weasels. They were an extinct species of European ferret, completely hunted down, extinguished, but somehow resurrected in captivity to be household pets for people like him and his two sons who were allergic to cats. Artificial weasels. So they called them Polly and Esther. Arnold hated the joke too. Arnold liked cats, even though they made his eyes red and itchy. But when his two boys started sneezing and wheezing, the extinct European weasel seemed an intelligent alternative. They were furry like cats, but their long bodies moved snakelike, and they climbed up people by digging in their needle claws. Arnold hated the feel of them on his shoulder when they would stick a ratlike nose in his ear as though to try to sniff out his brains. . . .

The community was built on a fragile, marshy wetland, and to preserve the environment everything was kept off the ground. The houses were built on stilts and instead of streets, there were raised boardwalks. The ground had been the terrain of foxes, deer, and raccoons. Everyone loved the deer and the raccoons, but the foxes, like Polly and Esther's European ancestors, were heartless predators, and so were wiped out. Once the last fox died some thirty years ago, there was no more hunting allowed, and the deer, a fecund lot with plentiful food and no natural enemies, were gradually filling the island. They ate leaves, with a noticeable preference for willows. They also ate carrots. Almost every home had carrots ready to feed the deer. The island's small ferret population—a number of sneezy residents had given up on cats and turned to these silken weasels—would become angry when household members started feeding carrots to the deer. But the ferrets were not foxes. They were too small to do anything about deer.

Arnold walked across the springy boards to Billy and Lena's back deck, which adjoined his, eager to tell them that he had decided to—or had finally talked Alice into letting him—put his house on the market. But when he arrived, Billy, who was blotting Caribbean brochures with paper toweling, instead gave Arnold the startling news that they had decided to go to the Caribbean for the winter.

"It's just for the winter. Just a quiet place with something besides beaches. Have any ideas?"

"St. John? It's a U.S. national park."

"Isn't that where they killed those people on the golf course?"

"No. I think that was St. Croix."

"Any volcanoes?" asked Lena. She had made no decisions. The search for a sudden and painless end was just an intellectual game to distract her from her itching legs. But it definitely had to be something that didn't leave her body behind. Maybe this thinking about the body was a way of not thinking about the real issue. How sacred was life, anyway? Now that Alice was here, they could talk about it. Something Lena never admitted to anyone was that her friend and neighbor Alice annoyed her. But she was in the mood for Alice. Alice, who worked in a hospital, hated all the things science had developed to hold on to life. It seemed clear that hospitals were keeping people alive who should be dead. They were doing it to make money. Medicaid, Medicare, Medi-everything paid millions of dollars to keep dead people alive. Her job was to advise patients, and frequently her advice, or so she said, was to die.

It seemed to Lena that Alice had no appreciation of the tenacity of life, the determination of all creatures to cling to it. There must have been something a little dead in Alice that she couldn't see this. That was what Lena used to think until recently. She looked at Billy trying to make the best of his damp Caribbean brochures, and she thought what she would never say: It was his fault. It was Billy who had never wanted children. She had to be married to him for sixteen years before she could convince him, and by then, she was too old. They either died soon after conception or developed abnormally. Finally she actually killed one, "terminated the pregnancy"—what phrases they found for these things!—because she was unwilling to raise a strange, deformed creature, which was all she seemed able to produce. Life was not the sacred thing she thought it was. Alice was right.

"Evelyn!" Lena suddenly gushed as though at the sight of someone unexpected and deeply loved. She picked up a plastic packet and stepping under the railing, walked off through the scrubby pine after a doe, who was trotting away uncertainly.

"I'm not sure that's Evelyn, dear. Isn't that Leslie? You already gave Leslie her shot."

"No, it's Evelyn."

"Billy, I'm putting the house on the market."

"What's that on your leg?!"

Arnold jumped to his feet. But the insect jumped even faster. Maybe a flea, but not a tick.

"That's terrible, Arnold. Who's going to get us our blueberries?" Arnold was immune to the ubiquitous poison ivy and could wander freely and pick the wild blueberries that grew alongside it.

"Lena might as well gather berries if she's going to go after the deer like that," Arnold said.

Lena's legs were constantly erupting with itchy rashes because she wandered in the brush giving shots to the does. Only a credible birth control program would stave off the Long Island hunting lobby. She didn't want hunting in their community. A rabbi from upstate New York had offered to take some of the deer to his farm, where deer were ritually slaughtered for a Manhattan kosher restaurant that was reputedly the most expensive restaurant in New York. Another group had proposed reintroducing foxes. But since Lena had gotten involved in the birth control program, she had become one of the hard-liners who would not accept the killing of any deer. She had gotten to know them all. Once you give something a name, you can't have it killed. She had named forty-five does and twenty bucks. Lena, Billy thought, had a genius for naming. But she hadn't ever had a name ready for their child—except the first time. She learned after that. This time she almost got to the name. Passed the first three months. Just a test with a big needle. Then she would have known the gender, she would have started thinking of names.

"What do you think of Jamaica, Arnold?"

"I can't afford this house. I just can't pay these taxes anymore. It went up again. I'm paying ten thousand dollars a year."

"Well, that's the storm last year. It cost more than a million to build the dunes back." Billy was a landscape architect.

"Why so much?"

"They had to bring in all the sand and plant all that reedy grass to hold it down. It takes money."

Alice came over. "Poor Polly and Esther. Two bucks started looking in the window. Makes them so mad. Where's Lena?"

"Down there giving a shot to a deer."

Lena returned with an air of triumph. "It was Evelyn. I got her."

"No babies for Evelyn this year?" Billy was instantly sorry he had said that. Lena walked up to the deck slowly, trying not to think of it. Alice was talking.

"I told him, 'You've got to let your mother go. Tell her she can die.' She was just lying there in agony, and all those ghouls were ready with tubes and wires, and she refused to die. She thought she had to live for the son . . ."

Arnold was watching Lena—something about the fleshiness of her thighs, the tightness of her khaki shorts. He had never had these thoughts about Lena before. It was disturbing and enjoyable. What had brought it on? It was the tight khaki shorts, the outline of her underwear. It was called a "panty line." He had once attended a shoot for a travel poster, and there was a great commotion because the model had a panty line. Arnold thought that maybe he liked panty lines. Perhaps he had a thing for them. Maybe he was a panty-line freak. He liked to imagine himself as slightly perverted, a boy with a good secret.

Arnold looked up to see his other neighbor, Tom Larkin, coming down the walkway. Tom wrapped his knuckles on the wooden railing as though it were a doorway.

"Tom, come in," said Billy.

"Sorry to bother you. But it's fire inspection time. I noticed your shovel isn't in plain view anymore."

"It's hanging right around the side."

"Oh, sorry, I didn't notice. I'll just have to inspect the dates on your extinguishers."

"Help yourself. Say, Tom? Have you ever been to Jamaica?"

"Not me. Too dangerous. Isn't that where they killed those people on the golf course?"

"No," Arnold said with patience. "That was St. Croix."

"So where do you go?" Billy asked.

"Puerto Rico."

"Isn't that dangerous?"

"Never been a murder on a golf course there," said Tom.

"It seems strange to leave New York for another island full of Puerto Ricans. . . . Damn!" Billy swatted his arm. The others stared at him. "Just a mosquito."

"I took one off of Arnold last weekend," said Alice.

"I had one on me too," said Lena.

"Just make sure you don't have a rash around the bite," said Alice.

"You'd never find it on Lena." Billy chuckled.

"It's a different-looking rash," said Alice. "Why? Have you been feeling sick?" She thought Lena did not look well.

"No, it's just poison ivy. I should wear long pants. But it makes it itch more."

"Besides," said Billy, "I like you in shorts."

Billy liked to say things like that because it implied that he was lusty, but Lena found it very hard to believe that Billy really cared what she wore. She thought that probably nobody really looked at her that way anymore. The ability to produce healthy children is not the only thing that was lost at forty. In fact, everything gets worse and goes on getting worse, so unless things were really good, how much point was there in seeing it through after forty? All your real possibilities have been used up. "So Arnold," Lena asked. "Which islands have volcanoes?"

"Martinique and Guadeloupe."

"The French don't like us," said Billy.

"Maybe St. Lucia."

"Oh, Lena," said Tom as he left, apparently satisfied with the fire extinguishers. "Have you heard, the hunters now say they only want a bow season? Bow and black powder. You know, muskets. That way it will only be the really dedicated hunters. No maniacs blasting away in the neighborhood. Just good, serious hunters. Bow hunters are different. It takes skill. It's not like a bunch of drunks with rifles. One buck permitted per license."

"How much skill could it take? Aren't you with us, Tom?" Lena demanded.

"I don't know. I like nature, but there are an awful lot of deer right now." Tom was aware that two bucks with warm black eyes were staring at him. "Just a lot of them."

"They keep coming up with one stupid scheme after another, and if we start losing votes, they are going to be able to pass one of these dumb plans. What about you two?"

"I wouldn't let anyone shoot them," said Alice. "It would be like shooting Polly and Esther."

Arnold tried to chase that mischievous thought from his mind. "I have to think about this," he said. "Right now I'm in favor of whatever is good for property values."

Alice wished the men would leave. She wanted to talk to Lena. Something was wrong.

"What about Haiti?" Arnold suggested. "Less expensive, beautiful places."

"I think it would be too depressing," said Alice.

"It's the only life they know."

"I suppose people in a place like that don't hold life as dear as we do," said Billy.

"They probably do," said Lena with a barely perceptible slyness to her smile.

"What's depressing for them is no tourists," Arnold asserted. "They just wish more people would come and spend money."

"Does Haiti have volcanoes?" Lena asked.

"The main thing"—Billy chuckled—"is to make sure it doesn't have golf courses. Who wants a beer?"

Arnold dressed in his running clothes and a new pair of running shoes with a complex, senseless pattern of purple and turquoise stripes, which the salesman assured him would compensate for his tendency to favor the outside of his feet. Polly and Esther were hungry, and Arnold grudgingly dropped pieces of last night's leftover steak in their cage. The ferrets growled as they ripped up the meat. It wasn't very good, anyway. Arnold would have liked the steak charcoal-grilled. But that was illegal. The risk of fire.

His youngest boy was on the back deck with a stack of

carrots. A fawn and three does approached, long necks extended. The boy held out carrots one by one. Each deer waited her turn for a carrot. Two bucks, more cautious, watched in the pines. Arnold's son fed the carrots tip-first into the deers' mouths as if feeding them into a grinder. They were silent creatures. They had arrived without so much as a snap of a twig. Now they chewed in silence, working knobby facial muscles, big-eyes staring some-where else. The boy reached over and stroked a white streak along the deer's nose.

"No-o-o!" Arnold shouted, and the deer all silently trotted away. His son was upset, and he had to comfort him. He took him in his arms. "How many times do I have to tell you? You can feed them, but don't touch them. They have ticks, and you can get very sick. You can get arthritis in your knees and you will walk like an old man. You want that?"

The boy agreed that he didn't want that. But it was hard not to pet them when they came up to you like that. Arnold walked down the main walkway until he got to the beach, which he had all to himself at this hour. It was the only time that he liked this island—alone with a dark slate sea rolling in softly, the dunes empty except for three confident bucks with four- or five-point antlers, huge, useless racks sticking out far above their heads. The bucks were grazing, calmly munching on the grass planted to hold the new million-dollar dunes in place. To Arnold it was as though they were munching on his ten-thousand-dollar taxes. If a bunch of nuts with bows and arrows wanted to come shoot them, why should he say no?

That was one vote lost. Lena did not want to lose any more. She canvassed the island, checking over and over again that those who were against killing deer stayed that way. But she was losing votes. Lyme disease had too many victims. Most of those who got it were simply sick for a few days and with antibiotics quickly recovered. But there was a twelve-year-old girl who got arthritis in her knees, and one fifty-year-old woman was left with her face drooping as though it had partly melted, a paralysis of some facial muscles.

"It is not the deer," Lena argued. "They just *call* them 'deer ticks,' but the ticks only feed on the deer. The ticks are infected from mice. It's the mice, not the deer!"

Alice researched this at her hospital and discovered that Lena was exactly right. She informed the community at a meeting that they should be killing the mice, not the deer. But Lena didn't want mice killed either. She argued that it would be unhealthy to leave some kind of rodent poison all over the island. It would probably make the deer sick. Then she found the answer. It came in cardboard tubes and it was called Haverlex. It was poisonous nesting material. The tubes were to be left around and the mice were to recognize their contents as irresistible home-building material. The poison wouldn't kill them. It would only kill the nymphs on them that would otherwise turn into deer ticks. Only tick nymphs were to be killed. It was a perfect solution—completely humane and natural in the view of even some of the residents who were starting to waver. Billy laughed and said, "Lena, I'm surprised that you will stand by and let them murder tick nymphs."

Alice was more skeptical. She did more research. There was only one study claiming Haverlex worked. The study had been commissioned and carried out by the Haver Laboratories, makers of Haverlex.

Billy and Lena decided on a forty-square-mile British colony. It had an independence movement but nothing violent. The beaches, blackened from the volcano, were unappealing, and on the Atlantic side there was no swimming at all. Lena worried that Billy would want to hike the black-soiled mountain interior to the volcano with her. He hated strenuous activities, especially in hot weather. But he had the annoying self-assurance of a man who could never imagine that his presence was not welcome.

A perfectly circular red patch, like a raspberry-colored poker chip with a dot in the center, appeared on Billy's left thigh, resolving this problem. Soon Billy had all the symptoms of flu, but with the round spot on his leg the diagnosis was clear: Lyme disease. At first he seemed to respond to antibiotics, but he remained weak and tired for weeks and tests showed that he was suffering from an inflamed heart muscle. His slight potbelly, which he had worn like an emblem of his good nature, was vanishing, and he was looking smaller and more fragile. Winter on a Caribbean island was the prescribed treatment, but "no hiking or strenuous activity of any kind."

Lena would hike to the mouth of the volcano and from a rocky precipice stare into a simmering pool of red-hot liquid rock, and in that instant she would know if she wanted to go on living. There, in front of the most dazzling sight of her life, she would know. Would it be a straight drop—a few seconds to endure on the way down and then she would vanish? Or would it be a difficult jump to make? She had been a good diver when she was younger. Still, not a great diver.

You are remembered by what you leave behind.

When staring into the molten lava, she did not want to have any thoughts about that. The lava would make sure that a cadaver was not left behind. And of course, there would be no children left behind. No need for a will. Everything would automatically go to her husband. More important to Lena were the things left in the house. People would go through her things. She burned her autobiographical novel that she had written ten years earlier but had never shown to anyone. Nor could she leave the diary on which the novel was based—especially some of the pages about Billy.

She thought about how wasteful it was that every idea she had grasped, every concept she had struggled to understand, would be gone with her. And yet the crystal sea otter

Billy had given her and she had always hated would survive her. Only things would be left. How strange it was to think of the things left behind. The most insignificant objects are more durable than people. They survive, are passed on, are sold in flea markets, become part of other lives, survive those lives too. She had heard environmentalists warn that plastic can last thousands of years. Her credit cards and makeup case and assorted refrigerator magnets could be examined in a millennium.

They closed up the house for the winter. It seemed to Lena that more than a dozen deer were watching, knowing that they were losing their protector. That had been the only unfinished business. The hardback notebook in which she recorded her deer census complete with first names was carefully placed on a table to be found. At the mouth of a volcano she would be free to leap except for this one thought: Who would protect the deer? But that last obstacle, her only remaining responsibility in life, had been removed when pro-deer lost their initiative by fourteen votes. The state wildlife officials would come to the island and execute twenty does death-squad style with a bullet to the head. There were still arguments about the meat—the bodies that would be left behind.

The cottage had a view of Soufrière. Lena was intrigued by the fact that in the afternoons, the tip of the peak, the mouth of the volcano, was covered in low clouds, as though draped for privacy. The rental agent for the cottage confirmed that the volcano was still active. He showed them around the area, including a golf course, which Billy eyed suspiciously, and then he questioned the agent about the independence movement. The rental cottages, in spite of their spareness, were called "villas," and they were in an area not unlike Saltaire. They were on a slope instead of flatland, and there were real roads—windy switchback asphalt trails with occasional cars. But as in Saltaire, almost all of the houses on the mountainside were only seasonal, winter instead of summer, and the occupants were mostly affluent New Yorkers who didn't even think about how close to one another the cottages had been built on an underpopulated island. Billy and Lena even noticed that two nearby households had pet ferrets, but while there were no deer, there were mongooses, and they were disturbingly similar to the ferrets, more brown than white, low-built serpentine streaks across the grass. The mongooses had also noticed the ferrets and seemed to frequently pass by the houses where they lived.

Billy, who loved their home in Saltaire, was happy in their winter cottage in the tropics with its comfortable view of the mountains where Lena would spend her days hiking. He found other amusements, such as watching small-island cricket, which made little sense to him but lasted all day and was a good place to meet other people with nothing to do. They rented a car. It was fun driving on the little roads. At first it seemed there were no traffic laws at all, but one day Billy was in town and a policewoman walked up to him and said, "That left turn you made on Parliament Street Tuesday last was illegal, sir." Billy liked that, because it, too, reminded him of Saltaire. But he was mostly happy that Lena seemed to be enjoying the hiking, leaving after breakfast and returning at nightfall. It seemed to Billy that they were having an exceptional winter.

All trails in the mountains began at an abandoned sugar estate. The windswept road climbed into wet, low-hanging clouds. At the spot where tropical sunlight and white, opaque mist mingled, the eighteenth-century ruins, evidence of slavery, glided in and out of focus—the caved-in remnants of the boiling house, the round turret of a windmill, and the circular wall of a cattle-driven one. Lena thought it was a perfect example of something someone should not have left behind to be remembered by.

The air filled with sulfur. She climbed over yellow, red, purple, and white rocks to what was said to be a dead volcano. But if dead, why did it bubble and hiss and belch steam? Why could she hear the molten earth rumbling below the surface? The live volcano peak could not be far away. How could anything be far away on a small island? But nature seemed tightly packed into these slopes. She found bamboo forests and high waterfalls pouring into dark, cool jungle pools. She discovered that days could be spent hiking in the steep, slippery, wet mountains down into hidden, cloud-covered valleys and up to spectacular heights—all of that without really having gotten anywhere. She couldn't get lost. The interior was uphill and the road was downhill. The uphill trails were steep and very wet and muddy, and at times she would find herself climbing on hands and knees to keep from sliding down. But she always had to return before dark, and she never found the volcano mouth.

She would return to Billy, hot, sore, and mud-soaked. Billy was secretly stunned by the look of her, the scent of her, the wetness of her shirt clinging to her breasts, her put-up hair falling down, drops of sweat running down her neck, dollops of mud drying on her arms or rubbed on the side of her cheek. She smelled like sex, and he wanted to inhale her. But she always arrived talking of how tired she was and dreaming of a bath, and Billy always let the moment pass prompted by some misguided gallantry. He would compulsively watch the sky to make sure he was back before nightfall just for the sight of her coming into the cottage. And he would marvel at his fortune that he could feel this after so many years. But the only thing he ever managed to say about the way she looked was that "a woman alone should be careful on an island like this."

"Afraid the natives will get out of hand?" She laughed.

"You know what I mean."

After dinner she was so weary from the day's hiking that she quickly slid into deep sleep, and another day had passed. For Lena physical exhaustion worked into her heart like a balm. By nightfall she was numb. In the mornings, she would wonder if she was in the early stages of death. For just a few minutes she was too groggy to feel the pain of life. Then it was back, life as it was.

One afternoon she found herself heading downhill but not toward the road, and she realized that she was lost. She climbed to get another view of the blinding blue Caribbean, which, once located, she would head toward. It was always over there somewhere on her right. She kept sliding down in the muddy trail that was no wider than her foot. By the time she got high enough to see the ocean, the sun was low enough to cast a shadow on every ripple—a hard corrugated cobalt sea. No trail pointed toward the coast through the thick tropical growth.

She stood on the wet slope catching her breath and dreaming of a machete that could chop through jungle. She had seen this many times, although only in movies. She did not even recognize the flat chime of the blade—half smack and half bell. Howard Justine appeared, cursing at a donkey and clearing his path with a broad, two-foot long blade.

Howard was lean and tall with ageless, weathered charcoal skin, so dark that with the afternoon light behind him, he appeared to have no face. He moved easily and naturally on the steep, slippery, narrow trail as though it were flat, dry land.

"Hello!" shouted Lena a bit too loudly while waving with too much enthusiasm. Howard cursed something at his donkey, who jumped forward two quick steps.

"Which way to Soufrière?"

Howard said nothing but seemed to be staring at her.

"Soufrière, the volcano? Do you know where it is?"

"Blackwell's Soufrière."

"What?"

"It's called Blackwell's Soufrière, miss. The one you are looking for. They are all called Soufrière."

"Then how do you know which one I'm looking for?"

"The live one. You can't get there today. It's almost dark. I can take you there tomorrow. I'll take you down to the estate now. Get on."

He helped her onto the donkey, which was much wider between her legs than she ever imagined. The donkey's spine was hard and uncomfortable and the whole back moved, and not knowing which way to shift her weight, she found the ride was more work than she ever thought sitting on a donkey would be. The donkey never missed a step as he went down the trail so steep she struggled not to slide down his neck.

That sleepless night planets, unexpectedly numerous, like shards from shattered glass, filled a black, translucent sky. She looked into all those fragments above the opaqueness of Soufrière's silhouetted crest, Blackwell's Soufrière, searching once more for constellations, and as always happened, she could only find the Big Dipper. God knew where the Pleiades were nestled and which six stars marked them, and it was very possible that she would die without having ever located the North Star. Tomorrow she would be on the precipice of all her recent fantasies and she would know. She could do it. She might do it. The great advantage of jumping was that the boisterous debate inside herself would end. To not jump would resolve nothing. Except maybe if she didn't jump, if she stared into a red-hot end and chose not to take it, she would then know that she wanted to live. She just wanted to know.

In the morning, Howard Justine and his donkey were waiting half in and half out of the mist that covered the ruined sugar estate. Lena greeted him and stroked the donkey's long, velvety nose. "What's his name?"

"It's a donkey, miss. It doesn't need a name. Get on, please, and we can start."

"Oh, I think I would like to walk for a while. See, I spent all this money on these hiking boots." She looked at her expensive, thick-soled shoes, some new leather surface still showing through the layers of mud, and then she saw that her surefooted guide was wearing loafers separated from the soles in the front, his bare, dark toes sticking out and looking more leathery than leather, tape wrapped around the left loafer to hold it together. She got on the donkey. She was thinking about her life, and she wanted to talk about it. She could not stop talking, and Howard Justine was as silent as his nameless donkey. His silence made her talk all the more, as though the silence was a space that had to be filled. She told him how she and Billy lived on an island even smaller than this one, about the deer. She wanted this man at this historic moment to understand, to be a part of her life, not just someone she was paying for a job. He hadn't even said how much she should pay him. "Whatever you feel like. I need to buy some things," was all he said. She gave him fifty dollars before they started, and he seemed to understand being paid in advance. It was almost as though he knew. She thought there was a wisdom in his surefooted silence. She heard only his clucking and cursing noises when he prodded from behind and saw only his back when he led. She was talking to a torn khaki shirt and muddy pants too large for his narrow waist, his gangly hips moving in rhythm with the muscles on the donkey. "Do you have children?" she asked.

Without turning back, he held up his right hand twice, the second time with the thumb tucked in.

"Nine. You have nine children? Where are they? Do they live in these mountains too?"

"They live everywhere. London, Toronto, New York. Boston, Miami."

She thought she had found an opening. But he didn't say anything more for two hours. Then as they moved into a dark valley of thick trees and heavy vines, he said, "You can get down if you want, miss." A small black river ran over smooth rocks. Selecting a broad, thick callaloo leaf, he folded it until it resembled a large scoop and filled it with water, which he carried to her. She drank the cold water as he held it. The water had a slightly sulfurous taste. She could now see his face. He was older than she was.

"Miss?"

She could see that at last he wanted to talk. Maybe they would talk for an hour or so before going up.

"Miss?"

"Yes."

"You have big feet for a woman."

She laughed. "At least you didn't say a big mouth."

"When you leave, before you leave, can I have your shoes?"

"My shoes? I don't know when I am leaving."

"Before you leave."

"Yes, I guess you can."

He nodded and started up the trail again.

He did know. It was one more thing to leave behind. It meant she would have to take off her shoes and stand barefooted before she decided. But she very much liked the idea of leaving this man her shoes. It was the best thing she was leaving. He would probably wear them, four sizes too small, for the rest of his life.

They stopped again on a high slope, a rich, volcanic plot of land with a well-tended, though somewhat wild garden. He carefully inspected the christophine on the trellises, throwing back the pumpkin vines so they wouldn't run under the brush, yanking out weeds. He showed Lena his dasheen and cucumbers and green beans.

"This island you live on—you have land?"

"No."

"You own the island?"

"No, just a house."

"No land?" He stared at her.

"What's wrong?"

"Why would someone rich and white live on some itty-bitty small island when they didn't even own the land. They have rich people on this island. Mr. Bramford Austin. You heard of him? He's rich and he lives here. But he owns half the island. He owns this land. I pay him eighty E.C. dollars a year to work this land."

"I don't know. We were in the city. We wanted to be more in nature."

"Nature is something wicked. Nature is a worse landlord than they have in town. But he charges less rent." For the first time Lena saw Howard smile. "Yeah, I lived in town. Eight years I was the boss of a government road crew. I earned money, but I had to live in town, and it was hard to buy enough to eat with that money. So I moved up here. And I got some fish from traps down there. I built a house. Had plenty to eat. Sold food to buy things I needed. Then comes your friend Nature. Hurricane Eunice. Takes my house, my fish traps, half that bamboo. There weren't even leaves. Thing only stayed twenty minutes and did all that. So now I'm what you white people with no land call 'a vegetarian.' I eat fresh cucumber slices with a little salt and pepper. That's good too, you know. I'm still living better than when I had a job and bought everything and paid taxes."

Lena did not know how to respond to that. After several moments of hissing wind in leaves, Howard nodded and said, "It's right up there. About a fifteen-minute walk up that trail. Gets pretty steep, but then flattens out. I imagine you want to go by yourself."

Lena examined the lean, ragged man in front of her, but she saw no answers.

"Man, I don't really understand white people."

"What don't you understand?"

"You all go off to die like cats. Why don't you want to die at home?"

"You mean there have been others?"

"Seven, eight. White people used to come to the islands to get rich. Now nobody can get rich here even if they are white. They just come here to die. To get divorced and to die. Sometimes both. I had one man who went to Haiti and got divorced. Then he came here to die. Don't they let people die in America?"

"Some people say they don't. Tell me. These seven or eight people all—did they all go through with it?"

"You come here to be alone with strangers. You don't have to mind what other white people do. That's why you came here." He pointed again at the trail.

She started and it soon was very steep, and she was pulling on roots and branches with her hands to help herself up. After a few minutes, the land seemed to level off and there was only a little brush. On all sides was the Caribbean, sparkling polished blue, but white swirls were curling in, and soon she would be veiled in the afternoon clouds. Should she wait for it? She could feel a rumbling under her feet, and it excited her. And she could smell a vague hint of sulfur. But there were no cracks, no reddish glow. She ached from months of not crying. It could all end. She could imagine it ending. She really could. What would it be like for Billy? Easy. Nothing to do. She had vanished. He could just go home and get on with his life without a depressive to weigh down his natural happiness. Would he make trouble for Howard? There he would be, wearing her shoes, trying to explain what had happened to her. Maybe he wouldn't say anything. Then one day the shoes would be recognized. Maybe it was a bad idea to leave the shoes. It would be better to jump with them. Why hadn't she just bought him a pair of shoes?

Howard Justine waited patiently in his garden. He repaired a cracked piece in the trellis and carefully rearranged the christophine vines. Without even looking up, he could feel the clouds sliding between the trees, slowly filling in until it felt cool and dark. Then he walked up the trail. When he got to the top, Lena was still walking from place to place staring at the ground for signs. She stared at Howard Justine. Was he after all just a useless idiot clumsily plotting an elaborate and hopeless scheme to get her money without even knowing where the volcano was?

"This way, miss." He walked over the rocky top to a wide indentation filled with rocks, a kind of crude gravel pit.

"This is the mouth of the volcano?"

Howard smiled. "I can give you your money back if you want. What did you imagine? You thought your friend Nature would just lie, excuse me, with its legs spread open for visitors?"

"I thought this was a live volcano."

"It is. But it hasn't gone off in fifty years. It will some-day. You'll hear her if she does it."

He took Lena back to the sugar estate with her question unanswered. If people were given the choice to be born, she wondered, how many would go ahead with it? The dif-ference between her and Howard Justine was that she thought life was a series of choices. Howard did not expect to be able to choose. When they parted, she wanted to say something to him so that at least he wouldn't think she was a fool. But she didn't know what to say, and they stared at each other.

"Don't forget the shoes. You can leave them at the food store in town."

"I'll remember. But how else can I thank you?"

He nodded his head. "When I told Mr. Austin I was moving in here and wanted to rent some land, he said, 'Agriculture is not the future of the island, Justine. Get into the service sector.'" He slapped his donkey and turned back into the interior. Lena heard him say, "You wouldn't have done it."

"How do you know?"

He didn't answer. He only repeated, as though to the donkey, carefully chewing each syllable, "de-ser-VICE-sec-TOR." Lena supposed it was a professional judgment, the kind Alice made.

She did leave the shoes in March, when she and Billy left. She thought she would return to the top of Blackwell's Soufrière from time to time. Saltaire seemed mostly the same.

Arnold and Alice and their ferrets were still in the next house. No one had met Arnold's price. He blamed it on the deer. That and the taxes. Arnold thought Lena was looking very fit and appealing. Some of the does, including Evelyn, Lena didn't see anymore, and she assumed that those were the ones that had been killed. No one seemed to care which ones she had already made infertile. They just picked out a certain number and killed them. One thing Lena was sure of—none of the deer would have chosen to die.

But then she wondered why she imagined she could know what a deer thought.

Exactly two years later, smoke, rumbling, and an explosion marked the beginning of the eruption of Blackwell's Soufrière. The town was evacuated and is now buried in ash. Lena and Billy's cottage, along with the other "villas," have vanished on a blackened hillside. Howard Justine has moved to Toronto.

DESAPARECIDOS

In case anybody is interested, Coca-Cola is buying up Belize. They already have about twelve percent of the land in a joint venture with a Texas cattle-ranching consortium.

Belize, you always have to say at this point, is the former British Honduras. It is in Central America. Coca-Cola, on the other hand, never seems to require further explanation.

Belize looks like a composite third-world country made up in some writer's imagination and given a fictitious name. There are black English-speaking people in quaintly painted, falling-down wooden houses, and Mayan-speaking Indians—indigenous people—in a jungle with ancient ruins. Lots of jungle—space that looks as if nobody has ever been there. That is the stuff Coca-Cola is buying, thinking it will make good orange groves.

I was having a pretty good day in Belmopan, which also sounds like a fictitious name but *is* actually the capital.

Belize City—a town with an even phonier-sounding name—was the original capital. But the ocean continually flooded the town, and so it was decided to build a new capital inland. One- and two-story buildings were quickly put up in a jungle clearing. Some of the buildings looked prefabricated. Signs posted on these buildings identified them as one ministry or another. A quickly bolted together two-story structure—only the second story prevented it from looking like a trailer—provided offices for the prime minister. That made it the capital building. It was pictured on the Belizean one-dollar bill.

When I set out that morning to arrange an interview with the prime minister, I did not recognize the new makeshift building from the dollar bill and had to drift for a while reading the signs on the far sides of buildings. They placed the building labels as though for someone coming out of the jungle into this clearing that was the capital. When I happened into the right one and climbed to the second floor, I saw a sign on a door that said, "Prime Minister." So I knocked. The prime minister answered the door, glad to grant a surprise interview in this lonely place.

Now it was lunchtime and I was eating at the Bullfrog, which was said to be the best restaurant in Belmopan. Everyone was always so insistent on this point that I have never found out if there are other restaurants in the capital. The Bullfrog has an open-air terrace with a canvas awning to shield customers from the tropical sun. I was lunching with the governor general. Lunch with a governor general in the English-speaking Caribbean ranks, journalistically, slightly above lunch alone. You don't have to bother taking notes while you eat, but you can feel as though you are accomplishing something. The governor general of Belize was a black woman with meticulously straightened hair and a posture that rejected curves. Her job was to represent the queen of England in Belize, and the queen's business in Belize was not very interesting—scholarship drives, fund-raisers, and other charitable gestures sponsored by the world's richest woman. But after—what was it?—I think nine weeks on the road, it was pleasant to have lunch with someone. I dutifully asked her questions while trying to sneak glances at a two-day-old *New York Times* at the next table, conveniently abandoned there by the baritone-voiced former U.S. ambassador who had retired and, naturally, now worked for Coca-Cola.

On page five was an article on Suriname, which was a rare event. This story was by Tom Serliac, whom I had first interested in going there over a late-night rum in Kingston. His story said that the little guerilla war was heating up and could turn into something bigger (you had to say that something might get bigger to get a Suriname story in the paper). According to local sources, increasing numbers of locals and even political dissidents in Paramaribo were simply disappearing. Also, some foreigners had been reported missing, including one American, Alan J. Hollins, a freelance journalist.

With a royal program for peasant women being outlined in the background, I read it again. "Alan J. Hollins."

Funny how your own name stares back at you from newsprint as though your existence had never been a fact before.

It was me. And I had disappeared. It said so in the *New York Times*.

It was September and I had not been in Suriname since the past December, when the dry season had made the river too dangerous. I had only been there two times, only twice convinced someone to send me.

What was Serliac talking about? I hadn't seen him and his blue, button-down-collar shirt that he wears even in jungles, in a year. As I thought about it, nobody had seen me in about four months—that is to say, no one who knew me. But that isn't the same thing as disappearing.

Trying to glance casually, I read on for more details of my disappearance. But no more details were deemed fit to print. Ideas sloshed and swirled in my mind while I picked at the almost black sauce of my *chilmole,* a chicken dish that, like many things in Belize, seemed like a watery version of something from somewhere else. The governor general was still detailing the queen's work in the former colony and, it occurred to me that she, too, might just be happy to have someone with whom to eat lunch.

Almost everyone I ever knew was a *New York Times* reader. Barbara read it every morning with coffee and fresh-squeezed grapefruit juice, both of which she bought at Balducci's. My wife, ex-wife really, did not even live in New York, but she still bought the *New York Times* every day from a thankless metal box on a curb. All my friends read the *New York Times,* along with every editor at every paper I ever worked for. All these people read it, and they believed it. I talked Serliac into going to Suriname because no one would send me back. If it was in the *New York Times,* then all my editors would decide it was a story again. When it is in the *New York Times,* it becomes a fact. So now I could be certain that my editors were not questioning Serliac's reporting. They were looking for a new stringer. They would probably send him to Suriname.

Every person I ever knew would be mourning me, replacing me, preparing to forget me. If I did not quickly contact a lot of people, I really would be disappeared—disappeared by the *New York Times.*

Back to Belize City, back to room 104 in the Fort George Hotel, which I reserved because it was one of only two rooms in Belize City that had air-conditioning. But it had no windows. Just harsh, blank, concrete walls. It suddenly occurred to me that the room looked like a place where a missing person—a *desaparecido*—might be kept.

The telephone was working well, and I was able to get Miami immediately, and I even got Serliac on the line.

"Hi, Tom." I said, pausing a dramatic two beats. "It's Al Hollins."

Serliac answered with no particular emotion, "Hi, Al. How are you?"

"Listen, I saw that article you wrote about me . . ."

"I didn't write an article about you," he snapped back.

"About disappearing in Suriname."

"Well, it is an exaggeration to call that an article about you."

"Okay, but . . ."

"It was a good story."

"But where did you get the part about my disappearance?"

"Sources. Reliable sources. Three of them. The story's good. Believe me."

"But, I'm here."

"Suriname?"

"No, in Belize City."

"Geez, you always go to the weirdest places. What is the story in Belize?"

"Coca-Cola is buying it."

"Geez. Some story. Look, nice to hear from you. I've got to go. I'm on deadline."

In the journalistic world, no one touches someone on deadline, or talks to them or argues with them. It is like the old yellow-fever-on-board flags that let a ship pass unchallenged. But I had to insist. "But, I'm here."

"Okay, good. Give me your telephone number."

"I'm leaving on Taca tomorrow morning."

"So, really, you are not there."

"But I didn't disappear in Suriname. I'm not even in Suriname."

"I'm glad you're okay. I've got to go."

"You are going to have to do a retraction."

"Look, I said you were reported missing, and you were. My sources said you were missing. I've got to go. Talk to them in New York if you want."

I took the Taca flight to Miami the next day. The plane ticket had my name on it as it always did, but this time I noticed it like some kind of discovered archival evidence. At the Miami airport, I stopped at the first bank of pay telephones. A group of tough-looking, thickset, short Salvadorans with straw cowboy hats had gotten off ahead of me and were now taking up all the telephones. I stood behind one waiting, hoping to make him uncomfortable, but he continued muttering conspiratorially in soft Spanish while running the lizard skin toe of an expensive, western-style boot on the blue carpet. When he was through, I called the *New York Times* and after being transferred to several people got the deputy foreign editor.

"I'm sorry, sir, but we cannot do a retraction on this." When an editor says "sir" in a newsroom, you know the person is making obscene hand gestures at whoever passed the call over.

"Why not?"

"It's not appropriate. The story said you were reported missing, and you were reported missing. The fact that you have turned up does not make the story wrong. The appropriate thing would be a story saying you have turned up."

"All right. That would be fine." I didn't mean to be

yelling, but a Salvadoran on the next telephone was making a great deal of noise, angrily shouting, *"Escuchas bien,"* while pointing a gold-ringed finger at the telephone.

"Look," said the deputy foreign editor, "how many stories do you think we can run on Suriname? That sounds like *some* place. Pretty strange down there, is it?"

"Do you realize that everybody who knows me thinks I have disappeared?"

"I appreciate that. But the *New York Times* cannot be using its foreign space for announcements to your relatives. Why don't you just call them yourself? Anyway," he added with real sadness in his voice, "you're lucky. I never get to disappear anywhere anymore. Suriname, huh. Sounds like *some* place."

🐓

Al Hollins was exactly right about Barbara. She got up at nine, walked over to Sixth Avenue, and bought a plastic bottle of freshly squeezed grapefruit juice, picked up a *New York Times,* went home, and, with juice in hand, read the article that was not about, but did mention, the disappearance of Alan Hollins.

She hoped nothing terrible had happened to him, but it sounded as though it had. She shuddered. Poor Al. Sadly, ironically, it was an end. Barbara had not seen Hollins in five months. He had called several times, usually from airports. He hated waiting around in airports, so he always passed the time on the telephone. If this was a relationship, it was not her idea of a relationship. At first she had been anxious for his return so she could tell him that. In time, her life just went on as though it had all been said. She vaguely dreaded his coming back. She had met someone who had her idea of a relationship. Somehow, it had never seemed as though Hollins was coming back. Everything had moved on. Now it turned out that she was right. He was not going to come back. That awkward encounter would never happen.

Poor Al. That thought periodically crossed her mind in between thoughts of floating and fixed interest rates. She had decided to buy her apartment and had to settle on the financing. One day while she was thinking "Poor Al," the telephone rang.

"Barbara," and then a pause for the drama of it. "It's Al."

I could tell by the silence on the other end that Barbara had read the story and was upset. I reassured her that I was all right, that the *Times* was wrong. I tried to be comforting. Then I told her I was coming to New York.

"But how could the *Times* be wrong?" she said.

"I don't know. They were just wrong. The *New York Times* can be wrong."

"But they couldn't have just made it up," she said. She seemed upset. "There must have been some truth to the story," she insisted. I couldn't get rid of that pleading sound in her voice. Finally I offered to prove the story completely wrong by hopping on the American flight from Miami and showing up at her apartment.

This part I can't remember the exact wording on. Only the vague tone of it. Ambiguous words. She was "involved" with someone else. The whole thing was very "awkward." I remember getting indignant. After all, the article only came out three days ago. But Barbara explained that she had been seeing this man for "months."

How could it have been months? I hadn't been away for months. I had only . . . well, I wasn't sure. But I don't think it was months.

Then she asked me something funny. She wanted to know, since I followed world events so closely, if I thought U.S. interest rates were headed up or down? An odd question to ask someone just back from Belize.

I was not at all sure when it was that I had last seen Barbara, but I knew that I would miss her. I was still at the Miami airport with its vast stretches of blue and motley gray carpets and white pillars and shops with Florida oranges and Latin American souvenirs and Cuban coffee and French pastry—an endless shopping mall of the trivial. At first it looks like a place where you could amuse yourself for hours, but after only minutes you see past the illusion and comprehend that there is actually nothing there at all.

The Salvadorans had gone. But now there were Haitians flailing gangly arms and shouting at each other as they taped closed overstuffed cardboard cartons, huge, almost-waist-high boxes of Miami booty, which they slid along the carpet toward the gate, where they would try to convince the airline, against all logic, that this was simply carry-on luggage that they would store under their seats. The shouting was growing louder, and I moved on to a different bank of telephones. It wasn't only the shouting. I wanted to move, to go from one place to another, to imitate the sensation of having somewhere to go.

I dialed the number for my wife—that was what I called her, though we had been divorced for . . . for a number of years. I cannot remember exactly how many years. She lived in Rhode Island near the Connecticut line in a flat town of stone walls and white houses. This was her description. I had never seen it. It was the way she had always said she wanted to live. I had always assured her that she would be bored after two months. Now, years later, she was still enjoying it.

On certain corners in this Rhode Island town, you could buy the *New York Times* from a metal box for two quarters. But on that day she had been going to the drugstore anyway to get medicine for her son's sore throat. She had read the article because she remembered Al talking about Suriname. She could not recall anyone else mentioning the name. The news had made her sad, worried, and then angry, because she was feeling just as she had when they were married. She thought how fortunate it was that this had not happened when they were married, when it would have been devastating. How glad she was that they were no longer married. Also, she was worried about the right dosage for her son and she was studying the label when the telephone rang.

"I'm glad you called. I was really worried," she said. But then she started thinking about her husband, who had just gone off to work in the morning, leaving her to figure out what to do about their son's sore throat. Well, at least he didn't keep disappearing and reappearing like this one. "So keep in touch," she said. Should she take her son to the doctor or just try the medicine?

I could tell that the whole thing had put her in a bad mood. This wasn't a good time to be talking to her. I remembered those moods. The way she acted distracted when she was really upset.

During the conversation I noticed two gray-haired women and a white-haired man, looking very tired, sitting like three half-filled sacks, all eating large ice cream cones. They stared in my direction, and their tongues seemed to move in unison. There was something unnerving about it.

I moved on to another bank of phones, where a group of Cubans were carrying a banner sprayed with red and silver glitter that said, *"Estamos acá, Hernando."* I got my editor on the phone and immediately told him that the *Times* story "was completely unfounded." But he never listened when I knocked the *Times*.

"Their Belize story?"

"No." Wait a minute. "The *Times* had a Belize story?"

"I hope not. Where is ours?"

They wanted to run Belize on Sunday. I could file it tomorrow afternoon. I would file it from . . . somewhere. I was starting to feel as if I would still be in the Miami airport. It made me feel disconnected to have no assignment and no plan. Could it be that this spot, the blue-carpeted Miami International Airport, was where I finally ran out of ideas?

I bought three newspapers and sat down with them at a bar. And there it was, this time in the *Miami Herald.*

The headline was THE DIRTY WAR WON'T GO AWAY. The dateline was Buenos Aires. The military had been overthrown in both Uruguay and Argentina. But thousands of disappeared, *desaparecidos,* were still missing, and their friends and relatives would not give up looking. An American "human rights activist" based in Montevideo had documented ten thousand cases and was quoted as saying, "This represents only the tip of the iceberg." His name was Alan Hollins.

It was only eight P.M. Miami time. There was still plenty of time to catch the midnight flight to Buenos Aires.

It was energizing to get out of syrupy tropical air and to breathe something light and scentless in a country where cities don't look as if they grew there by chance and where buildings were solid, as though built to be permanent instead of having just somehow survived.

Uruguay and Argentina are separated by a river so wide it looks like an ocean. As the ferry carried me across, I thought about the bodies in the river. There might be freshly installed democracies on both sides, but the bodies from before kept bobbing to the silvery surface. That morning's paper had an article about twenty corpses that had just floated up in a lake in Córdoba. And unmarked graves were still stumbled on. It was hard to keep it all buried—ten thousand missing or twenty thousand. Some said thirty thousand just in Argentina. There were fewer in Uruguay. But at least in Argentina there were trials. In Uruguay there was an agreement to forget. And in neither country was anybody certain of the exact number of *desaparecidos*. Everyone thought there were more than those on the lists.

I wondered about the others. The people who were missing but were not listed anywhere as missing. There was no husband to say, "My wife never came home." They were people who were gone but nobody saw them taken and nobody noticed their absence. That was as disappeared as a person could get.

Montevideo was a hilly town of snack bars and large, antique American cars—classic '50s Chevies and rounded bulky Oldsmobiles. I made an appointment with the other Alan Hollins for five o'clock, only identifying myself as an American journalist writing about *desaparecidos*. The voice on the other end did not sound American. There was that vague Italian lilt like an Argentine's or Uruguayan's. The *Herald* must have been wrong about his being an American.

He lived above a *parrillada,* where families were already gathering around large tables with platters piled with steaks, chops, and innards. Insatiable carnivores, these people. I climbed two sets of dark stairs and knocked on the door. A thin man wearing long, straight black hair, a scraggly black beard, corduroy pants, and a sweater answered the door. "Welcome. Alan Hollins," he said, extending his hand and flipping on a large, unconvincing smile.

Was he saying, "Welcome, I'm Alan Hollins," or was he welcoming Alan Hollins? I wasn't sure how to introduce myself. "Nice to meet you," was all I said. He led the way into a small dark room with a table in one corner. On the walls were photographs—thousands of snapshots in color, black-and-white, five-by-seven, wallet-sized, passport size. There were pictures of graduations, birthdays, weddings— bland pictures with forced smiles or unexplained seriousness. Many were of children—little squares with a blurry face that had been cut out of larger family photos. They all looked like normal people passing through the banal rites of an average life. But they were all missing, and this Alan Hollins had files on every one of them, documenting when they were last seen. Some had even been seen being pushed into cars or taken out of their homes in a confusing late-night raid.

This Alan Hollins talked on, pointing to different photos, telling what he knew of their story. "I came here because no one is doing it here. There are people in Buenos Aires . . ."

But for some reason I did not quite believe this assertion. For some reason I was certain this other Alan Hollins was in Montevideo instead of Buenos Aires because it was more out of the way. Or was I just assuming an expertise on people named Alan Hollins?

"You know the *parrillada* downstairs?"

I nodded, still trying to identify the accent.

"A woman was eating in that *parrillada,* four weeks ago. She was—" he started looking around the photos on the walls. "There!" he said, pointing to a dog-eared color snapshot of a husky young man in a pale blue soccer uniform. "It was his wife. They were both arrested together. Then a man with a mustache took her away for what he called questioning. Worked on her for days. She never saw her husband again. But she was in the *parrillada* four weeks ago eating steak and she sees the man with the mustache at the next table eating kidneys. She sees his face and she starts quivering. She can't talk. Can't eat. Can't leave. Can to do nothing."

Can to do? "Where are you from, Mr. Hollins?" I asked.

The other man smiled and pushed his straight hair out of his face with his left hand. "I am American," he said. The smile seemed like his idea of how an American would smile, meaninglessly, just because he was good-natured and American. Then he added, "New Jersey. I am from Hackensack, New Jersey"—only he pronounced it New Yearzee. Hackensack, New Yearzee.

"And your name is Alan Hollins?" I asked, appearing to be writing it all in my notebook. "Is that Alan J. Hollins?"

"Yes," answered the other Hollins, "Alan Yay Hollins."

I could not help snapping the next question at him. "What does the *J* stand for?"

"Yon," he said, not at all off-balance.

"I'm sorry. Is that Juan?"

"John."

"The reason I was asking is that—I am Alan J. Hollins too."

The other Hollins, with only polite interest, asked, "And what does the *J* stand for?"

"Julian. It was my grandfather's name."

"Yes," he said reflectively. "That's much better." Then, as though shaking off a thought, he pushed his hair away again, smiled, and said, "My grandfather was Yon."

When I left, I had learned nothing. I would have to spend more time. I would call some papers, get some money, stay here a week.

It was nighttime now, and the city was very quiet. The large, rounded old cars were gone from the streets. Only peasants from the countryside remained, driving horse-drawn carts, the clop of hooves echoing in the streets. It was a comforting sound, and back in my hotel room I quickly fell asleep to it.

In the morning there were big Chevy engines and no more horses. The change of sounds woke me at sunrise. How should I confront him? "Who are you really?" It seemed a ridiculous question. After all, who am I? At the window I could see the benign grinning monster faces of 1950s cars climbing the uphill street. And on the sidewalk stood a man with graying hair and a green shirt—my green shirt.

It was not only that he was wearing the same shirt as I and the same khaki pants, but he also had a notebook and two pens in his shirt pocket as though he were trying to look like a journalist. It wasn't the other Hollins. Someone else was trying to look like me. I ran out of my room, and without waiting for the narrow elevator, began leaping down the stairs. This person could tell Barbara—well, Barbara didn't care—could tell anyone he was me. He could—he could steal my newspaper strings!

By the time I got to the street, I realized that none of my newspaper editors had ever seen me. Anyone could say he was Al Hollins and get my assignments. He didn't even have to impersonate me. He didn't need to wear my shirt.

My name was simply a name. Couldn't it be merely a coincidence that someone else had the same name? Just like the man on the street with the same clothes? Yes, this Hollins was a coincidence. We didn't even have the same middle names.

I was beginning to feel better. I had arranged to return to Hollins, pretending to be interested in his cases, but really wanting to investigate him. But now I was looking for stories and was interested in his cases. Having understood that the name was just a chance pairing, I was calm. I was working.

But then, I saw him again, and he started smiling his American smile. I sat with him in his office and we had coffee while I asked him about his work. He said that he started with a photograph, which he pinned on the wall. Then he began gathering what he could.

"So you start with a face, not a name?"

"I start with what is known. In your case, there is your name and your face. And then who knows you. Who saw you last."

"Suppose you think the name is false?"

"Then there is the face. But in some cases, even a face can be false."

I studied his face.

"I think I have a good story for you," he said.

"Really?" I had to keep playing this out until I could understand it. Just go along. "What's the story?"

"Small village. Only maybe sixty kilometers from here. Farmers grow vegetables. Nothing big, but they live all right. A farmer is plowing a new field after a few days rain, and he finds an arm. Then it turns out to be a body. Then it is five bodies. Three children."

The longer I listened to him, the more I started wondering if Spanish was his language. Maybe it was something completely different that I hadn't even considered, like Lebanese. He could be a Middle Easterner.

"The bodies were pretty badly gone, but one had this purple shirt. The mayor of this village always wore these purple shirts. They used to call him *Intendente Morado,* 'Mayor Purple.' And this purple mayor had disappeared with his family some eight . . ."

Intendente Morado, he said it perfectly, with a nice roll on the r. All the books I could see were in Spanish. Was there any writing on his desk? As he talked, I looked for clues, but I didn't even know what kind of clues I expected to find.

Once again, I left without really learning anything. That night I could not sleep at all and listened to the horses. If I was going to stay, I had better do some stories. In the morning I bought several newspapers and read them in a café, went back to the hotel, and made some appointments with official people.

The following day I called my paper with six good stories to pitch. I got the foreign desk and landed with my feet already moving.

"I've got some really interesting things down here."

"Yeah, you sure do. That was a great piece. We got it on page one."

"What?"

"Purple mayor. That was great. If it wasn't for his damn shirt, they never would have caught those guys. It was like a good movie."

"Wait a minute. We have to talk about something here."

"What else have you got? We could take a whole series."

"Listen."

"Only I don't know what kind of telex or what you filed on. Why don't you move into some decent hotel instead of your usual dump? Get some good communication. We'll pay."

"You will?"

"Yeah, for a little while. Just save your receipts and keep coming up with stories like the last one. Hang on a minute, Bob Blackman wants to talk to you."

Then the deputy managing editor came on the phone to congratulate me. I had never gotten this before. It seemed they liked the other Al Hollins's copy better than mine.

I moved to the ninth floor of a hotel where the windows were so well sealed that you couldn't hear the horses at night. You also couldn't hear your own footsteps or the room-service waiter coming down the hall. There was thick carpeting on everything. The telephones, the fax, the telex, all worked perfectly, and the staff was always ready to help. The paper sent me clips every day, which were delivered to my door.

He was doing good work, and the desk was pleased. I was pacing the spongy carpet trying to figure out how to get out of all this. I no longer even cared if I understood it. I just had to get out of it. It was too late to tell the paper. But this couldn't go on forever. Then I realized that it wouldn't. He wrote only about *desaparecidos,* and there would be a limit to how many *desaparecido* stories they would take from Uruguay. I wrote up an expense report for the past week and faxed it. Expenses always made them lose interest.

He was losing interest too. He hadn't filed in two days. In fact, he wasn't answering his telephone. I went to the minibar and twisted open another tiny, expensive bottle. It would be over soon, and I was glad, ready to leave this well-carpeted hotel.

The next morning, another note of congratulations was slipped under my door along with a long story by Alan J. Hollins from Buenos Aires.

There was nothing I could do until he got back. What if he didn't come back? What if he was going to file stories all over South America? Or all over the world? Maybe he would win prizes and I would have to stand there and collect them. When was it going to stop? I should have stopped it in the first place. I didn't want this hotel. I hated hotels like this. I went to the minibar and twisted open another tiny bottle.

That afternoon Hollins called me. I suggested he come over to my hotel, and he said he loved that hotel and wanted to see the room.

Later, after I hung up the telephone, I wondered how he knew where to call me. But I resolved not to ask him because I knew that if I did, he would just answer with that smile. He arrived at the door wearing the smile and almost pushed past me to explore the room. Everything seemed to please him. He stroked the carpeting with his meticulously polished shoes. He picked up the remote control and flipped through the channels, pausing to nod approvingly at CNN. He knelt at the minibar, turned to me, and said, "May I?" Selecting a small Coca-Cola can, he opened it as he sat in a thickly upholstered chair. "This is the smallest can I have ever seen," he said admiringly.

"You've been very busy," I said.

"Yes," he said, savoring his miniature Coca-Cola. "It is good to be busy. And I will tell you something. I am very content as Alan J. Hollins. Perhaps you could go back to being Alan J. Hollins somewhere else."

I felt threatened by this man with the wrong smile and my name. Why should he say where I can be Alan Hollins? "Suppose I don't want there to be two of me?"

He smiled even more broadly. "Then one would have to be disproved. If it came down to it, with my experience maybe I could do a better job of proving who I am than you can. It is in my line, so to speak. Do you know how to prove that you are Alan J. Hollins?"

This wasn't working. Not turning out the way it should. I was having weird thoughts. If he is me, then who am I? It did not seem fair that he was getting me to ask such questions of myself. I was being outmaneuvered.

"I know your work. You are the same Alan J. Hollins who writes for *Esquire* magazine," he offered, as though trying to help me with my own identity. I thought that was condescending.

"I wrote one article for them."

"Yes. About Guatemala."

"Yes."

"I read it. I liked it very much. I also liked your name very much—Alan J. Hollins. It is a good name. It sounds like somebody, but it could also be anybody."

"You might think that, but it's different for me."

"Yes. Of course."

He *was* being condescending.

"I was just coming here. Just starting this work. And— well, I needed a name. So I used Alan J. Hollins."

I stared at him. He was still smiling, though I could not imagine why. Now I understood why he seemed to have that edge over me. I had merely stumbled into being Alan J. Hollins. He had made a conscious decision. It was an unmistakable advantage in the clinches. He looked very happy collapsed in the big chair, drinking the little can that made him appear to have a huge hand, rubbing his feet on the carpet.

He loved this hotel. Why shouldn't he stay here until the paper took it away? "How much do you plan to write?"

"As much as I can."

"Everywhere?"

"I'm only interested in *desaparecidos.*"

"The paper will lose interest. They always lose interest. Something else happens somewhere. They can't think about too many things at once." But until that happened, I told him, the hotel room was already in his name. I showed

him how to send in the receipt for the hotel bill. Suddenly
his face transformed, and for the first time, I saw his real
smile. I started packing.

"By the way," I said, handing him a large menu, "room
service to midnight."

"I'm a vegetarian."

A vegetarian? He wasn't from here! People here ate a
cow a day. "They have a vegetarian platter. You just dial
three and they bring it up." He looked very pleased.

"And French wine?"

"French or Italian." I had made him happy. "So you
were in Suriname last month."

For the first time, he looked confused. "You mean
that—Dutch Guiana, that place? I've never been there."

"Look, the *New York Times* said Alan J. Hollins was
missing in Suriname, and it wasn't me. See, I am not missing! It must have been you!"

He smiled again, not the real one. "I am not missing
either. Listen, Mr. Hollins. Do you know that I am looking
for two Horacio Mendoza Casaluccis? No relation to each
other at all. I have four Jorge Diazes."

"So you think a third Alan J. Hollins went to Suriname
and disappeared?"

"Well, in this disappearance business you have to look
at the facts. I am here. You are here. What we know is that
an Alan J. Hollins has disappeared. You just have to find
out which one."

Fort George Hotel. Room 104. I stared at the cream-colored concrete where the view might have been, if the architect had thought to put a window in the wall. The air conditioner grumbled like a rude and hungry man. A few phone calls confirmed that it was over, the deal had gone sour. Coca-Cola had pulled out. It was a good thing I had filed the story while it was still true. There were no stories in the paper now from either Alan J. Hollins. I suppose they just lost interest in the *desaparecidos*.

It was hard to say what to do. Belize City was full of people roaming the streets and never asking questions like that, so why should I? I went to a small upstairs restaurant and had peas and rice. The other choice was rice and peas, and the waiter explained this without the slightest suggestion of irony. One had the beans on top of the rice. The other was all mixed up and cooked together. Tonight maybe I will try rice and peas. Maybe I could just stay here . . . well, for a while. Maybe I could meet a woman, get involved. Become a Belize expert. Even without the Coca-Cola Company.

But I have to be careful, because now I know how easily you can disappear just by accident, just a misunderstanding, or someone else's whim. I really needed Coca-Cola to be here because that was the story and without the story you can disappear. I guess that's the importance of bylines. But a byline is just a name. It could be anyone.

All the people crowding into the rickety streets of Belize City with no Coca-Cola, no story, and they weren't worried about it. Why is it that they could all be here eating peas and rice without ever being at risk of disappearing and yet, every day that I stay here I am running the risk of turning up missing?

THE WHITE MAN'S GLOSSARY

bacalaitos—a fritter made from a batter of salt cod. (See **beignet**.) The batter is made by adding flour to the water used in soaking the dried salt cod. Then the salt cod itself is crumbled into the batter. In Puerto Rico traditional cooks add local herbs, garlic, tomato. The additions are chopped into small pieces and give little flecks of bright color to the fritter when it is fried. But not everyone adds them. Some cooks add baking powder to make the fritter puffier. Others make it flat. There are endless variations of *bacalaitos*. But water, flour, garlic, and salt cod are the essentials. In the Puerto Rican diaspora—places such as New York, Hartford, Boston, and Chicago—a *bacalaito* is often nothing more than these four ingredients. The batter is then dropped into hot corn oil. Some of the island fritters are made from a thick batter spooned into the oil to make a ball-shaped piece. In the Bronx and other points north it is often a very liquid batter ladled into a skillet of hot oil and the fritter comes out almost pancake shaped.

banane—a green, unripened banana that is eaten as a vegetable. Bananas, the bud of a bush of southeast Asian origin, are usually eaten green, as a vegetable, in the Caribbean. After the 1870s voyages of Lorenzo Baker, a Cape Cod sea captain, bananas began arriving in Boston ripened yellow into a fruit, and Americans began eating them that way. The choice is clear between a starch or a dessert, since a green banana is mostly starch with very little sugar, and a ripe banana is just the reverse. There are more than one hundred varieties of bananas. There is no botanical distinction between the fruit and the vegetable. Plantains, sold in the U.S. as a distinct vegetable, ripen into a yellow fruit the same as other varieties. If banana buds are cultivated, the plant, in spite of the appearance of seeds, is sterile and new stalks must constantly be planted. In Haitian food, *banane* on a menu usually refers to *banane pèsé,* flattened banana. The bananas are sliced and fried in oil until browned. Then they are drained on paper and flattened with a broad knife or small machete, placing the blade over each slice and pressing. Then they are put back into hot oil and fried again, only about one minute on each side. *Banane* and *griot* is a standard combination. (See **griots.**)

beignet—the French word for *fritter.* The Creole word is *accra.* A salt-fish beignet is an *accra de morue,* which resembles a *bacalaito* but is usually smaller and round. At the cocktail parties in Kourou, they are served as little finger hors d'oeuvres. (See **bacalaito**.)

blans—Creole for "white," *blans* are simply foreigners, non-Haitians. The word is used in the same sense as some Puerto Ricans use the phrase "white people" to mean non-Puerto Ricans.

bokor—a man skilled in the more marginal practices of Afro-Caribbean religion. He is not a religious leader, but he is an expert in the uses of herbs, potions, and spells. The fact that his skills are considered less spiritual than those of a priest is indicated by a tendency to refer to the *bokor's* practices as magic. It is magic for hire, and he will often do evil as well as good—anything for a price. *Bokors* are often feared, and since they are skilled in the uses of poisons, it is a reasonable fear. (See **obeah**.)

callaloo—the leaves of *Colocasia esculenta,* a native of India that, like many Caribbean people, traveled to the Caribbean by way of Africa. The broad green leaves, up to three feet long and sometimes nicknamed elephant ears, are cooked as a vegetable. The roots, called dasheen, taro, or malanga (see **sancocho**), are also a staple of Caribbean cooking. The most celebrated callaloo dish, claimed by most of the English-speaking eastern Caribbean, is callaloo and crab. Onions and garlic are chopped and wilted in oil, then the chopped callaloo leaves are added and cooked until wilted, and finally crab meat is tossed in. A little pepper sauce or a touch (literally) from a cut scotch bonnet pepper gives some flair.

Callaloo is one of the few green vegetables commonly eaten in the Caribbean. The traditional Caribbean diet includes few greens and a great deal of fat. (See **sofrito**.)

cas-cas—a tall grass planted around the sides of cane fields to keep topsoil from eroding off the field. It used to be a defining image, the typical look of a country road in Barbados and some of the cane-growing eastern Caribbean, but now, not coincidentally, *cas-cas,* like good topsoil, is seen less often.

challef—a knife made for slaughtering animals under Jewish dietary law. The law demands that the animal die painlessly and that its blood be entirely removed. A challef is a particularly well-sharpened knife designed to cut the jugular vein of the animal so that it dies instantly and its blood is completely drained.

chilmole—somewhat of a Belizean national dish, though, no doubt, not a Belizean invention. *Chilmolli* was mentioned by Bernal Diaz, the chronicler on Cortez's expedition, to describe an Aztec sauce that today in Mexico is called a *mole*. Mole clearly belongs on a shortlist of the great sauce ideas of the world. It is generally associated more with Aztecs and the indigenous people of Mexico's central highlands than with Mayans and the indigenous people of the lowland of southern Mexico, Yucatan, Guatemala, and Belize. But once the Spanish discovered it, they were quick to create their own versions. The most famous mole, mole poblano, was invented by monks in the Mexican state of Puebla in 1533. An 1877 book on food in the State of Puebla gave forty-four different mole recipes. Mole is a sauce made from grinding a staggering number of ingredients—chilis, spices, herbs, seeds, and, in a few recipes, chocolate—into a thick paste, then sold in blocks and added to chicken stock to make a sauce. Someone, either European or indigenous, introduced Belize to a mole negro, a mole made from black chilis, and this sauce over chicken—with other things added according to whim, such as boiled eggs, tiny pork meatballs, or green jalapeño peppers—has ended up being a fixture in Belize even among the coastal people of African origin. The paste is liquified in chicken stock and then sometimes thickened by burning corn tortillas and grinding them to a powder that is added to the sauce. You might marvel at the logic of taking the trouble to make tortillas from cornmeal only to grind them back into cornmeal again, but tortillas are only good fresh and something needs to be done with the leftovers.

christophine—*Sechium edule,* also known as *chayote* and in certain French and Creole areas, as *mirliton,* is a relative of squash and pumpkin, and native to Central America. Christophine was cultivated by pre-Columbian Aztecs and grows in runners that will climb thirty feet or more if left alone. The pear-sized fruit, unlike most of its relatives, has a single pit, but the flesh is not unlike a squash's. Roots, leaves, and young shoots are also eaten.

cuatro—like the *tres* in Cuba (see **tres**), the Puerto Rican *cuatro* is an island invention, a local guitar created at a time when it was too difficult and expensive to import guitars from Spain. It is made from local hardwoods and strung in double-string chords. It is called a *cuatro* because the original instrument had four sets of double strings. In the twentieth century, the *cuatro* evolved into a five double-string instrument, which is only one of many examples of the dubious growth that has taken place in Puerto Rico under the Americans.

coo-coo—a combination of *funchi* (a cornmeal pudding similar to Italian polenta) and okra, which is the unripened fruit of a plant native to Africa and related to cotton (see **giambo**). *Funchi* is also mixed with mashed bananas, which is called *foo-foo*. All of these names are African, *funchi* meaning "mush" and *foo-foo* meaning "pale." To make *coo-coo,* steam okra, which has been scraped to remove fuzz, in enough water to barely cover, for six to eight minutes, and then, over a low heat, pour in a stream of yellow cornmeal, a little at a time, constantly stirring, until it is a thick dough that does not stick to the pot. Spread it out, about an inch thick, on a serving dish.

E.C. dollars—Eastern Caribbean dollars, a currency of small islands of the Eastern Caribbean. They failed to get Trinidad or Barbados, relative giants, to participate, and so the currency is backed only by a group of the world's tiniest economies spread throughout the lower part of the Caribbean archipelago, and yet it has been a surprisingly stable currency, often faring far better than the large-island currencies.

gandules—in English known as pigeon peas and in the English speaking Caribbean, congo peas or goongoo peas, it is a bean of either African or Indian origin. This is one of the world's oldest crops. It was eaten in Egypt four thousand years ago. It is the *pea* of peas and rice. (See **peas and rice**.) According to Puerto Rican legend, always a risky source, pigeon peas were brought to the island by Moorish soldiers in the Spanish army. The word *gandules* is said to be from an Arab word meaning lazy, because the plant seldom stands alone but leans on whatever is available. The peas are sometimes eaten green but more commonly when they ripen to a wine color. They are soaked for more than an hour in water with salt, pepper, thyme, garlic, onions, and one or two cured ham hocks, cracked. Then it is all slowly cooked and *sofrito* added. (See **sofrito**.)

giambo—this word appears to have the same origin as *gumbo,* the Bantu word *gombo,* which is related to the word *ochinggômbo,* which means "okra." (See **coo-coo**). A gumbo or *giambo* is a stew (in the case of *giambo,* generally a chicken stew) that is thickened with okra. Thickening with okra is a tricky business. Scientific books say that the green pods are mucilaginous—a euphemism for mucouslike, slimy, slithery. . . . The more you cook them the slimier the stew gets. So I suggest adding it toward the end of cooking, but, of course, you have to allow enough time for thickening, the early stages of slime.

griots—in West Africa a *griot* is a wise man, usually an elder, but in Haiti *griots* are pieces of pork, marinated in lime juice and garlic and slowly fried until they become crisp on the outside and stringy inside. In Spanish-speaking islands the dish is called *masitas.* What makes *griots* work is either the pickled cabbage, carrot, and hot peppers that is called *piklés,* or the pepper sauce, one of the hottest, known in Creole as *ti malice,* "a touch of evil," which is made from garlic, lime juice, salt, onions, and scotch bonnet peppers.

guisado de bacalao—resembling a Basque dish of previous centuries, this is a salt cod stewed with various European and American ingredients, such as tomatoes, peppers, capers, ginger root, thyme, oregano. It is served with *coo-coo.* (See **coo-coo.**)

loas—"spirits" in Haitian Voodoo. They have complex personalities that, like those of mortals, blend both good and bad qualities. But they must be appeased, for they have powers. A believer can be endowed with some of these powers by becoming temporarily possessed by a loa.

métropole—a word in French used in colonies, former colonies, and overseas *départements* and territories to mean France, the mainland in Europe, the center of the imaginary French-speaking universe.

mondongo—tripe, which is stomach lining, soaked, flamed in rum, cooked very slowly with tomatoes, herbs, spices, and casssava (see **yucca**).

mofongo—mashed green bananas cooked in pork fat, sometimes with chunks of pork, always with garlic. On the west coast of Puerto Rico, in Mayagüez and to the south, *mofongo* is often served with crab mixed in or with conch. In the Dominican Republic, *mofongo* is sometimes mixed with salt cod, which is about as good as life gets.

montaña—ballads of rural life, sometimes called *jibaro* or peasant music. As Puerto Rican peasants were forced out of the mountains to urban centers of the island or the U.S., this country music became city music. Today it is more often heard in the Bronx than in rural Puerto Rico and seldom appreciated by young people.

obeah—*obeahman* is the word used on English-speaking islands for a *bokor*. (See **bokor**.) *Obeah* is his magic.

Oneg Shabbat—in Hebrew, literally "sabbath delight," it is a reception held after a Jewish sabbath service. The idea came from a famous Russian-born poet, Chaim Nachman Bialik. He held the first one in his home in 1924, the year he moved to Tel Aviv. It was supposed to be a reading and lecture series, followed by singing and some food on Saturday afternoon. But, increasingly, the American tradition has been simply a reception with food on Friday night.

parrillado—huge family restaurants in Argentina and Uruguay. Everything is huge—the rooms, the tables, the platters, and the portions. The name means "grilled," and they specialize in grilled beef and beef organs. Sometimes it seems that the entire animal is being served, a few pieces at a time.

rice and peas—pigeon peas (see **gandules**) and rice. This is served in every country in the Caribbean. I have always thought that the best peas and rice was in Jamaica where it is cooked in coconut milk.

sancocho—a stew of potatoes, yams, taro (see **callaloo**), cassava (see **yucca**), and bananas cooked with beef and beef stock.

sofrito—a tomato sauce that is the basis of many stews and sauces. It is made with tomatoes, green onions, garlic, green pepper, thyme, coriander leaves (cilantro), and annatto seeds (achiote). The ingredients are sautéed in pork fat, sometimes with olive oil. *Sofrito* means "sautéed slowly." Frying, which is an African cooking technique, dominates Caribbean cuisine. The choice of oil is always painful. Coconut oil and pork fat give these dishes wonderful flavor but are considered unhealthy, because of their high saturated fat content. Corn oil is healthier but adds little to the dish. In Puerto Rico, where the Spanish influence is felt, olive oil—the one healthy and flavorful oil—is sometimes used. But it is not traditional. No olive oil would be found in the Barrio Albizu.

stobá—a goat stew that reflects the international quality of the Curaçao market. The stew includes capers, onions, tomatoes, olives, ginger, thyme, cucumbers, shallots, cumin, and hot peppers.

tres—a guitar with six sets of triple strings. It is of Cuban origin and the most noted *tres* players are Cuban. Great *tres* playing is distinguished by its intricate finger work. (See **cuatro**.)

yucca—Spanish word for what is called cassava in English and manioc in French. It is a native American plant, one of the few indigenous Caribbean staples, and as such is often used in the speeches of Caribbean political leaders to invoke nationalism. It suggests authentic Caribbeanness in the same way the apple suggests America (though the apple, unlike the cassava, is not uniquely American). The root of the cassava is eaten as a starchy vegetable, or it is ground into a flour. It is also the source of tapioca. Some varieties of cassava root have a high concentration of glycoside linamarin, which breaks down into poisonous prussic acid. Columbus described being attacked by Carib tribesmen who shot poisonous arrows. The arrows were dipped in cassava poison. All the more reason for the symbolic importance of this root.

ACKNOWLEDGMENTS

My most sincere thanks to Nancy Miller, my friend and editor, who always makes it fun and exciting, and always makes my book better, and to Charlotte Sheedy, for her strength, grace, and huge heart.

To Virginia Peters, who believed in my writing when it seemed few did; to Kelvin Christopher James, a great writer and generous colleague; to Lisa Klausner, Bill Mooney, and Alex Webb, for their friendship and encouragement; to Jørgen Leth, for his hospitality and good sense of humor; to Henry and Laura Weil for their friendship and the stay in Saltaire; to Sarah Walker for all her help; and, most especially, to my dear friend Christine Toomey, whose enthusiastic reading was an inspiration to write this book.

And to Jack Ranson (1947–2000), the great friend of my youth with whom I laughed, cried, shared dreams, and played every sport known and a few invented. He made my life richer and more fun and was one of the most decent and gentle men I have ever known.